ALSO BY LAUREN BLAKELY

BALLERS AND BABES

Most Valuable Playboy

DARLING SPRINGS

It Seemed Like a Good Idea

A
WILD CARD
KISS

LAUREN BLAKELY

sourcebooks
casablanca

Published by Sourcebooks Casablanca, an imprint of Sourcebooks
1935 Brookdale RD, Naperville, IL 60563-2773
(630) 961-3900
sourcebooks.com

Originally self-published as *A Wild Card Kiss* and "A Wild
Card Night" by Lauren Blakely in 2022.

Cataloging-in-Publication Data is on file with the Library of Congress.

Printed and bound in the United States of America.
VP 10 9 8 7 6 5 4 3 2 1

To all of us who melt when a superstar athlete is also a good man.

CHAPTER 1

HARLAN

NEARLY EIGHT YEARS AGO

There are two kinds of men in the world.

Those who love suits and those who hate them.

Why love one? A well-made suit fits like a dream.

As for why you might hate one, don't ask me.

I'm a lover, not a hater. No one ever came to this guy for the negative on anything. Hate isn't my style.

But suits are, and I have a whole closet full of hand-tailored duds for occasions like the colleague's wedding where I'm headed tonight.

I pad across the carpet of my walk-in closet and appraise my options, flicking through the crisply pressed shirts hanging along one wall. I bypass the charcoal, midnight black, and dark blue, the paisley and the striped, until I reach a shirt in the palest of blues.

I slide it off the hanger, put it on, and smooth the front.

This color always wins the eyes of the ladies.

Now, for the suit. I've got more than a dozen custom ones to pick from. Comes with the territory—as a pro football player, I'm required to dress to the nines on game day. I consider my faves and zero in on the winner.

"Ah!" It's not your father's navy suit, that's for sure. No bankers would wear this color either. The deep, rich blue speaks up, gets noticed. It's a hue that says, *Let's have some fun tonight, sweetheart.*

And I am a fun kind of guy, so that's the romantic vibe I like putting out in the universe.

I put on the pants and a chocolate-brown belt, then head to the tie hanger. I opt for a pink silk one with tiny illustrations of playing cards scattered over it.

May luck be a very lovely lady tonight.

I grab the suit jacket, sling it over my shoulder on one finger, and spin around in front of the full-length mirror.

Yep.

"Well done, sir," I tell my reflection.

I am ready for the celebration. The bride and groom will say *I do*, and hearts will go a fluttering.

Ahhhh, yes.

Weddings—another thing I love.

Two people vowing to cherish each other for the rest of their lives. It melted my heart every time one of my sisters tied the knot, promising forever and fidelity.

Whether a couple can keep that promise, stay true to that vow…well, that's another issue.

I shudder, shucking off those unpleasant thoughts.

Not today, brain.

As I head down the stairs, I laser in on the best thing about weddings—for me, that is, as an attendee.

Weddings are the *best* place to meet women. Talk to women. Dance with women.

Three of my favorite things in the world to do.

Fuck this online shit. Swiping left or right and snapping this or that is not for me. I'm all about face-to-face chemistry and real-life chitchat. Weddings are perfect for a social cat like me as they're usually brimming with single women in the mood for a man.

Pretty sure I've never met a wedding where I haven't gotten laid, and I wouldn't mind keeping up that streak tonight.

I leave my place and head to the limo waiting at the curb just outside on California Street. I slow to survey the sleek, black set of wheels and whistle in appreciation.

The driver—a slim, efficient man in a black suit—pops out to open the door for me. "Thank you very much," I tell him. "And nice to meet you. I'm Harlan."

The man gives a surprised smile. "Darien. Pleasure to meet you too," he says.

I slide into the back seat to join my teammate Jones Beckett. "Damn, you look almost as good as I do," I say, checking out my friend in his Tom Ford suit.

The team's star receiver rolls his blue eyes. "Thanks. You look almost as rich as me."

I laugh as I smooth my hand down my tie. "Thanks for giving me a new goal."

Jones settles into the seat as the driver pulls onto Fillmore. "Thanks for being my"—he stops to sketch air quotes—"'date' tonight."

"Of course. Anything for the cause of love, buddy."

Jones sighs heavily and drags a hand down his face. "Fuck, man. I've got to figure this out and soon."

"No argument here."

My friend has it bad for the Renegades' lead publicist. He tried to keep it a secret from me and everyone else, and I understand why, but I put two and two together. Jillian's perfect for him— whip-smart and loyal. But Jones has been rehabbing his reputation, trying to shake off a checkered past, and he hasn't figured out how to bring their forbidden romance into the light.

More power to the two of them for running the relationship obstacle course. But just the thought of all those hurdles is too much for me. I prefer my dalliances simple, mutually enjoyable, and free of angst.

The strategy has served me well—*mostly*, I should say—for the last several years. I like to date, I like to have fun, and I like to fuck. But with my career still on the upswing, anything more compli- cated than that is not part of my playbook.

"I don't envy you, pal," I tell Jones as the driver swings onto Steiner Street.

"I don't envy me either. What am I supposed to do?"

"You could—just a thought—sort this shit out and have a relationship," I offer with a smile. I'm encouraging like that. But seriously, sometimes you just have to man up and do the hard things in life.

"I'm working on it, Harlan. And I think I've got a plan for telling the team and my new sponsor. But it'll have to wait until this weekend. Tonight, I just need a wingman so I can spend some time with Jillian."

I tap my sternum. "One fantastic, grade-A, top-choice wingman at your service." It's not my place to pressure him to come clean. He knows what he needs to do, and he's got to do it in his own damn time.

Plus, I know my role at this wedding.

I'm Jones's cover, and that's fine.

When the car stops on her block, Jones bounds up the steps and returns with Jillian a few minutes later. She greets me as they slide into the car, but mostly they make *I want to bang you backward, forward, and six ways to Sunday* eyes at each other as she snuggles up against him.

"Would you like me to just get in the front seat with the driver?" I offer, gesturing to the partition. "You can have a wham-bam while I chat with Darien. He seemed chill."

"You don't have to do that," Jillian says, ducking her head as a smile plays across her face. "We'll behave."

I scoff. "No need to behave on my account. I'm happy to shoot the breeze with the guy." I point to the speakers. "'I've Got You

Under My Skin" pipes through the limo. "He's got good taste in music."

Jones runs a hand along Jillian's bare arm, and she shivers. "Can't help myself," Jones says, "Haven't seen her in a while."

"I can tell. The sexual tension between you two would fill an ice cream tub. I could scoop it up and serve it in a cone. Sexual Tension Swirl, I'd call it."

Jones arches a brow. "Seriously?"

"What? I love sexual tension," I say with a grin.

"Everyone does, Harlan," Jones deadpans.

"Exactly. Marketing gold. I'll make millions. This idea is going to fund my retirement someday," I tease.

Jillian narrows her eyes and shakes a warning finger. "You better not retire anytime soon. You're only twenty-nine."

"You never know. That's why I'm always thinking ahead," I say, tapping my temple. "Plan for the unexpected."

Like how, a minute later, the car pulls over a few blocks from Jillian's place.

"We're just picking up my friend Katie," she explains.

I turn my head, glancing toward the sidewalk and—*whoa*.

Wait a hot, sexy, beautiful second.

I stare at the vision in pink heading straight for this car—a knockout with a smile that has me waving a white flag. Her dress clings to her curves in all the right places and swishes around her knees. Silver heels complete that *take me away to cloud nine* look she has going on.

Her lush blond hair falls in waves over her bare shoulders, which shimmer enticingly.

I whip around to glare accusingly at Jones, then Jillian. "Excuse me. Why did no one tell me that Jillian's friend is an angel dressed in pink, and the answer to my prayers?"

Jillian laughs. "Presumptuous much, Harlan?"

"Presumptuous a lot."

I hit the intercom. "Darien. I'll get the door."

"As you wish."

I push open the door, step onto the street, and sweep out an arm for the bombshell. "Your chariot," I say, gesturing to the car.

The stunning blond, with eyes as blue as the sea, flashes me a grin, with just a hint of naughty on her lips.

Mmm. Yes.

"What do you know? I was hoping for a chariot, and here you are." Her confident voice holds a touch of sarcasm as she slides into the car. I follow, sitting next to our newest passenger.

Jillian clears her throat and makes the introductions. "Jones, Harlan. This is my friend Katie."

Let's see if I can pave a path to her dance card tonight. "You're a goddess, Jillian, for inviting your beautiful friend."

"You know, she *also* has a good personality," Jillian says drily.

I narrow my eyes at the publicist. "Oh, hush. I already figured that no friend of yours would be a wet blanket." I turn to the blond, shooting her a big grin. "I bet you're a firecracker, Katie."

Her blue eyes go all kinds of flirty. "I'm the aerial fireworks, Harlan—the finale at the end of the show."

And I do believe I am officially in love.

"See? I knew that your sparkly personality would be perfect.

But let me give you a proper greeting." I reach for Katie's hand, clasping it to press a kiss to her knuckles. "How do you do tonight?" I ask, all refined, a hint of my Atlanta roots coming through.

"I do very well," she says. "And aren't you quite the gentleman?"

"Once a Southern gentleman, always a Southern gentleman. Especially in the presence of such a lovely, brilliant lady." Yes, I'm all manners on the outside, while on the inside I'm thinking, *holy hell, I've already met my dream wedding hookup.*

She rolls her eyes, but she's smiling, too, as she tosses a glance at Jillian. "I can't believe you didn't warn me about this one and his oodles of flirt."

Jillian shrugs. "I didn't realize Harlan would be in such rare form tonight."

"What would you have liked to know?" I ask. "That I'm patently charming? Terrifically entertaining? Possess gobs of sexy, endearing, can't-resist vibes? Also, I pour an excellent"—I stop to consider the bottles in the limo's bar—"tequila, whisky, or vodka. Take your pick."

"I'm a tequila girl," Katie says, laughing. "And maybe warn a woman she has to keep up with a master charmer."

"Sometimes surprises are fun." I grab a glass and pour her a splash, then do the same for myself.

Jones and Jillian opt for water, and the four of us toast, our glasses clinking as Sinatra croons about the way you look tonight.

"To weddings, wingmen, and wingwomen," I say, casting my gaze from Katie, to Jones and Jillian, then back to Katie. "And to new friends."

Her eyes twinkle as she taps my glass one more time. "I'll drink to all that, Mister Charmer."

I knock back my liquor, and she does the same. I sigh happily at the turn the night has taken. "Have I mentioned I can dance too? It's one of my many talents."

"What are your others?" she asks with that firecracker sizzle. "Besides running, blocking, and tackling."

Ah, she knows my skills. "I can catch a football too. Tie any kind of knot. And I can also bake pies like nobody's business."

She hums her approval. "I'll be saving a dance for you." She studies my face, the corner of her lips screwing up in a smile. "So please save one for me."

Oh, I like weddings very much.

CHAPTER 2

KATIE

I am a woman on a mission.

I have a message to deliver to someone at this wedding, and I don't intend to mince words.

That's why I said yes to Jillian's invite, and that's all I expected I would do tonight.

Now, though, I'm thinking this event is going to be a whole lot more fun—thanks to Mister Dreamy Brown Eyes, who makes no bones about trying to charm my ass off.

A hunk of man in a tailored suit who's quick with his tongue? Let me order a double.

He's precisely what I've been craving. I am done with bores and through with nitwits who can't hold a conversation.

As we exit the limo, I set a hand on Harlan's hard-as-iron bicep. "Nice guns," I tell him as we walk to the swank entrance of the hotel overlooking the Pacific Ocean.

"Thanks. I had them polished today at the gym."

I squeeze harder. I do love a firm body. "Well, I'd like to feel these arms when I take a spin on the dance floor with you."

He flashes a megawatt smile at me as we head into the lobby. "Be my guest. I will be counting down the minutes until that dance."

"Same here."

He leans in close, dusts a kiss onto my cheek, and whispers, "I'll save you twenty, sweetheart."

My heart flutters. And so do my lady parts. His voice, his kiss, his body—his confidence. I do like a man who knows his mind and uses his mouth.

It's been ages since I've had a decent date. My social life has fallen by the wayside these past few months while my sister and I have worked on our secret business plans. I've been mega busy juggling a day job and a burgeoning side hustle. Mornings and evenings, I grab any chance to teach extra yoga classes.

That means activities in the man department have been few and far between. The handful of dates I've snagged recently have been snooze-worthy.

Maybe that can change now.

Though, I don't have much time for flirting. My sister's flying up from Los Angeles tonight, and her plane gets in at eleven. But that still leaves a window for a dance or two. This gal will take what she can get.

Harlan turns into the row of seats, and I shamelessly check out his ass as he walks. There is just something about a man in a tailored suit, especially a man with a great butt. A butt I want to hold onto.

Stop, Katie Madigan, stop. You can't think filthy thoughts in front of a preacher.

Unless that's a justice of the peace up there, which I'm pretty sure it is. So, it's totally permissible to be a bad girl. JPs don't mind dirty minds during a wedding ceremony.

Harlan grabs a seat, then Jones sits next to him, then Jillian, and finally, I flank my bestie.

We settle in, and when Pachelbel's Canon in D Major begins, my heart rises to my throat.

Memories of other weddings claw their way to the front of my mind, and I force them away.

Stay present.

Focus on the here and now.

I zoom in on the bride and groom, though I hardly know them. They're Jillian's colleagues, and I'm simply her plus-one. Still, when the groom promises to love his bride so long as they both shall live, I choke up.

Ugh, emotions, you bedevil me.

I root around in my purse, hunting for a tissue. I dab my eyes, then steal a glance at Jillian. Even through the silky black hair curtaining her face, I see she's biting her bottom lip, holding in a tear or two, I bet.

I offer a few tissues, which she takes, mouthing, *thank you*, then swiping her cheeks.

Once the happy couple exchanges their *I dos* and their first married kiss, we stand and clap. They walk down the aisle, hands clasped, gazing all lovey-dovey at each other.

What would it take to get to that place where you know you want to be with someone forever and ever? I can't picture it. Didn't see anything remotely like that while I was growing up.

When the bride and groom leave the ballroom, I grab Jillian's arm and squeeze. "Thank you for making me your date. I don't know a thing about those two, but I'm so stinking happy for them," I say with genuine emotion.

"Me too. Weddings get to me," she whispers, then her eyes stray to Jones.

I squeeze her arm harder. "Maybe your guy gets to you," I tease under my breath.

She swats my arm. "Stop knowing me too well."

I shrug happily. "Can't help it. It's our curse and our blessing as besties." I tip my forehead to the exit. "Let's get you to the reception so you and Jones can play footsie under the table."

She arches a brow. "And maybe you and the running back?"

"Ha. Let's focus on you."

My first job tonight is to be her wingwoman. And my job as her friend is to deliver my message.

Once we make our way to the reception, I hunt for my opportunity. I've watched Jillian fall for this guy over the summer and into the football season, and he damn well better know exactly what he's got on his hands.

A prize.

When the dancing begins, I motion for Harlan to come closer so I can whisper in his ear.

"Hey, there," he says as he sheds his suit jacket, tossing it on the back of his chair. "You ready to cut a rug, sweetheart?"

"Not quite. But soon. First, though, I need to chat with Jones—and you're going to help me."

"Hit me up," he says, rolling up the sleeves of his dress shirt. His forearms—his strong, muscular forearms—are a little distracting.

Fuck, they're *a lot* distracting.

But I soldier on. "Make some magic happen for me on the dance floor. You take Jillian for a whirl, and I'll grab her guy, since I need a quick chat. And then you and I can dance together to our hearts' content."

"Whatever the lady wants," he tells me, his eyes traveling down my body, then back up, "the lady shall get."

"Are you mentally undressing me?" I ask, feeling quite bold.

"Seems I was," he says, unrepentant and confident as hell. "What do you know?" With a wink at me, he moves over to Jones and whispers something, nodding my way. Then they switch places, Harlan asking Jillian for a dance and Jones locking eyes with me.

"May I have this dance, Katie?"

"You absolutely may." We step onto the parquet floor, and I set my hands chastely on his shoulders as we sway to an Adele tune. "I was hoping to chat with you."

His eyebrows shoot into his hairline. "Let's talk, then."

Jillian is head-over-heels crazy for Jones, and she's about to go out on a limb for him career-wise. I need to make sure he's the kind of man who will treat her like a queen. "Listen," I begin. "I'm a ride-or-die kind of gal. I've known Jillian since college, and she's my girl. I've got her back anytime she needs it. You know what that means, Jones?"

"Means I don't want to run into you in a dark alley?"

I flash a big Texas smile. "You got that right, partner," I say, slipping in a touch of my once-upon-a-time Texas twang.

"I hear ya, boss." Despite our slip into comic stereotype, Jones gives a crisp nod of understanding.

"You better treat her well," I add.

Seeming earnest enough, he answers, "I will."

But I'm taking no chances. "I mean it. If she risks her job and her reputation for this romance, do not let her down. I know that you're a foot taller than I am and probably a hundred fifty pounds heavier, but I don't care. I will kick you in the balls if you hurt her."

He flinches. "Damn."

"Exactly." Jones seems like a good guy, but I am not messing around when it comes to my friend. "She is the best person I know, and she prizes honesty and integrity. If you make a play for her, it had better be for real. You better put your whole heart into it." I hold his eye with a knife's-edge look and flint in my voice. "Or you will answer to me and my steel-toed cowboy boots."

Jones meets my gaze without flinching, intensely serious. "You will never need to break those out with me." Then he nods in a that-explains-a-lot way. "I can see why you're her best friend."

"Then we have an understanding." I let go as the song ends,

stepping back to swipe one palm across the other. "That's done. Good luck with the game this weekend. I will be rooting my ass off for the Renegades like I always do."

Before Jones can reply, his handsome friend taps his shoulder, but Harlan's oh-so-charming smile is aimed at me. "Hope you don't mind me interrupting, buddy, but the lady and I have twenty dances to work through, and I'd like to start right now."

I'd like that too. My night will end far too soon, and I want to make the best of the next few hours.

CHAPTER 3

KATIE

Goodbye, Jones. Hello, Harlan.

"Let's see what your quicksilver feet can do," I say, and Harlan moves right in, sets his hands on my waist, and dips me.

I am going to have so much fun with this hottie.

From his million-dollar smile, to his lush, golden-brown hair, to his dreamy eyes, the man has heartbreaker written all over him.

And that's fine by me, since my heart isn't on the table.

"So, what sort of dancing are we talking about?" I ask. "Do you dance like *Magic Mike*?"

He tugs playfully at his tie, jutting out his hip à la dirty dancer. "If that's what you're looking for, Katie. I'm more than happy to offer you a lap dance."

The way he says that—a soft Georgia lilt returning to his voice once more—makes my skin tingle. Yes, he could definitely strip down for me in private sometime.

But just so I don't melt into a puddle on the dance floor, I turn up the tease. "But maybe I want you to do the polka."

On cue, he steps to the left.

I step to the right a half-second later, and we both do a hop. A few more impromptu polka steps and I'm laughing too hard to continue. "I'll admit, I did not expect you to know such an old-fashioned dance."

"You underestimate me, Katie. Go ahead, try another," he challenges. "Dance-stump me."

I can play this game. "Fox trot."

Harlan steps forward; I step back. I'm breathless with laughter again.

"My turn now?" he asks, all rumbly sexy.

"I did get two requests. Seems only fair to give you one."

"Then we need to tango." Harlan hauls me in close and with my hand in his, thrusts our arms out to the side.

No wonder this is the sexiest dance ever. You have to press your chest up against a hot man. Let's tango all night long.

We dance deliciously close for a minute on the edge of the dance floor. I like the feel of his firm body very much. "All right. I'll bite. Where did you learn to dance like that?"

"Chippendales," he says as we settle into a casual slow dance sway.

"You moonlight at a dance club? Is that after your football games?"

He winks. "'Course it is."

"Ha. Somehow, I doubt it," I say. "Even with your smooth moves."

Harlan smiles, runs a finger down my nose. "I'm from Georgia. A cotillion is mandatory."

"Aha. The Southern charm explained," I say, moving under the twinkling lights as the DJ cross-fades into "Never Tear Us Apart."

"I dip into the accent now and again for fun. I've been on the West Coast for many years, but I ham it up with the guys and lay it on thick at practice, so they can all bust my chops about my supposed *Southern drawl*."

I flash a grin. "Better watch out or you might lose the chance to dip into the sound for...*fun* all together."

He feigns shock. "Whatever will I do without my Atlanta charm?"

I shrug helplessly. "You'll just have to switch to San Francisco charm. Speaking of, how long have you lived here? You've been with the team for six years."

He arches a brow, impressed or perhaps appreciative that I know that about him. "I have indeed. Before then I went to college in Washington."

"A Husky?"

"Go dawgs," he says.

"So, you've been out of the South and accent-free for quite some time now."

"I have—ten years, to be precise—but when I'm with my sisters and Mom I sound all peachy again," he says.

"And I probably sound like a...bluebonnet," I say, sliding into the accent I lost long ago.

Harlan blinks, pulls back. "Whoa. I'd never have known you were from the Lone Star State."

"Born and raised, but truth be told, we moved to California when I started high school. Though, you can never entirely take the Texas out of the girl."

"And who'd want to? Your personality is as big as that state," he says.

"You have a line for everything, don't you?"

"Hey, now. Who said it was a line, sweetheart? I like your sass, and I like talking to you."

He's too much, but I'm completely taken by that, especially when my last three dates were so very, very lacking in…everything that Harlan has. The most recent guy explained, in depth, the ins and outs of his job manufacturing windows. The man before that waxed on about his favorite episodes of *Barney Miller*, and his predecessor debated the whole time whether his ex-girlfriend was a bitch, a big bitch, or the biggest bitch.

So, over-the-top or not, Harlan is galaxies better. "Fine, fine." I fake a grudging admission. "I don't mind chatting with you either."

"Good. Now here's something I want to know." He curls his hands tighter around my hips, a move that sends a zing through me. "Hypothetical situation. You walk into a trendy ice cream shop. You have to pick one of two flavors based only on the name. Are you getting a pint of Swoon or Sexual Tension Swirl?"

A laugh bursts from me as I rest my palms on his big shoulders. "That's easy. I'll get a double scoop, one of each."

With dark eyes that glimmer with heat, he gives me an approving nod. "A woman after my own heart."

"Oh. Your heart thinks a lot about ice cream?"

Letting go of my hips, Harlan spins me in a dizzying circle, then yanks me close against his big wall of a chest. "It thinks a lot about a lot of things."

He slides a hand up my back, and I can't even fashion a comeback. That strong hand feels so good.

And it hasn't just been a while since I've had a good date. It's been a while since…well, a lot of things.

I generally try not to think with my libido, but my libido is pounding its fists and pitching a fit, wanting to take the wheel. When his fingertips coast across a sliver of bare skin near my spine, I shiver, and a breathless, wordless whisper stutters over my lips.

He's quiet for perhaps the first time. A few seconds later, he lowers his voice to a husky murmur. "And what does *your* heart dwell on, Katie?"

I try to think beyond the pleasure racing over my skin. "Dancing," I answer low as I brush my fingers over his shoulders, indulging myself in touching him, just like he's doing with me. "I believe in fashion, friends, family, and…flirting."

His eyes never stray from mine, and they're full of daring. "Tonight, you shall have that last one till your cup runneth over."

That sounds like a pretty good deal.

What's not good is that it's past nine and I'll have to take off at ten thirty. I can't change the countdown, so I vow to make the most of dancing and flirting with this man.

We stay on the floor for another few songs, talking and flirting, then he hooks his thumb toward the bar. "Glass of champagne to quench your thirst?"

"I'm in."

We make our way to the bar, passing a terrace overlooking the sea. Everything from the sparkling lights to the swoony music to the ocean waves crashing in the distance makes this night feel like it could go on forever.

But it can't.

CHAPTER 4

HARLAN

With champagne flutes in hand, we head to the balcony—alone. It's deserted out here, and I'm over the moon because I'm eager to gobble up more time with her then find the perfect moment for a kiss.

After that, I'm hoping we can kick it up more than a few notches at my place or hers. I've got a feeling Katie is game for that too.

I clink my glass to hers. "To weddings."

"To wedding kisses," she adds.

Yup. Perfect night.

I take a drink and she does too. We set our glasses on the terrace wall at the same moment, then she puts her pink purse next to them.

"You truly can't beat this view," she declares as she gazes at the ocean. "I'll miss San Francisco."

"Wait. Hold on. Are you leaving the city?"

Quickly, she shakes her head. "I mean *if* I leave. I'd miss it. That's what I meant to say."

I arch a dubious brow. "Are you sure? Are you Cinderella, planning to take off at the stroke of midnight?"

She laughs, a buoyant sound that kind of turns me on. "I promise I'll leave behind a glass slipper if I do."

My eyes coast down to her shoes. "They're silver, Katie. Not quite glass."

"But close enough?" she asks, like she's hoping the answer is yes.

"Do you want to be Cinderella?"

"I have no desire to be in a fairy tale." Her eyes flicker with hints of naughtiness. Or maybe I'm just seeing my own wishes reflected back. "Unless…it's the dirty kind."

Ah, and naughty hope wins the night. I step closer, brushing her hair off her shoulder. She trembles, and I don't think it's from the night air. "And now we're talking the same language."

I savor the anticipation in this moment.

The moment *before.*

There is little I love more than teasing a woman, than drawing out the high of expectation.

I play with her hair, running the strands through my fingers, then dart my thumb to her cheek, stroking a soft line across her jaw.

She breathes a shuddery sigh, and I inch closer but still don't touch. I wait, staring at those glossy pink lips.

Katie lifts her chin slightly. "My language says kiss me. What does yours say?"

I slide my palm over her shoulder, then down her bare arm.

Goose bumps rise in its wake. "Same, but a gentleman should ask, Katie," I say. "May I kiss you?"

"Get your lips on mine."

"You're my kind of woman," I tell her, then I shut the fuck up. I close my eyes and brush my lips across hers.

A jolt of pleasure slides down my spine as I taste her—lip gloss and sweetness and a hint of champagne.

Sugar and sparkles.

So damn fitting.

I start slow, exploring her lips with a gentle sweep of mine, letting the moment expand, enjoying every sensation—from the hitch in her breath, to the jut of her hips, to her soft hands traveling up my chest.

I cup her cheek, running my thumb along her face, then I thread my hands into her hair. Soft strands slide through my fingers as I flick my tongue across the seam of her mouth, pressing a little harder.

She parts her lips, inviting me in.

Her eager hands fall to my hips, and in one swift move, she jerks me against her.

Yes, ma'am.

Wrapping a hand around the back of her head, I draw her lips close and her body closer. As we kiss, my other hand skims down her back to her ass.

I squeeze, savoring the handful of flesh.

This full-body kiss causes my bones to hum. She makes the sexiest sounds—little murmurs and sighs as our tongues get to know each other. Katie kisses like she talks—flirty, fiery, and full of sass. She doesn't simply relax as I take the lead. She kisses back all hard and rough, and I love it. Love it even more when she draws my bottom lip between hers, then nips me.

It's like a zap of pleasure.

We break apart for a second. "Do I have a biter in my arms?" I ask.

Her eyes blaze with a *yes*. "Maybe a little. Promise I won't hurt you, Harlan," she says, a little coy.

"Maybe I like a little hurt. A nibble here or there would do the trick."

She tests me by running her lips along my jaw, then nipping. A sizzle of pleasure shoots through me.

"Oh yes," I rasp as I grab her ass harder.

With a throaty purr, her lips journey up my neck, peppering me with hungry kisses. When she reaches my ear, she nips on the lobe, then lets out a little roar like a lioness.

I believe I have met my match.

She's the fire to my fire. I want all her passion, and I want to give her every ounce of mine.

I let go, back her up against the terrace edge, and meet her heated gaze. "You like it the same way, sweetheart?" I ask, my voice low and smoky.

"Seems I do," she says, reaching her hands around my neck, playing with the ends of my hair as I crowd her against the stone railing, my whole frame lined up with hers.

So she can feel me.

Know how aroused I am.

Experience what she's done to me.

I slide my hands down her sides, savoring her curves—enjoying, too, the wild look in her eyes as I touch her body. She shudders, and the sound urges me on. I drop my lips to the hollow of her throat where I can lick, kiss, suck. As I move along her sweet-and-spicy skin to her collarbone, I graze my teeth over her flesh.

"Ohhhh," she says on a shiver, trembling in my arms.

I nip a little harder, push my pelvis against her, meeting her move for move, moan for moan, giving as good as she gave.

Tit for tat.

Speaking of…

Letting go of her hip, I roam a hand upward over the pink silk, then up a little higher, then higher still.

Katie gasps—a needy, sexy sound.

A lovely plea inviting me to indulge.

So I do, cupping a breast, filling my hand. I squeeze, and she lets go of my mouth, tosses her head back, and moans against the night, "*You.*"

Indeed.

I'll take that as a compliment, thank you very much.

But I want more. I want to please this woman to the stars and back. It's my kink, my passion, my pleasure. *Giving.*

"Katie, tell me what you want to do tonight," I murmur. I don't want to lead her into temptation. I want her to find it from within.

She pouts. "I want you to take me home, spread me out on my bed, and do dirty things to me all night long."

Yes, there is a God.

"Taxi," I say, then bring my fingers to my lips like I'm about to whistle for one.

"But…"

That word is the door slamming on all my wedding fantasies. "Aww, why does there have to be a 'but' when I want to deliver everything you want?"

She smiles softly, but sadly too. "I have to leave soon. My sister, Olive, is flying in tonight, and I need to pick her up in an hour. We have a meeting tomorrow morning for a new business venture."

That sounds exciting.

And thoroughly cock-blocking.

But if I've learned one thing playing pro ball, it's that the play doesn't always go the way you planned. Sometimes your quarterback hands off so you can run with the ball. Sometimes he calls an audible and passes. Your success depends on how quickly you react to the action on the field.

"Let's see, then," I say, because I can react damn quickly. "It's Thursday night now. I'm on game lockdown Friday through Sunday. I have a sponsor event Monday night. How's Tuesday?"

She blinks, taking a second to catch up to my question. But she quickly does, and her blue eyes twinkle.

To be sure, though, I add, "By 'Tuesday,' I mean I'm asking you on a date. I want to take you out on the town. Have a good time with you. Then do to you all those decadent things that are racing through my head right now."

Katie's nimble fingers make their way up my tie. She tugs,

yanking me closer. "Tell me *one* naughty thing. Wait. Hold on. Tell me where you're going to take me out first," she says, letting go of my tie to run her palms down my chest, covering my pecs. "Then you can tell me something deliciously dirty."

Oh, I like the way her mind works. She knows her worth.

My fingers wander across her stomach, making playful circles as I answer. "I bet you'd like to do something a little competitive, a little showy."

Her eyebrows rise. "I'm showy? You think I'm showy?"

"I sure do, and I think it's sexy as hell. Now, let me finish, woman."

She rolls her eyes. "Fine, fine. Finish."

I tap my chin like I'm deep in thought. "I could take you out bowling, ballroom dancing, or to play my second-favorite sport."

"Sex is your second-favorite sport?" She bats her lashes ever so innocently.

I toss my head back, laughing. "Sweetheart, sex is not a sport. For it to be a sport, it would require rules, regulations, and competition. And sex should never be a competition."

"What is it, then?"

I don't answer right away, but shoot her a sly, knowing grin. Then I speak the truth from the bottom of my heart...and cock. "Sex is a *devotion*, ideally to the woman's pleasure."

She murmurs her approval. "Ultimate Charmer. That's you."

"I will wear that title with pride. Now, as I was saying, my second-favorite sport. Want to know what that is?"

"You know I do."

"It's only one letter different from the one I play for a living…" I trail off, eager to see how quickly she'll figure it out.

She furrows her brow, and then one, two seconds, later, her eyes pop. "Foosball! I love foosball." She pokes my chest. "Bowling and foosball, pretty please. Then…*devotion*," she says, all low and seductive, like a phone sex operator.

"Tuesday night, Katie. It is on." I haul her in for another hot, passionate kiss, and we seal our plans for the best kind of date. I swallow her sighs, devouring her sounds.

Maybe I'm a player. Maybe I came here tonight with my one-track mind on a mission. And yes, I desperately want to get Katie naked and writhing under me, but I'm also having a fantastic time talking to her.

I've got a feeling with her, one I've never had before.

A feeling that there's something brewing.

Something that sparks with fresh and daring possibilities.

But tonight, the clock is ticking, so I break the kiss. "When do you need to go, sweetheart?"

She reaches for her purse from the wall, clicks it open, and takes out her phone. "I should leave in fifteen minutes." Her blue irises flicker with mischief. "You know, there's a lot we can do in fifteen minutes."

How did I get so lucky and this woman so amazing?

I must have been a very good boy in a past life.

CHAPTER 5

HARLAN

One minute later, we're in the bathroom.

It's one of those classy hotel bathrooms. Only one stall, with its own tiny lounge area with a carpet and mirror. Katie closes the door with a quiet snick, then locks it, pressing a finger to her lips. "Shhh."

"Not sure I can be quiet," I tease as she sets her purse on the counter.

"You better be, Harlan," she whispers. "If word gets out that you're the one getting blown at the sports reporter's wedding..."

Yup. Past me was clearly a choirboy. An angel, even.

But hold on.

"Wait. What if I want to make you see stars?" That's my playbook. Give a woman pleasure. Then do it again, and again, and again. A man shouldn't even think about coming until she's ridden to the moon and back three times. Minimum.

That's just polite.

"You can save that for Tuesday, big guy." There's nothing unclear about her intention when she undoes my belt, wiggles a brow, and licks her lips lasciviously. "I know what I like. And when I felt you press this fantastic hard-on against me earlier, I kept imagining what you'd taste like. Will that work for you?"

My brain goes haywire.

Yup.

Officially, it's one hundred percent nuts up there. All the circuits are frying, all the lights flashing and the sparks flying.

"But I want to make you feel good," I say. Only, it's a feeble protest because, holy hell—I don't think it's in my DNA to turn down a blow job from a gorgeous woman, no matter how badly I want to give her O after O. Not after she unzips my slacks, then sinks to the floor. "Well. Happy Thursday to me, then."

"That's the idea." The blond beauty gazes up at me with sex in her eyes and dirty deeds on her parted lips.

"Oh, sweetheart. You look so fucking good on your knees."

"I feel good on my knees too," she says, tugging down my black boxer briefs. My cock springs free.

Katie's eyes pop like she just got everything she wanted for her birthday. I'm certainly glad she seems to think so, because I'd like her to gift wrap my dick with her mouth, lips, and tongue.

"Mmmm. You're like hard candy." She wraps a soft hand around the base. A quick burst of pleasure pulses through my body as she squeezes and strokes.

"I hope you like your candy good and long," I tell her.

"Very, very long," she says, pumping my cock in her fist, wasting no time.

She dips her face to my dick and sucks the head between her lips. My blood surges. My fingers weave through her silky blond hair while she flicks her tongue along my dick and pulls me deeper into her decadent mouth.

"Can it be Tuesday right now? Because I want this again," I whisper, my voice already rough with lust.

My legs shake as Katie smiles wickedly up at me, the wild look in her eyes saying she wants this as much as I do.

That she relishes *giving*.

It's official. I have met my match.

"Your mouth is incredible," I murmur, electricity crackling along my nerve endings.

The sight before me is out of this world.

Sure, I left my home tonight a hopeful motherfucker, but I didn't imagine a beautiful, fun, feisty woman would haul me into a bathroom and take me to town with her throat.

This is one helluva night, even for a guy who likes to have his fun.

And that's me.

I'm the player.

The good-time guy.

I don't lie, I don't lead women on, and I don't hide where I stand. And right now, I'm standing with my pants at my thighs while the most captivating woman I've met in ages worships my dick and blows my mind too.

And yet I'm also pretty sure something new is happening. Already, I'm positive I want more than one date with her.

Maybe even more than a handful.

With Katie, I could maybe see many wild nights like this, nights when I'm not a player at all. But as she flicks her tongue along my shaft, I lose my focus on the future. I am only interested in the here and now. "Fuck, yes. Won't take me long, sweetheart," I rasp out.

In a second, she sucks harder, deeper, with the fervor of a zealot.

I succumb to the build. To the bliss barreling down my body. The delicious swirl of an orgasm that's not far off.

But the gentleman hasn't left the building entirely. "Just want to warn you. In case you don't want to swallow," I mutter.

She hoovers.

Holy hell.

My toes curl in my shoes as she sucks even more intensely, the head of my dick hitting her throat.

My brain jumps into sexual overdrive.

I rock my hips, losing myself in the caress of her tight, hot lips. My climax pulls me under. I shudder, ecstasy wracking my body as I come hard in her mouth.

The world around me blurs. "Yes, fucking yes!" I grunt.

I nearly black out from the crush of pleasure. I sink against the wall, savoring the aftershocks.

A few seconds later, she's standing, smiling, looking more than satisfied. I open my eyes, reach for her, and bring her close.

"So, was that good?" she asks, a little nervous, hopeful too.

Is she for real? Does she not know? "Katie, that was Christmas cookies and a Vegas jackpot and a fourth-down, game-winning touchdown all on the same night. I want to get naked and explore your gorgeous body with my tongue and fingers and cock so badly, I would do just about anything to delay your sister's flight." I make a flourishing gesture, flicking an invisible magic wand. "Abracadabra."

She sighs with a smile, which is the best way to sigh.

Wait. Second best. Sexy sighs while kissing are the first.

Her baby blues sparkle. "Can you? Delay her flight an hour?" Then she holds up her hand, changing her mind. "Wait. Nope. Don't. I don't want to rush sex with you. I want to bask in it. I feel like I could be very greedy in bed with you, Harlan."

I rub my thumb along her lower lip. "You should be greedy in bed. I want you to be." I glance at the clock on the wall. "That took seven minutes, start to finish. How about we see how good my skills are?"

Her lips part, and her eyebrows rise dubiously. "I'm going to let you in on a little secret. I kind of take a while."

I can't resist.

In a flash, we've swapped places and I press her back against the wall. "Challenge accepted."

The countdown is on.

CHAPTER 6

KATIE

For the record, I didn't come to the wedding to, well, come.

But I won't turn down a chance at an O from a hottie.

Especially since I have a theory. The better the kisser, the better the kisser. The man's lips already drove my mouth wild. I can only imagine what he could do between my thighs.

Trouble is, I need to be lying down, naked on a bed, thrashing around. I know myself. I like my oral sex, and I like to enjoy every second of it. It's not bad standing, but it's much better when I can get all the way into it while horizontal.

So when Harlan kneels, I grab his hand and tug the big guy back up. "Let's save that," I tell him.

He taps his temple. "Tuesday night. Ten p.m. Go down on Katie for a full hour of pussy worship. There. It's on my calendar." He presses against me, hikes up my skirt, and cups the lacy panel of my panties, making me shiver. "And this is on my agenda right now."

A tingle pulses between my legs as he pulls my panties to the side. The tingle morphs into a tremor of pleasure as he strokes my wetness.

"Oh, sweetheart, you're so ready to come," he rasps.

He's not wrong.

In seconds, I'm moaning under his touch, gasping as his fingers glide across my pussy.

I do my best to be quiet, to keep my sounds and murmurs all to myself.

But Harlan is just what I need.

He's the antidote to my busy days and nights.

He's the opposite of my dating life.

Interesting, confident, entertaining—he's a bright, shining star in a dimly lit night sky.

Hot sex with a handsome stranger who's hardly a stranger?

Yes, please.

The man's hands are masterful. Long, strong fingers stroke me, teasing at my clit, rubbing in tantalizing circles.

Ohhhhh.

So good.

Yesssss.

I don't have to help things along with a finger on the pink button. This man knows his way around my body. Everything he's doing is just right—so right that I'm vibrating with pleasure.

I grab hold of his arms, clasping his big biceps. "I'm so close," I whisper, squeezing my eyes shut as his fingers fly.

A shudder speeds through my body on a breakaway sprint. My

orgasm has a mind of its own, building strength, intensity, then…
exploding in one delicious, mind-bending frenzy of bliss.

I cry out, but before more words escape, his lips are on mine.
He swallows my cries, keeping me quiet as he kisses me through the
wild spread of pleasure.

As my orgasm ebbs, I open my eyes, woozy and sex drunk, then
meet his gaze.

He's smiling, looking satisfied and happy.

Harlan drops another kiss to my lips, all soft and sweet. "Thank
you for giving me the best fifteen minutes I've had in ages."

I grab my lip gloss and reapply it. "Those fifteen minutes were
pretty darn good for me too."

Harlan walks me to the hotel lobby, standing outside with me while
I wait for my Lyft.

We're quiet until he reaches for my hand. "I can't wait to see
you again. I want you to know how much I'm looking forward to
getting to know you."

The feeling is so very mutual. Sure, Harlan's a playboy, if I
believe the media and gossip blogs. And yes, I've seen pics of him
with beautiful women. But I'm not bothered. Why wouldn't he
enjoy the perks of his fame? A gorgeous, talented pro athlete beloved
by the city? He's not hurting for offers from the fairer sex.

Good for him.

And now, good for me. I can handle whatever *this* is, whether
it's a date or a prelude to sex.

"Me too," I say.

Though, a tiny part of me is curious if he'd be interested in more. Maybe another date, maybe seeing what comes of it?

A pang in my heart is hungry for a little something more.

I wince.

"What's wrong, sweetheart?" Legitimate concern imbues his tone.

It's so real, so tender, and I like it so much. Perhaps he also feels all this yummy possibility.

"Nothing," I say with a smile. "Just had a good time tonight."

"Me too," he says, grinning back, then he brings me close again, tucks my hair around my ear. "I mean that. And I truly do want to see you again. We're going to have a great time."

"We are absolutely going to."

A red Nissan pulls up. As I check the plates, Harlan says, "Give me your number."

Quickly, we exchange digits, and then he kisses me goodnight, and puts me in the car. The driver pulls away. Already, I miss Harlan.

I don't have room in my life for more, and yet I just might want it.

As the driver pulls onto 19th Avenue, making his way to the airport, my phone beeps.

I expect it to be my sister. But it's Harlan.

Harlan: Call me crazy, but that was the best unexpected first date I've had in ages.

It's like he can read my mind.

Katie: Me too.

Harlan: Also, I have your lip gloss. You left it behind. And it's in a glass tube. Fitting, Cinderella.

I grin like an idiot.

Katie: Tonight was kind of like a dirty fairy tale.

Harlan: It sure was, sweetheart. Let's turn those pages some more.

I can't get Harlan out of my mind, but I have to the next day when my sister and I meet with a potential business partner about our yoga studio and the new style of classes that we've brainstormed.

It's an incredible meeting, and now I'm feeling all kinds of fairy-tale-ish—in business and in romance.

Everything seems possible.

CHAPTER 7

HARLAN

The best night ever is followed by a great weekend.

Texting with Katie.

Flirting with Katie.

Winning a football game.

Making plans for Tuesday.

I'm not in the market for a relationship, but there was something about her that was impossible to ignore. A spark. A possibility.

A connection I want to explore.

I haven't felt this in a long time with anyone.

When I leave the field on Sunday and head home, I'm ready to crash, but I send her a text first.

Harlan: Still can't wait to see you.

An hour later, she replies.

Katie: I can't wait to see you too. But I can't make our date this Tuesday. The business partner wants to fly us both to Los Angeles to look at possible studio space there. She loved the classes that we've planned.

Harlan: That's fantastic news! And no worries, sweetheart. You let me know when you can reschedule.

Katie: I promise, sexy man. I need that lip gloss. Need you to mess it up for me.

Harlan: And I will. We'll have that double scoop of Sexual Tension Swirl and Swoon.

Katie: *licks lips in anticipation*

A couple nights later, another text lands on my phone.

Katie: Sooooo...the business partner made us a crazy-amazing offer...the kind of offer that sweeps every other plan off the drawing board. This is last minute, but I'm mov-ing to LA. *This weekend.* Rain check sometime?

Whoa.

Harlan: *Moving* moving? As in moving to LA...now?

But even as I send the text, I know the answer. She's made it clear, although I still can't quite believe it.

42

Katie: Yes! I'm excited, but I'll miss our date, and you. We have to do a rain check.

My shoulders sag, and I sigh. The sad kind. But what can you do?

Harlan: Definitely.

I don't hear from her again, but that's okay. It was one night. I don't text her, either, because there's no point. Nor does she text me. But I hear from Jones and Jillian that she's happy in Los Angeles, building her yoga empire with her sister.

So it goes. Sometimes you have one perfect night, and that's all.

And sometimes you meet again more than seven years later.

The next time I see Katie, I'm a single dad with a six-year-old daughter, and it's Katie's wedding day.

CHAPTER 8

KATIE

PRESENT DAY

I wasn't one of those girls who imagined her wedding day from the time she was small.

Or at any time.

I didn't fantasize about walking down the aisle and into the arms of the Prince Charming of my dreams.

No way.

For one, I was agnostic about the existence of Prince Charming. And two, I was emphatically atheistic about princesses.

Didn't believe in being one, acting like one, or becoming one.

When I was growing up, my dreams were pragmatic—make friends, be awesome, and kick unholy ass.

I blame my dad.

He instilled in me a belief that I could do anything I set out to if I used my brain and heart.

Getting married was never on my vision board.

But today I am *that* person.

It's my wedding day, and I just can't wait to say *I do*. Hell, I've been floating on air since Silvio proposed four months ago, after two mere months of dating.

"Fair warning. You three are going to have to stop me from running across the lawn and into Silvio's arms," I say to my crew as we get ready, my hairstylist working on my updo.

"Ah, so you're going to be one of *those* brides," Emerson quips as she fishes in her makeup bag in the suite at the Legion of Honor, where I'll be doing the aforementioned forty-yard dash into my tall, dark, and handsome groom's arms.

I smile, owning it. "Yup. It's going to be so cheesy, but so romantic, and none of you will be able to stop me. In fact, you'll all melt into puddles of swoon," I say.

Ever so briefly, a memory rushes over me.

A pint of Swoon.

But I push away the imaginary ice cream flavor. It's bad form to think of past men on your wedding day, even for a second. And why would I when my main man might as well have stepped straight out of Central Casting and into the role of my Romeo?

My heart flutters.

I'm getting married.

The girl who never fantasized about dresses or *I dos* is ready to skip to her guy in about an hour.

Hold me back, world.

As my stylist clips the sides of my hair into a silver barrette, I can't stop smiling stupidly at my reflection in the mirror. Karissa surveys my peeps—Jillian is perched on the couch; my sister, Olive, sits on the desk; and Emerson stands next to her, still sorting through a makeup bag. Skyler ran out to refill a water bottle, but she should be back soon.

"Say the word, and I'll arm wrestle Katie till she stops waxing on about her groom," Karissa says to my friends.

Jillian taps her chin, deep in thought. "I'm tempted simply because of the arm-wrestling match."

I pinch Karissa's toned biceps. "She'd win. She's got Gal Gadot arms."

"I moonlight as Wonder Woman," Karissa says as she runs a flat iron over one of my blond curls. My hair has darkened a bit over the years. It was bright blond when I was younger, golden in my twenties, and now it's heading into a dark blond palette. Seems fitting—I still feel perky and bold, but stronger, surer of myself, and maybe a touch more vulnerable too. Time has done its thing. So, letting my natural color shine through fits who I've become in my mid-thirties and who I want to keep being—the best me possible.

"But seriously, I am so happy for you I could cry rainbows," Karissa says as she squeezes my shoulder. "You're going to be the most gorgeous bride in all of San Francisco. I swear, Silvio won't know what hit him."

"I don't know what hit *me*." I lean back in the chair, catching Emerson's knowing look as our eyes meet in the mirror.

"What hit you is a smoking-hot Italian artist who's a real-life Romeo," my good friend says. Her smile tells me she's thrilled for me. She has been since he swept me off my feet the night I met him—New Year's Eve.

Jillian straightens her shoulders, tucking strands of silky black hair over her ear. "And who treats you like the goddess you are."

"And who's almost too good to be true," Olive chimes in as she ties a bow around a bouquet of sunflowers. She holds it up for praise. "What do you think? Maybe if the whole numbers thing doesn't work out, I could become a florist."

"Hey! Don't panic the bride on her wedding day," I say, only part joking. "I need my numbers wunderkind."

"I would never abandon Sassy Yoga," she replies and ties the twine in a bow just so. She can't help herself. She has a penchant for crafts. "But if I was to start a floristry side hustle, I would never sell sunflowers. They kind of stink."

"Mom begged me to have them," I say with a shrug. "She said they'd be perfect, and pretty much got down on her hands and knees. It was easier to let her have her way than to argue. I'm not a big flower person, anyway."

"You're a tiger lily," Emerson announces. "That's what you should have."

"Thanks. I'll have tiger lilies at my next wedding," I deadpan.

Emerson crosses the suite, stops in front of Jillian, then swipes the brush down my college bestie's nose. Emerson taught herself classy wedding makeup through YouTube tutorials. No surprise— she loves YouTube.

47

And I love my friends.

This is my dream come true. A pack of women. Good friends through thick and thin.

"I'm so glad you're all here," I tell them, love and happiness rising to bring a shine to my eyes.

"You say that like we'd be anyplace else," Olive quips, adding a *ta-da* when she finishes another bow.

"Well, you have to be here. You're family," I say to her.

"So's Mom, technically, but I'd say she doesn't *have* to be here." Olive laughs drily.

"C'mon, you know she can't resist a wedding," I tease.

"Who can't?"

I tense everywhere as my mom's voice carries across the suite. Is she a freaking cat? I didn't even hear her enter. But now she saunters in, head held high, clasping a pretty white ribbon and a garment bag, which I presume holds her mother-of-the-bride dress.

I hope she didn't hear me. She'll go full drama llama, tears and all.

"No single *she* in the universe can resist a wedding." Olive jumps in, and I could kiss her for taking that grenade for me. If my mom knew I'd thrown shade on her love of weddings, she'd fling a hand on her chest, fall to the floor in a fit of tears, and demand to know what she'd done wrong.

I can't. Not today.

She hangs the garment bag on the hook on the door. "I love weddings. I just do," Mom says with a dramatic sigh, and maybe she's why I never imagined my own nuptials growing up. I witnessed too many of hers.

But this is not the day to think about her four failed marriages.

Today I will zoom in on my *one* marriage, and the only wedding I plan to have.

My mom crosses the carpeted floor, her dyed red hair styled in a stunning updo, clearly professionally done. She flicks a hand lightly against a few wisps, drawing attention, silently fishing for compliments.

"You look great," I assure her.

"Thanks. The mother of the bride should look stunning."

Olive rolls her eyes.

"But do you think I should add this white ribbon to my hair?" she asks.

"No. White is for the bride, Mom," Olive answers.

Mom ignores her, then parks her hands on my shoulders and plants a kiss on the top of my head. Karissa snaps her gaze up from the front of my hair. "Careful, there. Don't want to knock a hair out of place. Just let me finish."

Mom pulls away, scoffing. "I didn't mess it up. I just gave her a kiss."

Karissa shoots Mom a sympathetic smile. "Of course you didn't mess it up. But we want the bride's hair to be fabulous."

"Her hair looks perfect," my mom says, bristling, as Karissa silently returns to her work.

The suite goes quiet. Too quiet.

My friends know not to argue with someone who's always right.

But my mother can slice through any silence with her voice. "Anyway, let me know what else I can do as the mother of the bride," she says to the room. Then, to me in the mirror, she adds, "Since, apparently, I can't give you away."

Again? We're doing this *again*? "Because no one is giving me away," I say calmly. I'm opting out of some rituals. "Just like I don't have a dowry. Just like we both have engagement rings."

"And I disagree. Your father and I should give you away. Wouldn't that be fair? Aren't you a feminist?" Mom asks, like feminist is the equivalent of a nose-picker.

But I won't take her bait.

"Sometimes I am. Mostly on Wednesdays. On Wednesdays, we smash the patriarchy," I say with a shrug.

Olive snickers.

Jillian reins in a laugh.

Emerson just smiles.

"But it's Saturday," my mother points out, flummoxed.

I sigh. "I know. It's a saying. My point is, *this* is what I want." I won't let her win this battle. This is her tenth time trying. "I'm paying for the wedding myself. No one is giving me away. I'm an independent woman. I'm good with this, Mom. The only thing I want that I didn't get is axe-throwing at the reception."

She scoffs at me. "Who would do axe-throwing at her wedding?"

"Who wouldn't? It's crazy fun." I had suggested it to Silvio for the reception, but he politely declined. He also politely declined my suggestion that we have a small wedding by the Pacific Ocean, then do bowling and sushi with our closest friends. But hey, I can't complain about the Legion of Honor and champagne. Or a honeymoon in Dublin, visiting the countryside to take pics, rather than Kauai doing an adventure tour.

"I doubt it's that enjoyable," Mom says about the axe-throwing.

"We'll go do it together sometime, Mom," I offer as an olive branch. I'm in the mood to spread love, not spew snide. "I swear, you'll enjoy it more than giving me away."

"Fine. Don't let me give you away. I'll survive," Mom says as Karissa runs a brush down my bangs, giving them a wispy look. "But I ask you this, darling—are you one hundred percent sure you want to marry Silvio?"

I flinch and hold up a hand to ask Karissa to stop. Then I turn around in the chair, eyeing the redhead who raised me. "Why are you asking this now?"

Olive wheels around from setting the smelly sunflowers on a table. "Yes, Mom. Why?"

My mother squares her shoulders. "It's important to be certain. Isn't that what you two preach in your yoga practice?" She gestures from Olive to me and back.

I answer in a rush. "It's not a religion. We don't preach it. Also, our brand is yoga that doesn't take itself too seriously." There Mom goes again, winding me up, getting me off-topic. "But why are you asking if I'm certain about Silvio?"

Her question irks me. Earlier this year, I'd asked myself plenty of times if he was the one, but that's normal—it's smart to make sure you're making the right choice. I asked myself over and over if yoga was the right business for me before I launched my company. Natch, I'd do the same for marriage.

51

My mom scans my crew. "Do your friends think it makes sense to marry him?"

Ugh. Now she's trying to throw me off via my friends?

Jillian cuts in firmly, handling Mom like she handles an out-of-line question from an unruly press gaggle. "We think Silvio is great."

"We were just talking about what a sweetie he is," Emerson adds. "How well he treats Katie."

Skyler strides back into the suite at the tail end of that, water bottle filled and eyes curious.

My mom's lips curve down. "Does he, though? Does he treat you how you deserve to be treated, honey?" She squeezes my shoulder again.

What is going on? Why the frick is my mother trying to dissuade me from getting married an hour before the ceremony?

"I don't understand why you're asking," I say. Maybe my wedding reminds her of her own marital belly flops, the quartet of *I dos* that didn't work out.

With a worried sigh, my mother clasps her hands, her fingers fidgety. "I'm concerned. That's normal. It seems like it's all happening too quickly. It seems like you might not really know him that well. Or yourself."

What the hell? Just because we had a whirlwind courtship doesn't mean I don't know him well. I met him at a restaurant when our reservations were mixed up, and we dated for two months before he proposed.

Do I know him well?

As well as I need to.

I don't believe you need to spend years with someone before you walk down the aisle.

Sometimes love happens quickly, even if you don't like the same music, food, or wine.

Who cares about that stuff?

"That's not an issue, Mom. I know he gives excellent foot rubs, he loves to snuggle, and he'll probably take at least ten minutes to tie his bow tie even though he's been watching YouTube tutorials for a week. His favorite book is *The Little Prince*, he loses track of time when he works on his murals, but he showers me with kisses when he comes home from his studio. And I feel like I know myself even better too, now that I'm thirty-five. I trust my instincts. I would love it if you would trust me too."

By the end, my throat has tightened like a noose squeezing my neck, and tears sting my eyes but don't fall. I can't believe she's doing this to me on my wedding day. Maybe this is another reason why I never imagined a wedding as a kid—because she'd find a way to ruin it with an ill-timed warning.

But screw it.

I'm not going to let her.

I suck in the threat of tears, swallow them down, and raise my chin. "I love Silvio and he loves me, but I appreciate your concern."

"If you say so," Mom says, letting the words hang in the air like a cloying, passive-aggressive-scented air freshener.

My friends step in like superheroes. Olive grabs my mother's hand and escorts her out of the suite, and Jillian swoops in with a tissue. "Don't let her get to you on your wedding day, or any day ever. She wants to be the center of attention, so she's looking to make it all about her."

I take the tissue and dab my cheek, but I don't think a tear sneaked out. Ha. Take that, Mom.

"Coffee, yoga, and wine, coffee, yoga, and wine," I say, repeating one of my favorite mantras as Olive returns, shutting the door loudly behind her.

"And tonight, there will be wine," Olive declares.

Cheers erupt, and we sing an impromptu homage to wine.

That gets my mother out of my system.

When we're done, Emerson sweeps a tinge more mascara on my lashes, I slide on some lip gloss, and Karissa declares my hair is fabulous. Skyler offers me a sip from the water bottle, but I decline.

"You're ready," Olive says.

I am so damn ready.

I look in the mirror, draw a deep breath, and catalogue the woman I see. Bold, honest, strong, and outgoing. The dress is my best me too. A chiffon A-line, it swishes around my ankles, with cap sleeves showing off my arms. It's simple, white, classy.

We'll exchange our vows at five against the backdrop of the ocean and the Golden Gate Bridge, then we'll head into the art museum for a reception, surrounded by more than seventy Rodins in the galleries.

No axe-throwing, but hey, I like art, too, so it's all good.

A deep, fortifying breath lets me put my mother all the way behind me.

Time to go.

My friends and I make our way through the Legion of Honor toward the lawn. But nature calls, and the last thing I want is to think about peeing while I'm saying my vows.

"Let me just pop into the ladies' room," I say to the bridesmaids when I spot the restroom.

Emerson slashes an arm in front of me like a human stop sign. "That one is too close to where the men are getting ready." She turns me by my shoulders and ushers me down the hall the other way.

"We definitely don't want to bump into them. Whatever would we do?" I ask in exaggerated horror. "You superstitious creature."

She shrugs impishly. "I am what I am."

"I'm not worried if I see him before the wedding. I don't believe in all that stuff," I say as we reach the other restroom.

I stop with my hand on the door because faint voices carry from the end of the hall.

A man and a woman.

Sounding…worried.

They're familiar, but muffled, so I strain to make them out.

"I tried," the woman whispers.

"Of course you did," the man says, gentle, caring.

Ohhh.

That's definitely a voice I know.

I swallow roughly, trying to understand what they're talking about.

Emerson asks me questions with her eyes, and I bring my finger to my lips.

Gathering up the skirt of my dress, I pad as silently as possible to the corner, where I can hear more easily.

"So what now?" the woman whispers.

"There's only one thing to do," he says.

The rustle of clothes. The sound of lips touching lips.

My skin crawls.

The hair on the back of my neck stands on end.

All the breath flees my lungs when I peek around the corner for confirmation.

It's twenty minutes before my wedding, and the man who's supposed to become my husband is kissing another woman.

CHAPTER 9

HARLAN

Elvis Presley is in the house!" I shout as I crank up the volume to "Hound Dog," and Abby lifts her chin to howl at the moon.

I clap, keeping rhythm as my six-year-old uses a wooden spoon as a microphone, crooning along with Elvis's tune.

She breaks off to grab a rubber spatula from the flour-and-cherry-covered kitchen counter. "You need a mic too, Daddy," she says, thrusting it at me.

I take the instrument and we slide into our best imitation of The King as we wait for the pie to bake.

We finish our daddy-daughter duet as the timer bleats, and Abby points wildly to the oven. "It's ready! We can eat it now."

I laugh, shaking my head. "You know the drill. You've only made, what, ten million pies with me? We have to let it cool."

"Ten million and fifty!" She bats her lashes. "But I was just hoping maybe this time."

I ruffle her curly brown hair, chuckling at her attempt to make me bend. "Hope is a good thing, little bear," I tell her as I turn off the timer. "But pies don't cool with hope. They cool with time. Also, you know this pie isn't for us." I grab a Rudolph the Red-Nosed Reindeer potholder, open the oven door, and slide out the cherry pie. I set it on a rack on the counter, then use my hands to direct the scent of sweet and tart fresh fruit and crumbly crust our way.

"It smells so good," Abby says, bouncing on her toes as she inhales.

"'Course it does. We made it. We rock. And your mom is going to love it."

Abby arches a mischievous brow. "What if I eat it all first?"

I bend to drop a kiss onto her nose. "Then you're going to have the biggest bellyache in all of San Francisco," I tell her, then rub her tummy.

"Fine. I'll wait. But I hope she lets me have some tonight," she says with a touch of worry. "I really, really hope so."

Ah, the dilemmas of youth.

I worry whether this city's NFL team will offer me a contract next season and if I'll even want it, whether my kid is making friends at school, and whether she'll want to find a new gymnastics class, since she decided to quit the one she was taking.

She worries about pie.

It's a fair trade-off.

An hour later, we're ready to go. I grab a pie box from the stash I keep, pop in the tasty treat, and tell Abby to find her overnight bag.

It's bowling night with the guys, so I'm dropping Abby at her mom's house. I don't always bring pies, but Danielle and her hubs dig them, so I try to do so as often as I can. Also, it does *not* suck making pies with my little girl. Win-win.

Abby snags her panda backpack from the hallway and slings it onto both shoulders. "And now I am officially ready."

I swing open the door. "Panda is on the back, so it's go time."

On the sidewalk, Abby reaches for my hand. I take her little one in mine and we head toward California Street.

She looks up at me, concern in her hazel eyes. "Are you sure you have to go to training camp next week?"

Okay, not all her worries are of the sugar variety. This kid misses me when I'm out of town, and I sure as hell miss her.

I throw her a them's-the-breaks smile. "I do. The Renegades won't let me play if I don't show up. But I'll talk to you every day."

"I know. I just miss you when you're gone," she says, matter-of-factly as we near the corner.

"I miss you too, little bear. Every day. And that's why I always call you from training camp, and away games, and every night when I'm on the road," I say.

She sighs, a little forlorn. "And I *always* can't wait for your calls."

Time to cheer her up. Remind her that we have a regular routine. That I'm around a helluva lot. Half and half—that's how the time split works with her mom. "Did you know I've been calling you from every single training camp since you were born? Even when you were *only* eight months old?"

Her expression turns intensely serious. "I remember that."

I bark out a laugh as we turn the corner. "You do *not* remember that. No one remembers stuff from when they were one. Or two, or three, or four, or five, for that matter."

"Well, I'm six," she says, like I don't know her age. Like I need the reminder of how seismically my life changed that November day more than six years ago. When she was born, this little bundle of joy and chatter and brightness upended my days and nights, and I learned in an instant what it means to love someone so much it hurts. It hurts so good to love like this.

"I am well aware that you're six and sassy. But still, you don't remember me FaceTiming you from the Paleolithic era."

She crinkles her nose. "What's pale licks?"

"A long time ago. When dinosaurs roamed Earth."

"Daddy!" she shouts in a fit of laughter. "I'm not that old, and you're not either."

"Oh, I'm pretty old. In football years, I'm definitely a dinosaur. But not a T. rex, because they can't do anything with their teeny arms," I say, flapping my left arm like it's as useful as a big dino's, while holding the pie high in my right hand like it's a football.

Abby's eyes widen to pizza size. "Be careful!"

I thrust the box even farther away with my outstretched arm. "Did you or did you not see my one-handed, game-winning catch in the Super Bowl this year? My second Super Bowl win, Miss I Remember Everything."

But she's lasered in on the pie, and only the pie. Back to sugar worry. "I just *really* don't want you to drop the pie."

"And I *really* didn't want to drop Armstrong's thirty-three-yard pass," I say, taking her back to that beautiful day in February. "So I didn't." I put her out of her misery, hauling the pie box back to my chest. "Better?"

A long sigh of relief is her answer. "I've been waiting all day for that cherry pie. But it feels like I've been waiting a year."

"I know what you mean, but it'll be okay. Promise," I say. Because kid time is eternity.

We weave past a goateed guy pushing a sleeping toddler in a jogging stroller.

The guy stops. "Taylor? Harlan Taylor?"

"That's me," I say, hoping he's a fan, not a hater. We have our share of both in this city. Any team does, and you never know who you're going to run into.

But the dad breaks into a wide grin, pressing his hands together in a prayer. "Thank you for that catch. But please re-sign this year. If we lose you to another team, I will die."

He's exaggerating, of course. But he sure does sound like he'd be devastated if I went elsewhere in free agency. But it's not up to me. I have no idea if the Renegades will re-up with an ex-running-back-turned-receiver who's nearing the end of his playing days. I'm thirty-six, already on the long end of a long career.

"I'll do my best to make sure you live," I tell the fan as I offer my free palm to high-five. He smacks back, then continues on his way.

Abby and I do the same.

"It's weird that you're famous," she says, reaching for my hand and swinging ours together again.

I scoff. "I'm not famous."

"Please, Daddy. Don't be silly. You're sooooo famous. All the kids at school say so."

"I'm only *kind* of famous. And only locally. And only with sports fans."

"That's still famous, then," she insists, and I can tell I won't win this battle with her, so I relent.

"Fine. You win."

"But you don't seem famous when we're at home," Abby points out.

"Good. That's how it should be."

Soon, we turn onto Danielle's block and head up the front steps to her Victorian home.

Abby pushes the doorbell, but Danielle's already swinging open the red door, letting her in.

"Hey, cutie-pie," she says, scooping up our daughter and peppering her cheek with kisses. Then to me, she says, "Hey, you."

"Hi, Danielle. I brought you your favorite pie."

"Cherry!" She makes grabby hands. "You're a godsend. Jamie and I have friends coming over tonight, and I was going to rush out to the bakery and grab a cake."

"There is never a need for cake when you have me around," I say, then make my way into her home.

Her husband looks up from the dining table where he's drawing a pig, or maybe a duck, or possibly a cat, with their two-year-old.

"Hi, Harlan!" the little kid shouts.

Jamie lifts a hand. "How's it going? You ready for your last season?"

My mind snags on the word *last*. Is he trying to trick me into confirming the rumors?

Love the dude, but I swear he's got a bet with his buds he'll be the first to reveal what I do at the end of the season.

Hell, I'd like someone to reveal it to me.

Danielle comes to the rescue, setting a hand on her husband's shoulder. "Honey, you're a broken record. Maybe find a new topic."

Jamie shoots her a confused look, his gray eyes narrowing. "Like what, sweetheart? The new surgical technique for reattaching a retina? And football is starting soon. Football *is* the topic."

Danielle tosses her hands in the air. "How about the latest restaurants in Hayes Valley? Or maybe interesting tech news? Perhaps baseball?"

"Hmm, the new Thai place or whether the city's star receiver is going to stay or go… What's more interesting?"

Danielle shrugs helplessly. "Football fans. What can you do?"

Jamie smiles and stands, gesturing to the kitchen and the deck beyond. "You want a beverage, Harlan? Soda? Bubbly water? Beer? We're grilling later if you want to join us." He lowers his voice to a stage whisper. "We can talk about baseball. How about those Dragons?"

"They look good this season. Maybe they'll finally win a World Series," I say, happy to shift to another sport.

"Home run!" the two-year-old shouts.

"And a bubbly water would be great," I add.

"I'll grab it," Abby calls as she sweeps into the dining room, clutching an early reader book from among the many lying around. "And I like football better, Daddy."

As the girl joins her mother in the kitchen, Danielle pats Abby's head. "I wonder why."

After Abby returns with a raspberry LaCroix, I catch up with Jamie, chatting about the Dragons' chances of making it to the Fall Classic. When we've shot the breeze for thirty minutes, I stretch my arms and tell them I need to take off.

Danielle walks me to the door, motioning for Abby to stay behind.

"Thanks again for the pie, and for the school check," she says softly.

"Of course," I say, but I kind of can't believe she's thanking me for paying for Abby's school. What else would I do?

"I appreciate it," she adds.

"Danielle. C'mon. It's a given," I say.

Her expression softens. "I don't take it for granted."

"You never have, and I never thought you would," I say, since friendly is how we do things.

I met Danielle at the University of Washington. We dated our freshman year of college, but then she transferred to a school with a better pre-med program. I ran into her again the night I won my first Super Bowl. She was at a post-game party, and we hit it off again. I gave her a hard time about her preferring the San Francisco Hawks over the San Francisco Renegades. Then I gave her a hard time between the sheets, and we said our goodbyes in the morning. A few weeks later, she learned she was pregnant.

A Super Bowl baby.

The Southern gentleman in me reared his head and asked Danielle if she wanted me to marry her.

I'd never heard a woman laugh so hard in my life.

"We're not in love. That was a one-night stand. No, sweetie. I just want to know if you're interested in helping raise this baby. It's hard being a doctor and a mom."

Was I interested?

Absolutely.

I wasn't going to be a deadbeat dad.

"Of course I am," I said.

"Are you sure? A lot of athletes aren't."

"I'm not a lot of athletes." Sure, I'd been the good-time guy. I was still a helluva ladies' man back then.

But I also damn well knew what family was, thanks to my mom and the way she looked after all of us after my dad walked out.

I was not going to do that.

So, we agreed to raise Abby together as friends, as co-parents, and as equals.

A few years later, she met Jamie, a fellow surgeon, and married him. Abby and I went to their wedding together.

Now, in the doorway, I give Danielle a serious look. "It's not only my job to take care of her. It's my pleasure," I tell her. "And you, if you need it."

Danielle lets out a sigh of relief. "I never want to assume."

"You're a sweetheart, even if you prefer the Hawks. Glad you're her mom," I say, then I cup my hand over my mouth and call to Abby that I'm leaving.

She runs over and leaps into my arms, clutching me like a koala. "Bye, Daddy."

"I'll miss you, little bear. But I'll call you tomorrow night."

"Just like you did when I was one." Abby stares up at me, her hazel eyes big and serious. "And I remember you sang Dolly Parton to me as a lullaby."

Holy shit.

Does my kid have a weird-ass memory from being an infant? How is that possible?

I narrow my eyes in suspicion. "Wait…"

Abby cracks up, swatting my shoulder. "Got you! Mommy told me you did that."

"Dolly's the best," Danielle adds.

"That she is," I agree, and then I tap Abby's nose. "Let me know if you want to do gymnastics somewhere else in the fall."

"I'm still thinking about it."

"Take your time," I say gently. But I know how much she loved it, so I hope she'll want to go again.

She looks away briefly, then nods, resolute. "I will. And I'll let you know. Promise."

"Love you, little bear."

"Love you too."

I say goodbye, humming "Nine to Five" as I make my way across the city to a bowling alley to meet my buds.

For the next few hours, I have a blast throwing strikes and gutter balls alike with my friends until, one by one, they peel off. As the clock ticks closer to ten, it's just Cooper—my quarterback—and me, and we chat as we make our way out, passing the bar inside the bowling alley where my gaze catches on a woman in a formal white dress.

That's odd enough to rate a look, but something about her feels achingly familiar.

Possibilities nag at me all the way to the exit, then won't let me leave.

At the door, I tell Cooper I'll see him at training camp. "I swore I saw someone who looked familiar. I'll catch you later. I need to go check on something."

He lifts his chin in a goodbye. "See you at camp."

I turn around, the blond profile triggering a memory that tugs me back to the bar.

Could it be?

Is that...her?

A tingle of excitement coasts over my skin at the mere possibility.

When I reach the bar, I take a deep breath and look in, then I shake my head in amazement.

The woman in white is none other than someone who, seven years ago, I desperately wanted to see again.

And she's wearing a wedding dress as she orders another shot of tequila.

CHAPTER 10

KATIE

A FEW HOURS EARLIER

*N*o.

This is not happening.

This is a nightmare.

I'm seeing things.

As my stomach crawls up my throat, my brain tries to rearrange the picture in front of me.

They're hugging? They're planning a gift for me?

But I don't want a gift.

I want my almost-husband.

Who is sucking another woman's face.

"Are you…" I can't go on. Emerson squeezes my arm, and the encouraging touch from someone I trust drives me on. My face burns as I gear up to try again and spit out, "Are you kidding me?"

The man in the tuxedo breaks the kiss, wrenching away from the woman in his arms.

My mother.

Bile rises in my throat once more. How could she? How could she actually do this?

I pinch the bridge of my nose, shake my head, but the reality doesn't change. "I cannot believe you," I say to the woman who gave birth to me. Emerson grips my arm tighter, helping me to get through this horror.

I am livid and devastated.

Ashamed and enraged.

Shocked and disgusted.

I never thought it possible to contain all these awful emotions at once. But then, I never imagined I'd find my fiancé making out with my about-to-be-officially-and-finally-estranged mother.

Fight-or-flight indecision holds me frozen. I need to get the hell out of here, but one thought echoes in my head and won't let me leave.

Say something before you take off.

My mouth feels like glue. The woman who raised me just kissed the man I was going to marry.

I dig down deep, searching for the right words, in the right order, but come up empty.

My mother reaches for my arm. "Darling, I tried to tell you it was a bad idea," she says, getting the first word in, beating me to it.

"Don't, Tracy," Emerson hisses at my mother. "Don't you dare."

Like I've inhaled secondhand strength from my friend, I seethe.

My mother gets my fiancé and the last word?

My gaze drifts down to her fingers on my arm.

She is touching me.

She was kissing the groom.

No fucking way.

I recoil, jerking my arm away from her like she's diseased.

"We're in love," my mom declares, gazing into the green eyes of the artist I was about to marry.

He shrugs in surrender, his crow's feet crinkling, giving away the five years he has on me. "It happened so quickly. I didn't even expect it. I barely had time to think of what to say." Silvio meets my gaze. "But I wanted to tell you, love. Truly, I did."

Love?

He's calling me love, like he always has?

I snap out of my surreal, sluggish haze.

I laser in on the slithering tuxedoed snake of a man. "I'm sure it was difficult to find the time to say four whole words—*I'm fucking your mother.* But maybe in the ten minutes it took you to tie your bow tie, you could have called me and delivered the news."

I inhale sharply, gearing up for another round of zing, and swing my gaze to *her*. She's no garden-variety snake. She's an anaconda. "By the way, wear the white ribbon. I bet it'll look great on your wedding day." I thrust the bouquet at her. "And feel free to use these sunflowers. I get why you wanted them so badly, and since they smell like crap, they'll go great with your secondhand groom."

I turn on my heel. Emerson wraps an arm tightly around me.

"Let's get out of here," she whispers, and I'm so damn grateful for her because I don't even know which direction to go.

My eyes sting.

Tears prick at the back of them, threatening to let loose geysers.

I grit my teeth.

I will not let them hear me cry.

I will not let them see me fall apart.

Oh hell.

The waterworks are coming, and I can barely hold them off.

Thank God Emerson is here.

I yank up my skirt and we run like the Legion of Honor is on fire.

Through the hallway, toward a side door—somewhere along the way Jillian, Olive, and Skyler join us. Jillian's on the phone, giving instructions about the car.

When I reach the exit, my friends are still running by my side. We race down the long entryway steps, and I don't even risk a glance at the lawn or rows of folding chairs. I can't bear the thought of guests gawking, pointing. I must look like a runaway bride, only the opposite is true.

A few more steps, and I'm nearly there. My father waits for me by the limo, right at the edge of the car park.

I stumble into his arms, and I fall to pieces.

———————

Go.

Just go.

That's literally the only thing I can say, over and over.

We pile into the sleek vehicle—my dad, my sister, Emerson, Jillian, and Skyler.

My crew.

But Jillian stops before she gets in, her hand on the door. "Katie, why don't I take care of all that?" She gestures to the lawn.

Ugh.

The freaking guests.

All those guests milling about in their pretty clothes, waiting for a ceremony. They're here for my stupid wedding that isn't happening. Soon, they'll be able to whisper about the time they went to a wedding where the bride was stood up at the altar.

"Thank you, Jillian. That would be great," my father says, answering for me.

"I can help too," Skyler offers.

A sob wracks my throat and I nod savagely. "Just take care of it, please."

"We'll take care of *all* of it," Jillian assures me, going full badass, problem-solving babe as they stay behind to clean up the mess my mother and fiancé made of my wedding day.

We peel off, away from the gorgeous art museum, high on the hill. As the Golden Gate Bridge looms closer, another burst of tears rains down my cheeks. I can't believe what just happened.

I truly can't.

My dad's seated next to me, and he rubs my back gently. "Honey, I'm so sorry. But you've got to know—none of it is your fault."

My heart clutches, and even through the tears, I do know the truth. "You're totally right," I say between sobs.

"Good. Glad you know that. Now, where can we take you? What do you need? Do you just need to cry it out some more?"

Those are all great questions.

I have no idea what to do next.

My heart thuds heavily. My hands are clammy. Hurt rages, clouding my thoughts. "I don't know," I whisper with a shrug.

"We can just drive," Olive says from the seat across from me.

I look up, meeting their gazes. These people who are here for me. My sister, my best friend, my dad.

I should try—really, I should—to answer their questions. But I just want to get as far away from my old reality as possible.

"We could go out on your boat," I say to my dad, casting about for options. Maybe that's what's next?

"My fishing boat? You hate fishing," he says with a sympathetic smile.

He's not wrong.

"We could go eat veggie burgers," I say to Emerson, since that's her thing.

Her brow knits. "You're not a stress eater."

"Maybe now is the time to start," I say, my voice hollow as I try to figure out what the hell to do after being ditched. "Maybe that's what I need to do. Scarf down french fries and wine. I bet that's what you're supposed to do when you've been jilted."

My dad squeezes my hand. "If you want fries and wine, that's fine."

"Gah, I love you," I say, all choked up. One of my parents understands the value of salt and liquor—the other stole my fiancé.

My phone bleats. I jerk my gaze to the device in my hand. My mother's name flashes on the screen, and hate roils through me. I death-grip the device and lift my arm, poised to chuck it at the window.

My dad stops me with a hand around my wrist. "She's not worth the cost of a new phone," he says, gentle but firm.

I huff. I growl.

But he's right. She's not worth so much as a dime.

"And believe me, too, when I say this—you never need to talk to her again," he adds.

Letting the phone fall to the seat, I drop my head into my hands. "My life is a telenovela," I say. But after a moment, I look up, determination kicking in, replacing the self-loathing. Apparently, emotions for jilted brides ride seesaws.

Who knew?

"I know what to do."

Emerson leans forward in her seat, eager. "Tell us."

I've got a plan. Something my ex-groom would hate. Something his floozy would despise too. And, most importantly, something I love.

———————

Twenty minutes later, the limo pulls over to a too-trendy axe-throwing brewery. I march inside, dress still on.

Ready to take on the goddamn world with my axe.

With a clenched jaw, I head straight for the lumberjack in green flannel at the check-in desk. "My fiancé left me for my mother twenty minutes before my wedding," I bite out. "I need a big-ass bucket of axes."

The bearded man blinks, his brown eyes etched with sympathy. "It's on the house."

For the next hour, I toss axes at a target.

It's cathartic until Olive's phone rings, and she steps away from our throwing stall.

"Hey, Jillian, what's up?" she asks softly.

I turn away from the lane, my ears pricked, eager to hear what's going down at the crime scene where my marriage was pronounced dead on arrival at four forty-five on a Saturday.

Olive's jaw drops to the wood shavings on the floor. "For real?"

I groan in misery, my axe in hand, my heart in my throat. What now? I don't know how this day could get worse, but I'm certain it's about to.

Olive hangs up, takes a bracing breath, and says, "They're flying to Dublin right now. They're taking your honeymoon. He just posted it on social. They're at the airport on their way." She winces in sincere sympathy. "I'm sorry."

But fuck sympathy. Fuck my mom. Fuck my ex.

I see red. I see all the bull's-eyes in the world.

I turn to the target, raise the axe over my head, channel all the rage, and throw. The blade slices deep into the bull's-eye.

Then I spin around, dust one hand against the other, and adopt a smile.

Apparently, I am making my way through the seven or seventy stages of getting-left-at-the-altar grief, lickety-split.

And right now, I've entered the burn-his-stuff-down phase.

"Can you guys go to my apartment, get rid of all of Silvio's things, change the locks, and then bring me a key?"

The answer from everyone is a resounding *hell, yes.*

A few hours later, the deed is done.

My ex-fiancé has been kicked out of my place, where we lived together for the last month.

Good riddance. The man can't tie a bow tie but can untie the knot like Benedict Arnold.

I push open the door and enter my now emptier apartment, fearful of how much it'll hurt.

I brace myself as I drink it in.

His stacks of hardcover biographies are gone from the coffee table.

His framed photographs of moody skylines are nowhere to be seen.

His paintbrushes have vamoosed from the kitchen.

What's left are my pink and purple pillows scattered across the couch, my *Wine is my friend* corkscrew on the kitchen counter, and my *For Fox Sake* collection of pun art hanging on the walls.

This home is for someone who doesn't take herself too seriously.

Only, I did take commitment seriously.

I sure as hell did.

And he did not. So I suppose I'm glad he showed his true colors now. Glad he revealed his trickery before I said *I do*.

Maybe that's why seeing his stuff gone doesn't lacerate me. Maybe I'm a little bit lucky.

I turn around and meet the eyes of my crew. "Thank you. I appreciate this so much."

"Do you want me to stay the night?" Olive offers, all kind big eyes and giant heart.

"Anything you need, I'm here for you," Emerson adds, and my other friends chime in with similar sentiments.

"Thank you, but I'm good," I say. I love them, but I need a break from sympathy.

"Do you want to stay with Janice and me in Sausalito?" my father offers; he and his new wife have a lovely home on the water, with a view of Richardson Bay from the guest room.

"I appreciate the invite, but I'll stay here," I say, because it sort of feels like mine again.

And mostly because their pitying looks—though well-intentioned—might drive me crazy, especially when I'm feeling the tiniest bit of this-is-a-blessing-in-disguise.

"Call me tomorrow," Emerson says, making her way to the door.

"And don't answer your mom's calls," my dad adds.

"Not a problem. I blocked her already."

"Good girl," he says, and they leave.

Once I shut the door, the walls instantly close in.

I'm all alone.

The silence is claustrophobic.

I was wrong. This is the last place I want to be.

Even with all his things gone, I can't stand being here alone. I don't want to be by myself, but I don't want to be with friends right now either.

What *do* I want?

To be with this city.

Yup. That's what I need.

I kick off my stupid white satin heels, march into my bedroom, and yank open the closet door, scanning for something to wear that's not this dress.

Maybe a cute V-neck, or some jeans and cowboy boots. Something that's the opposite of a wedding gown.

I pluck at the chiffon.

But damn. I like this dress. Hell, I love it. I bought it because it's my style. It's fun and pretty.

Screw it.

Might as well make some new memories in this dress.

I'll make it the perfect outfit for a solo night on the town with *these* babies. I grab a pair of fuchsia cowboy boots from the closet, tug them on in a flurry.

Yup. This is me now.

My dress, my boots, my style. From a shelf, I grab a purple wristlet that Emerson gave me for my birthday. *Go Ahead, Underestimate Me* adorns one side in a curlicue font.

Indeed, world.

Underestimate me.

I am not staying in.

I am not curling up and downing a carton of Häagen-Dazs.

I am taking myself out in my goddamn dress.

Stuffing my phone into my colorful clutch, I get the hell out of my apartment, hitting the sidewalk on a Saturday night.

I wander through Russian Hill, weaving unnoticed through crowds. Across the street, a woman dressed as a leprechaun skips down the block. As I round the corner, a man in a porkpie hat rides a unicycle. No one gives the woman in the wedding dress a second look as she wanders the city solo.

San Francisco is awesome and wonderful, and this is why I loved and missed this city when I was in Los Angeles building my business.

I walk, and I walk, and I walk into the night until I see a sign for Pinup Lanes advertising a Saturday-night special on tequila and bowling.

I'll take what's behind door number one, thank you very much.

I head inside. It's so old school, and this is what I need right now.

Brimming with orange Formica and fifties tunes, this place is nothing at all like the Legion of Honor, my mural-artist almost-husband, or the ceremony I didn't have.

I head to the bar, order a shot, and knock it back.

It burns all the way down.

I order one more, and when the bartender sets it down, I notice footsteps growing louder on the linoleum behind me.

I turn my head. Glance over my shoulder.

Is that…?

No way.

Tonight, after all these years, my eyes land on the guy who got away.

CHAPTER 11

HARLAN

Holy smokes.

She is a sight.

As sexy as Katie was more than seven years ago, she's somehow even more stunning today. Her hair is all done up and clipped back, with lush, dark-blond strands curling over her shoulders. Her skin shimmers. Her high cheekbones slant in fantastic contrast to her pert, freckled nose.

The last seven years have been very good to her.

And yet, everything about the woman is incongruous. It's not a stretch to imagine there's something wildly wrong tonight. A woman doesn't wear a wedding dress solo to a bowling alley bar on a Saturday night in July without a reason. But I don't want to make any assumptions. Hell, her groom might be in the little boys' room, taking care of business.

Or waxing a big, old bowling ball.

Or playing a speed sesh of Pac-Man in the video game lounge.

But a quick glance around tells me she's not here with the mister after saying *I do*. The place is mostly empty with just a few groups of old dudes in bowling shirts left of the crowd, and no one who looks like he got hitched today. So I'm thinking Katie and her man didn't rush off to Pinup Lanes for an ironic game of bowling to celebrate their nuptials.

Just to be safe, though, I go in nice and easy. I'd like to avoid hitting on another man's bride.

What am I saying? I'm not going to hit on her, period. I'm merely saying hello to an old flame.

I close the distance, leaning a hip against the bar. "Hello, blast from the past. And happy…Saturday night?" I arch a brow, give a crooked smile, hoping maybe that's the start of what she needs. A friendly face. Someone to lighten the mood.

Katie turns to me in slow motion, taking her sweet time. Her blue eyes are edged with sadness and fury. But when they lock on mine, recognition sparks, and a wide range of emotions dance across her face.

Surprise. Embarrassment. And maybe a touch of excitement?

"Or we can be more precise and call it Happy Just-Escaped-Marriage-to-a-Cheater Day," she deadpans.

Whoa.

Someone does not mince words.

Who the hell would do that to her?

I blow out a long stream of air and scrub a hand over my jaw.

"They ought to have cards for that," I say, trying to match her mood. "Say goodbye to the double-crossing, duplicitous dick."

She lifts her shot glass, a tiny laugh escaping her lips. "Yes. And the inside could say *Congratulations to the jilted bride*," she says, hurt leaking into her tone now.

My heart screams for her. "I hate that this happened to you, but I'm glad you got out in the nick of time." I park myself on a stool and do the one useful thing I can—I lift two fingers at the bartender. "I'll take a shot too."

"Coming right up," he says.

I turn to Katie. "I cannot let you drink alone. Not on your wedding night. It's just not right. I refuse to do it. So you have a *just escaped marriage to the traitor* drinking buddy."

She pats the bar, heaving a sigh. "Then drink up, partner."

The bartender slides over a tequila for me. "Here you go, sir."

I slap down some bills. "And I'll take care of her bar tab tonight," I say.

Katie shakes her head. "I've got it."

I scoff, patting my chest. "Gentleman here. It's the least I can do on your Great Escape Day."

She holds up her hand in surrender. "I have no argument left in me. Thank you."

"You are most welcome. And by the way, on behalf of all men everywhere, I'd like to apologize for whatever that dickhead of a guy did. He is clearly an asshat of the highest order, and he does not deserve you. That's just a fact."

She lifts her glass in agreement, then downs the shot. "He is, but that's not the worst of it, Harlan."

"Oh, you remember my name?" I tease before I knock back my drink too.

She narrows her eyes, shoots me a *c'mon* look. "Did you think I wouldn't?"

"I'm just happy you did...*Katie*." It comes out flirtier than I expected. But maybe flirting is what she needs tonight?

Her blue eyes widen. "Are you trying to impress me by remembering mine?"

"Did that impress you? If so, check out the other details I remember." I count off on my fingers. "You're from Texas, you love fashion and flirting, and I sorely missed the chance for a second date with you."

I put that last nugget out there because...why the hell not? Maybe tonight is the perfect time to let the woman know she was wanted something fierce.

Katie shoots me a skeptical glance. "Now you're just blowing smoke up my skirt."

"I assure you, no smoke is being blown. But I do like your skirt." I curl my fingers to beckon the rest of the story from her. "Go on. You were about to tell me what is the worst part of today. Also, if you need to punch anyone or anything, my chest is a brick wall." I pat my pecs, inviting her to toss her fist my way. "Feel free to take it out on me."

Another small laugh falls from her lips, and I feel like I'm winning at something—at making a woman who's had a terrible day feel a tiny bit better.

Katie breathes deep, yoga-style, like she's inhaling a *namaste* to form the next words: "I walked in on the groom kissing the mother of the bride."

What?

The revelation spins my head around, horror-movie style, with shocked disbelief.

That can't be true.

"Tell me that's a joke," I say. Because how could it be anything else?

She sighs and shakes her head, her lips quivering slightly. My heart lurches toward her.

"I'm not joking," she says in a terribly sad whisper.

I can't resist giving her some comfort. I reach for her arm, squeeze it, rub my palm along her soft skin. "That is the worst. People *say* things are the worst—bad parking spot, terrible coffee. But this scenario is the actual worst, and I am so damn sorry it happened to you."

"Thank you. I really appreciate that. My friends and my dad tried to help comfort me today. They were helpful, but even though I asked them to leave, when they did, I discovered I didn't want to be home either. So I wandered around the city alone until I stumbled across this place. It seemed"—she stops to survey the retro room—"fitting in some way. It's the complete opposite of my wedding." She plucks at the fabric of her dress. "Maybe that's why I left this on. To wear it for a completely opposite purpose. Just for me on a random night."

What she's saying makes perfect sense. "You're reclaiming it in a way."

She seems to consider that, then nods. "Yes, maybe I am."

I point to the door. "Did you want to be alone? It'll be hard for me to go, because there's a part of me that doesn't feel like I can abandon you. But if you need to be alone, I'll leave."

Her eyes drift down to my hand on her arm. "No. Actually, I don't want to be alone." Her voice dips quieter. "I can't believe this is even real." Katie drops her forehead into her hand, drawing a shuddery breath.

I slide my arm around her, rubbing her back. "Sweetheart, he doesn't deserve you. She doesn't deserve you. You are light years better than those two. Look at you."

She lifts her face, curious. "What do you mean?"

I gesture to the bombshell sitting next to me in her yards of white finery and bright-pink boots. "Your ex-fiancé should have to wear a sandwich board for the rest of his life that says *I lost out on a fantastic woman because I'm a stupid, shit-for-brains numb nut.* Also, those boots are hot."

With a small smile, she kicks out her right foot, showing me the fuchsia boots. "Thank you. Suffice to say, they were not part of my official wedding costume."

That gives me a fantastic idea. "How about we call this your bowling dress?" I say, gesturing to her outfit.

She smooths a hand along the white fabric. "Why yes, this is, indeed, my bowling costume."

I eye her dolled-up hair. "And I see you did up your hair for a night of fantastic tequila drinking with a football player."

She rolls with the make-believe without missing a beat. "I so did."

The smile that sneaks across her face makes me feel damn good. That is my job tonight—to cheer her all the way up.

Hell, I feel like a superhero, an agent called in for a vitally important duty. My mission, should I choose to accept it, is to cure Katie of her getting-left-at-the-altar blues.

If anyone can do it, it's me. And if anyone deserves to feel a helluva lot better, it's this gem of a woman.

I slap my palm on the bar. "I'm declaring it. We are having a *just saved from the dickhead* party. How about that, Katie? Are you in or out?"

She rolls her eyes but laughs lightly. "I'm all the way in."

"It's a *congratulations on not marrying a flaming pile of dog shit* event," I add with an emphatic bump of my fist on the wood counter.

She gets in on the game, raising her glass high in the air. "It's a celebration of freedom from a backstabbing, lying, cheating, awful, terrible groom and his brand-new snake of a girlfriend as they enjoy my honeymoon."

Oh, no. Say it isn't so. I grimace. "He took her on *your* honeymoon? Today?"

Katie lets out a resigned sigh. "He sure did. And I hope she enjoys taking boring, moody pictures of the Irish countryside or what-the-fuck-ever."

That's it. There's nothing I won't do to take her mind off her Officially Awful-est Day. I sweep my arm out. "Then we are celebrating you being Indiana Jones and escaping from that fiasco of a marriage one second before the boulder came rolling down on you and locked you up with a ring."

She considers that, her brows knit. The bartender strolls by, waggles the bottle, and we lift our glasses, asking for refills.

"If I'm Indiana Jones," Katie counters playfully, "I need a hat, don't I?"

This woman. Even on a terrible day, her spark and fire haven't left her. "You sure do. We'll make it our mission to procure an Indiana Jones hat for you," I declare.

She hums, tapping her chin. "Do you think there are any hat dealers open in the city right now?"

Where there's a will, there's a way. Plus, we aren't living in the middle of nowhere. Presuming she lives here again. I can't resist finding out, even on her not-wedding night. "Are you back in the Bay Area?"

"I sure am. Moved back seven months ago."

That makes me happy, but a little sad too. I growl, crossing my arms. "And you didn't even look me up."

She waggles her hand, showing me her engagement diamond. "I met him a week after I moved. Also, I'm going to sell this and donate the money. Plus, hello! You have a kid. Jillian mentions you from time to time."

"I do have a little girl," I say, grinning as I picture my little bear. "Abby is the apple of my eye and the love of my life. I'm great friends with Abby's mom—we get along like thieves. But just because I have a kid doesn't mean I'm off the market. Au contraire. I'm as single as the day is long."

Holy hell, I am flirting shamelessly with a woman who was about to walk down the aisle today and tie the knot with another man.

That ought to be the yellow flag to end yellow flags. And yet, I'm just as eager to chat with Katie tonight as I was seven years ago.

Riddle me that.

"You're single?" The woman in white leans closer, lifts her glass, whispers conspiratorially. "What do you know? So am I. Cheers to that."

She clinks her shot glass to mine, and I tap back.

It feels like a legitimate toast, like we're both truly pleased to be free.

Hell, considering her ex-fiancé, maybe she *is* glad to be unhitched.

We both drink some liquid fire, breathe out hard, and put the glasses down at the same time. "To being single in the city," I say. "And you know what? This is San Francisco. I bet there is someplace in the city where we can get you a hat and a whip."

She runs her thumb over the empty glass, her smile a bit naughty. "Well, I have no doubt there's someplace in the city where we could get a whip right now."

I wiggle my brows. "Would you like a whip, darlin'?"

Her eyes twinkle with mischief. "Oh, there you go again. Dipping into the accent for fun."

"Seemed the perfect time. You like the reappearance?"

She bobs a shoulder. "Depends on the reason it's making a reappearance."

"Ah, seems it sneaks back when I flirt with a gorgeous woman," I say, putting that out there.

Yup, I am flirting with a jilted bride, and judging from the happiness in her eyes, it seems like exactly what she needs.

Maybe it's what I need too.

But tonight isn't about me.

It's about her.

"So, you *are* flirting with me?" she asks, like she needs and wants the confirmation.

I smile. "Seems I am."

She takes a beat, eying me up and down. "Good. Keep it up."

CHAPTER 12

HARLAN

So, you swear this is the place to go?" Katie asks.

"Don't just take it from me. Take it from *Best of San Francisco Blog*. They rate it as the top costume shop in the entire city. Let's get you a costume," I say, as we turn into Daisy's Duds.

Judy Garland's "Somewhere Over the Rainbow" plays softly on the sound system. A statuesque Black drag queen, decked out in a tight, purple-sequin dress with an emerald-green feather boa tossed around her neck, waves to us from behind the counter. "Welcome to Daisy's Duds. I'm Daisy. Let me know what I can help you with in my palace of costumes," she says, sweeping out a muscled arm to indicate the plethora of options.

My eyes scan the colorful arrays of finery—glitter and boas, faux fur and leather, spangles and pasties, as well as all sorts of uniforms for cops, doctors, nurses, firemen, and soldiers.

"Daisy, my lovely lady friend here has a hankering for an Indiana Jones hat and a whip. Any chance you can deliver?"

Daisy cracks up, rolling her big brown eyes. "You say that as if I couldn't. *Of course* I have every Harrison Ford costume under the sun. I just love that man something fierce." She sashays through the store, taking us to a rack next to a mirror with dressing room lights flickering over it. Her hand glides over a Princess Leia bikini from her Jabba the Hut days, then a Ron Burgundy maroon suit.

"You really do have everything," Katie says, wide-eyed as she fingers a *Charlie's Angels* get-up.

Daisy clucks her tongue. "What did you take me for? A costumer you can stump? Darling, my job and my pleasure is to have everything your heart desires."

Katie laughs, and I am so damn glad she's smiling again and having a good time. "I like your style, Daisy," she says.

"And I like your dress. Let's get you a hat to go with that fabulous A-line on your gorgeous body."

Katie juts out a hip. "Why, thank you very much."

The drag queen doesn't question why Katie's wearing a wedding dress, and I have a hunch the not-a-bride appreciates that.

The owner roams her hand along a shelf, snags a hat, then grabs a whip. "It's a Saturday night. Who doesn't need some light bondage?" she says with a wink, then a snap of her wrist. "Giddy-up."

"Ooh, would we call that light?" Katie asks.

Daisy tuts. "Darling, we'll discuss heavy bondage another time. This whip is definitely light." She hands her the coiled leather just as the door slings open, and Daisy excuses herself to help the new customer.

Katie takes the whip, sets the hat on her head, and tosses me a saucy smirk. "How do I look? Like an adventurer escaping from doom in the nick of time?"

More like Indiana Jones's very naughty sister. "It looks like maybe you're a little bit kinky," I say, my voice dropping to a rumble. I'm not a kinky fucker, but I am a game-for-anything guy, so if kink is Katie's thing, I'm up for it.

Katie gives a light snap of the whip, her eyes twinkling with possibilities. "Maybe I am."

Her coy tone lights up my skin.

I just wish we didn't seem to have the worst timing in the world. Reconnecting with her on her foiled wedding night seems like Fate's way of saying we're all wrong for each other.

And yet, I'm not going to end this night any sooner than I have to. She's still the best company I've ever had, even when she's suffered the worst day ever.

Daisy finishes with her customer and returns to us, parking her hands on her hips and staring at me. "And what about you, handsome? You're not going to let Ms. Indiana Jones in a white dress be the only one looking fabulous, are you?"

Katie shoots me a challenging stare. "Yeah. C'mon, Taylor. What are you going to wear? How about a letterman jacket? You could be a football star."

She sounds so happy again, so sassy. It's a great sound, and I feel like a million bucks for restoring her faith in, well, in fun for a night.

I shake my head. "That's a bit on the nose, don't you think?"

"Maybe I think you'd look cute in it," she says.

Is she putting me on? "Cute?" I echo with a raised brow. "I'd look *cute*?"

Daisy sets a hand on my shoulder. "Take the compliment and tuck it away. Enjoy it."

"Fine. I'll be cute," I say, faking indignation.

Katie gives me a *so there* look. "Yes. You're cute. But..." She studies me seriously, tapping her chin. "I'm thinking you could be a fireman."

Interesting choice. "Does someone have a thing for firemen?"

"Who doesn't?" Katie asks.

Daisy points two thumbs at her ample bosom. "I'd love a man to rescue me." She spins on her silver shoes, and props to her for pulling off those heels at work. "And, handsome, now you have no choice but to be a fireman. I hope you have a good hose."

Katie's lips part into an *O* as she catches my gaze. "I hope you do too."

I crack up, loving that she's ventured so far into the flirty zone. My good-time superhero would do this for a damsel in distress—make her laugh. Help her flirt.

"I'll take a fireman helmet," I tell the shop owner.

"And what about turnouts and suspenders? I hope you're going to take that polo off and run around shirtless for the rest of the night," Daisy suggests.

Mischief sparks in Katie's eyes. "You have to do what Daisy says."

Five minutes later, my jeans and shirt are tucked in a plastic bag, and I'm decked out like a fireman about to do a striptease. I emerge from the dressing room, shirtless, as if I'm ready to work the pole, and I don't mean the kind you'd find in a firehouse.

I spin in a circle for Katie, and she wolf whistles. "You look fabulous, Harlan. This is celebrating being left at the altar in style."

Daisy's eyes widen, and she sets a hand on Katie's arm. "You were, sweetheart?"

"I was," Katie says, even and cool, then points to me, nibbling on the corner of her lips. "But he found me at the bowling alley bar. And now here I am, playing dress-up."

Daisy smiles, shaking her head, then beckons for Katie to come closer. "Girl, you know the best way to get over a man?" the drag queen asks.

"Tell me," Katie says, her tone dripping with interest.

Daisy points at me, circles her finger in my direction. "Get under another one. Like this handsome piece over here."

CHAPTER 13

KATIE

What's the protocol for jilted brides on what to do or say on their should-have-been wedding night?

Someone should write that manners guidebook.

Is it okay for me to feel a little flirty, a little dirty when my heart's been so recently stomped on?

Daisy certainly seems to think so, and who am I to argue with her?

Heck, if I were developing a yoga class for this situation, I'd call it How to Shavasana When You've Been Dumped on Your Asana.

And pose number one would be…on your back.

Just like Daisy suggested.

With her confidence and tell-it-like-it-is-ness, she seems to be exactly the type of woman you'd bank on.

Come to think of it, I'm not sure I've ever received better advice.

As soon as she voices those wicked words, I'm positive that's exactly what I need. A hot, toe-curling, no-strings-attached roll in the hay.

A good, old-fashioned screw can reset me to human again.

But I don't want a scorching one-night stand to be someone else's idea. I want it to come from that hunk of a man. I want it to be *his* idea to *Calgon take me away!* from this hellacious day.

So, I say to the gorgeous beauty at the costume counter, "I'll take that under advisement."

As soon as we leave, I point to a bar at the end of the street. Pink neon flashes on a marquee—*It's 80s night, oh what a night*—luring patrons with a retro playlist of Wham!, Madonna, Cyndi Lauper, and a-ha.

That's where I need to be. Dancing my dumped ass off. I nearly bounce in my boots. "That's got to be even better than axe-throwing."

"Was axe-throwing an option?"

"Oh, that's where my girlfriends and my dad took me earlier tonight."

"That makes perfect sense. And now you're thinking you want to shake it out?"

I'm giddy with the prospect of shimmying to classics from many decades ago. "I do. I really, really do."

Harlan flicks his suspenders against his hard, firm bare skin, then arches a cocky brow. "I'm always up for a dance," he says, and I'm up for staring at his pecs.

His carved, yummy pecs.

I wonder what they taste like… "And you look like you're ready for a striptease."

"If memory serves, I offered you a lap dance once upon a time. The offer still stands," he says, leaving that enticing possibility hanging in the night air.

And yes, I do believe I'm getting closer to my goal. For him to suggest taking me home.

C'mon, Harlan. Reel me in. I'm an easy catch tonight.

"Maybe I'll take you up on it," I say playfully.

He gestures to the club. "Let's go have some tequila, some Go-Go's, and me."

Oh yes. That sure sounds like he's game. Harlan can be the official antidote to my horrible day.

He feels that way already.

Somehow, running into him feels like the universe's way of saying *I'm so sorry for that shit sandwich I served you earlier. Here's an ice cream sundae to finish off your night.*

We go inside and after he drops his bag at the check-in, we head to the dance floor. Belinda Carlisle croons about having the beat.

Under the smoky purple lights, I shimmy, shake, and move my body to the old-school beat. Harlan swivels his hips, and we find a groove.

"You make a fine fireman," I say above the music.

"Have you got a fire for me to put out?"

I move closer, tugging my hat down so it doesn't fall off. "Maybe I do."

"I bet I can take care of it," he says, looping an arm around my waist and yanking me close to him.

Hello, reversal of fortune. It is nice to see you. And to feel this football god's body.

With him, I've nearly forgotten what sent me out tonight. The need to get away. But now isn't the time to remember this afternoon. I want the events of this day to fade far, far away into the past.

As we dance, swaying closer, I imagine the betrayal slinking out the door and vanishing into thin air.

It has no room in my night.

I'm too busy dancing to Whitesnake's "Here I Go Again," Van Halen's "Jump," and "Bizarre Love Triangle" by New Order.

In my wedding dress and his fireman costume, we dance it out. With every swish of my hips, I imagine leaving behind this afternoon's hallway encounter at the Legion of Honor. I picture saying *see you never again* to the two people who upended my plans.

And I see moving on in my near future.

It's as if I shed more of the pain with every single song. Did I even love Silvio? Were we too different all along? Did it happen too fast? Is this a blessing in disguise?

Maybe I was hoping he was the one when we truly didn't even have that much in common.

He didn't like bowling, or foosball, or Halloween.

Or fun.

Perhaps he was wrong for me.

I'll move on, I'll move forward, and I'll move away.

When Madonna's "Crazy for You" comes on, the ultimate 80s

tune, Harlan's eyes darken. "This is a damn good song," he says. "And you're going to need to slide even closer to me for this one."

I don't want to say no. Not at all. I want to sing all the yeses. Daisy was right. So damn right. "Let's do it, handsome," I say, and Harlan brings me up against him, looping his hands around my waist.

"Wrap your hands around my neck, darling," he says, that little hint of Southern drawl coming back.

My lips curve into a grin. "I hear your accent."

He leans in close, nuzzles my neck, whispers in my ear, "Maybe I save it for dancing too."

"I wonder if you save it for other things," I whisper, enjoying the feel of his chest against mine, his body pressed tight.

"I just might," he says, then murmurs softly against my hair, "This is a better dance for tonight, isn't it?"

I smile against his warm skin, getting his meaning right away. This dance with him is worlds better than a wedding spin. He's right. He's so right. "It sure is," I say.

"I like our celebration, Katie."

"I like our celebration so much better," I echo.

And I truly do.

It's crazy, in some ways.

How can I have shivers sliding down my spine after what happened today? How can I have flutters in my chest?

But they're here and they're real.

I was going to wait for Harlan, but screw waiting. It's time for me to take the reins.

I draw on those wild new sensations as I reach for the antidote. "I think Daisy had a great idea about tonight, Harlan. What about you?"

His lips crook into a naughty grin. "Are you asking me to engage in some red-hot rebound nookie?"

Those tingles turn into full-on sparks, igniting in the center of my body, pulsing between my legs. "I absolutely am, Harlan."

"Then the answer is… I'm at your service."

CHAPTER 14

KATIE

Ouch!" I hop on my left foot in the entrance to Harlan's home, holding my right one as a sharp pain radiates through my arch. "Did a tarantula eat my foot?"

Harlan rolls his eyes. "Dramatic much, sweetheart?" He bends, scoops up a pink plastic death device, and waggles it at me.

"Seriously. Stepping on a Lego is on a pain level right up there with childbirth," I say, then shrug sheepishly. "Or so I'm told."

He laughs as he sets the block on the entryway table. "Can't answer that one either. But I will corroborate your concerns. Last season, I was steamrolled by a three-hundred-pound lineman on a short pass and it hurt less than the time I stepped on one of these."

"So, I'm not dramatic, then," I say, chin lifted haughtily as I head into his home, having left my boots by the front door. My hat too. Also, my whip.

Harlan chuckles, shakes his head. "You're still dramatic, Katie," he says.

He flicks on the light for the living room, and I stop in my tracks.

Early-reader books and kid-size blankets cover the couch. Cartoon dogs dance down the fleece on one blanket, dinosaurs roam another, and astronauts fly through space on one more.

"Ah, sorry, I didn't clean up yet. We were playing library fort this morning before we baked a cherry pie."

My heart flies out of my chest, cheering in utter delight. I fling my hand to my sternum. "Shut up. Just shut up. You must stop talking now."

He furrows his brow. "Um, why are you telling me to shut it?"

Settle down, stupid heart. You're here for rebound banging. Not swooning over his dad skills.

But apparently, I don't listen to myself. "That's too cute. Too sweet. Too freaking adorable," I say, flapping my hand at the evidence on the furniture. "Library fort."

It's on the same level as a six-pack.

As dreamy eyes.

"Damn, you really do think I'm just cute," he says, with a faux-heavy sigh.

I park my hands on my hips. "Hey, why do you think cute is bad, mister?"

The tall, strapping fireman—he's still shirtless, lucky me—reaches for a hand, tugs me close. "I would think smoldering, sexy beast would be better. Try that, Katie."

I slide my hands up his bare chest, thrilling at the feel of his hard, smooth skin. I shiver as I trace his flesh. "Fine, fine. You're a very sexy beast. That work for you?"

His eyes glint with satisfaction. "Why yes, it does. Now, can I interest you in my bedroom? I think it might work better for my plans for you."

An idea pops into my dirty brain as I pluck at the suspenders. "You can definitely interest me in your bedroom. But do you think you could fling me over your shoulder and—"

In a flash, he hoists me up, tosses me over his shoulder.

"Oh, hello fireman carry," I say, a little giddy and a lot turned on as he heads up the steps, two at a time.

Hello, stud.

"Is it wrong of me to like this so much?" I ask, giggling as Harlan effortlessly eats up the stairs with his stride, his big arms wrapped around the back of my chiffon-covered legs. "You've got the whole big-and-strong thing down pat."

"It's absolutely terrible of you to objectify me for my body. The same one that earns me a damn-fine living to support my family," he says as he hits the second-floor landing.

My family.

The way he says those words—with masculine pride—sends sparks across my skin.

What is with me tonight? I'm turned on by his ability to take care of a kid I don't even know? Why is this getting to me?

Oh, right.

My emotions are a merry-go-round today.

But all I want now is to ride on the carousel of desire with him.

"I'm sooo sorry for objectifying your strength," I tease as he turns through the doorway to his bedroom, then sets me down on my bare feet.

The man stares at me, smolder in his irises. "Actually, you *should* objectify me all night long," he rumbles as his eyes roam up and down my frame.

I feel naked under his gaze, and I like it a lot.

Need licks at my skin.

Harlan peers at my dress. "Got a zipper on that?"

An idea bursts before me, bright and powerful.

"Rip it off," I urge.

He lifts one questioning brow. "You want me to tear off your dress? You sure?"

The idea takes a delicious, cathartic hold of me. I need this. I have to have it. I grab a handful of the chiffon skirt. "I'm not wearing this again. I promise."

"Do you want to sell it?"

Just like I need to have him tonight, I need him to shred this dress from my body. "No. I want you to tear it off me."

He gives a slow and sexy shrug. "What the lady wants..."

My shirtless football player fireman closes the distance, spins me around, sets his big hands on my back.

I shiver in anticipation.

This want feels exhilarating.

Necessary too.

I draw a breath, waiting for him to tug the fabric in one rip. His hands clasp around the top of the chiffon.

But instead, soft lips whisper across my skin.

"Oh God," I gasp, unbidden.

Unexpectedly.

His mouth travels across my back, dusting reverent, open-mouthed caresses along my body. I arch into his touch, craving more. "Yes," I murmur.

He roams along my skin to my shoulder, presses a hungrier kiss right there, then coasts those decadent lips over my neck. "Mmm. You taste delicious," he says.

I shudder as a pulse beats between my legs.

This man does things to me. He has since the night I met him. And he seems to sense my needs before I'm even fully aware of them.

Like he knew I needed gentle, tender kisses first.

He picks up the pace, kissing me harder, rougher. Then he digs his teeth into my shoulder. I cry out as he bites me, tossing my head back as the ache turns both sweet and sharp.

"Mmm. You still like biting, I see."

"From you," I add, since that feels important. I want him to know that *he* brings out this feral cat in me, who likes to play and nip. With Harlan, I seem to possess an animalistic desire to tussle.

"Is that so? You saved your biting for me, sweetheart?"

"I did," I answer as he lifts his face, then returns his hands to the top of my dress. He gives a gentle tug at first. "Ready?"

Funny, I want the ripping off of my dress even more now that he's marked my back with his sweet, greedy kisses.

Harlan wraps his fingers around the chiffon, then gives a fast, powerful jerk.

The sound of fabric tearing rends the air.

And heats my core.

Holy shit.

It worked.

I gaze down at the top, hanging at my waist in tatters. I'm wearing only a lace bustier and the bottom half of my wedding dress. "Mmm. Gorgeous," he murmurs against my neck. "Want more?"

"All the way," I say, breathless, urging him on. Pleasure rattles through me as he bends lower, one knee on the floor, then gives another hard tug.

Rip!

The white chiffon pools at my feet in pieces.

I turn around, wearing only the lace corset, a garter, and white, barely-there panties.

His eyes glimmer with desire. "Edible, sweetheart. You're so damn edible," he says, groaning in wanton appreciation.

His heated gaze sends pleasure spinning in me, dampening my panties so they're nearly soaked.

I slide my teeth along the corner of my mouth. "Then maybe eat me," I suggest, since I'm helpful like that.

"I've been waiting seven years to taste your sweetness."

His hands slink around my back once more, and he unhooks my bustier. It falls to the floor, and the groan that comes from him officially turns me into a hot, wet mess.

Exactly how I want to be right now.

But there's one more thing I want too. "What do you say we go for full-frontal nudity? From both of us," I offer, gesturing to him, still clothed in pants.

"I say yes, since you're better than my wildest fantasies," he says, staring shamelessly. His *eat-me-alive* gaze makes my skin sizzle.

In seconds, I slip off my panties. His clothes hit the floor, his cock springing free.

Oh yes.

He is mine tonight—all those yummy inches.

With hooded eyes, he takes a step closer, reaches for my garter, and slides it down my leg. "Everything off."

I step out of the garter, officially done with my wedding clothes.

Harlan flops down on the bed. "Now, come sit on my face."

Happy Just-Escaped-Marriage Day to me, indeed.

CHAPTER 15

HARLAN

I need to distract Katie completely from her day.

And I intend to do that with my tongue.

"Get up here now, woman. I am starving for you," I tell her as she straddles me, and I grab her hips.

With a laugh, she says, "I'm coming, I'm coming."

"No, that's what you'll be doing in a couple minutes."

She climbs up my body, naked and glorious, her fantastic tits bouncing, her soft skin glowing in the moonlight.

"Let's see about that," she teases as she reaches my shoulders.

I loop my arms around her, grab her ass, tug her close. "You doubt me? I can't wait to prove you wrong. You'll be coming in three minutes, sweetheart," I tell her, then give her no time to protest as I bring her sweet, wet pussy to my face.

I inhale the intoxicating scent of this aroused woman, and the first taste of her is incredible. My eyes roll back in my head, and I groan so damn loud. She's sweet and salty and sexy.

"You're so wet," I tell her, stating the patently obvious, but sometimes it needs to be stated.

"Seems you turn me on," she says, then presses her hands to the headboard and rocks.

Oh yes.

Fuck my face, babycakes.

Fuck me hard and good.

Only I can't say any of that out loud since my lips are so damn busy with a fantastic pussy right now.

My hands curl around her hips, and I rock her back and forth over my mouth, devouring her sweetness, tasting her wonderful heat.

The woman is silky and hot.

And…it turns out…*loud.*

"Oh God," she whimpers as she rocks shamelessly against my face. "Yes…please…more."

I've got a live wire here.

With a firm grip, I lavish love on her center, my tongue flicking against the delicious rise of her clit.

"Yes, oh God, yes. I love that, love it so much," she gasps.

My entire body goes up in flames.

Heat licks every corner of me as Katie goes to town on my face.

She's losing her mind, shedding any inhibition as she rides me like I'm her bucking bronco.

Yee-fucking-haw.

My hands clamp down on those hips as I lick and suck and

French kiss her until she's tossing her head back and shouting my name.

Harlan, oh God, Harlan.

Yes, yes, yes.

Her words turn into a dirty chant. A wild, desperate plea.

And I'm so goddamn happy as I rise to the occasion of my sex-superhero calling, devouring her till she's breaking apart on me.

Grabbing the headboard, she tenses. Everything goes on a sensual, heady pause. Until… "Yes!"

She starts up again, trembling, as she rides my face through her orgasm, her taste flooding my tongue.

Prides suffuses me, and wild desire too, infusing every damn cell.

I hold her tight as she pants and moans. As she comes down, I gently lift her off my face, setting her next to me on the bed.

A few seconds later, I stretch over her, pressing my hard cock against her soft stomach. "Want to make you come again, sweetheart," I say, pushing, rubbing, letting her know how hard I am.

"Yes, please, now."

I reach an arm to the nightstand, grab a condom from the drawer.

When I return to the beauty, she slides a hand down her body, traveling between her tits, heading for her mound. She parts her legs wide for me.

"Fucking beautiful," I moan in appreciation as I settle between those toned thighs.

"So are you," she says, reaching for my chest, her expression lust drunk, like she's still high on her first orgasm.

I roll on the condom, then rub the head of my cock against her slick heat. She arches, her body begging, her voice husky.

My dick throbs with anticipation.

But before I push in, I wiggle a brow. "So, how about an *I told you so?* That was less than three minutes."

Her grin is electric. "You're right. You're so damn right. You're so fucking right. Now give me that fine dick, and give it to me hard."

And I'm positive God is a Renegades fan and rewarding me for that last Super Bowl win.

Because this is heaven.

I slide inside, her heat welcoming me as I fill her to the hilt.

Her breath hitches. Mine escapes my lungs in a shuddery gasp.

Because she is divine. "You feel incredible." I grunt, savoring the tight warmth of her body.

Wrapping her legs around my ass, she whispers, "So do you."

She loops her hands around my neck and draws me closer. She's all vulnerable as she asks, "Will you kiss me?"

Wherever are my manners? I haven't kissed the woman tonight. "Shame on me for not kissing your lips before your sweet pussy."

"Shame indeed," she teases.

As I swivel my hips and drive into her, I drop my mouth to hers, catching her lips with mine. My eyes close, and we get lost in each other.

Our tongues explore.

Lips slide.

Mouths tangle.

She lets out a sensual sigh. "Mmm yes," she murmurs and I deepen the kiss.

"So good," I whisper, savoring her mouth as I fill her body.

We kiss as we fuck.

Long, slow, indulgent kisses mixed with passionate thrusts.

It's the perfect pace. Limbs tangled together, bodies connected, breath coming fast.

She bows her back, arching with me, moving like water as I take my time, enjoying this delicious, lingering rhythm.

A pace that soon seems to drive her wild.

She moans as she jerks me closer, wraps those long, toned legs around my body, rocking up with me. She's so in tune with herself. So connected with her own pleasure. It's incredible to watch her move, to feel her let go.

Her ankles hook around my ass, tugging me even deeper. A hot spike of lust shoots down my spine. "Mmm. Use me, sweetheart," I rasp in her ear, bracing myself on my forearms, my chest sliding against her firm tits.

"I am, oh God, I am," she murmurs, her fingers playing with the ends of my hair. "Deeper," she begs.

I love it when a woman asks for exactly what she wants—and when I can give it to her. I ease out, nearly all the way, then drive back into her.

"Yes, yes, yes," she moans, stretching her neck.

"You want me to fuck you good and hard?"

"I do, yes, I do."

"Then let me put you on your hands and knees."

Her eyes sparkle with dirty yeses.

In seconds we scramble around, shifting position. The beautiful woman lifts her hips, and I slide back home.

Stilling myself as her body hugs me.

Then I roam my hand up her back, grip her shoulder, and pin her in place as I fuck her deep and hard, with powerful, long thrusts that make her shake with pleasure.

She drops down to her elbows, and in seconds, she's gasping again.

Groaning.

Then shouting my name once more.

"Oh God, yes, oh God, yes," she moans, tensing, and a climax seems to tear through her body.

That's enough for me.

It trips my wires, and pleasure seizes me, taking me captive. I come hard.

The aftershocks radiate spectacularly through every damn cell in my body.

I dip my face, giving her a little bite on the shoulder.

"Mmm, nibble on me," she murmurs.

I nip her once more.

She laughs lightly. It's a great sound, and it makes me smile.

I roll to my side and ease out of her. "I've wanted to do that with you for more than seven years."

She turns her gaze to me. Her eyes are etched with happiness, but it reads a little temporary. "When I woke up this morning, this wasn't how I expected tonight to go," she admits with a touch of sadness.

My shoulders tense. Is she about to gather her things and fly out of here? I don't want her to go. But then, she can't truly take off. She has nothing to wear.

Hazards of jilted-bride sex, it seems.

Still, I want her to *want* to be here.

I didn't expect to feel so much *want*. Not tonight, and not of *that* variety.

"I'm sure you didn't," I say with sympathy. That's the reality of her day, and I can't escape it.

Hell, she can't truly escape it.

She was dumped on her wedding day.

My stresses are nothing compared to hers.

"But," she adds, running her fingers down my arm, "I'm weirdly, strangely glad I'm here."

A smile tips my lips.

All things considered, that's as good as it gets with compliments on a day like today.

And I'll take what I can get from her.

Oh yes, I will.

After we clean up, I bring her back to bed, nuzzling her neck. "Do you have to go?"

I hope she says no. I really want her to stay. It's been a while. A long while. No one's spent the night in ages, and having a woman in my arms feels too damn good.

No, that's not it.

Having *Katie* in my arms feels great.

She props her head in her hand. Fear flickers across those pretty eyes—worry too. "Do you want me to go?"

I hate what she's been through. That it may make her doubt… everything. "Hell, no. I want you to stay." I can give her that much—the truth, something her slimeball of an ex couldn't muster up. "And I definitely want you to spend the night," I add, even as nerves prickle along my skin.

What the hell? I'm not a guy who feels nerves. But I do with her, and I think I know why. She's tough on the outside, using her humor as a shield, her sex appeal as a source of strength. She's all confidence and guts, but she's also remarkably fragile.

I don't want to take advantage of her.

I don't want to be the kind of guy I was raised by.

Don't want to be the bad guy. That's my worry—the possibility that I could hurt her.

She's had more than enough of that lately.

"You want me to stay?" She sounds like she can't believe her luck.

"I sure as hell do." I sit up. "Wait, are you hungry? I haven't fed you. I should be ashamed of myself."

Her stomach rumbles. "I *am* hungry, and I want to stay."

With a smile, I swing my legs out of bed, stare at the wedding dress in tatters on the floor, then grab a T-shirt from a drawer and hand it to her.

She pulls it on, swimming in it. "How do I look?"

"Good enough to eat again." And that's the truth too.

After I tug on boxer briefs, we head downstairs, where I whip up scrambled eggs.

"You can cook," she says, whistling in admiration as she sits on a stool at the island counter.

"Isn't that like the equivalent of saying I can put down the toilet seat? Seems a basic skill."

She shrugs. "You'd be surprised."

I throw her a dubious glance. "Don't tell me Mister Jackass didn't cook?"

"Didn't cook. Didn't clean either."

I groan. Men. What is wrong with some of them? "Well, I have a person to cook for."

She sighs softly. "Tell me more about Abby. What she's like?"

A smile takes over my face. "Are you trying to win my heart? Asking me to talk about my little lady? Well, if you *insist*," I say, with an *of course I'll go on and on* shrug. "She's feisty and snuggly and smart. She wants to get a dog, but that's hard with me being on the road. She'd take a cat, though, she says. Or a hedgehog, if that's easier."

"Are hedgehogs easier on the road?"

I stop, raising the red plastic spatula, wondering what the hell the answer is to that. "You know, I have no idea about the care and feeding of hedgehogs. But I know this: She wants to name it Dolly. Cat, dog, or hedgie."

Her eyes pop. "Shut the front door. She's a Dolly Parton fan?"

I give her a look, complete with a full-on eye roll. "As if she'd be anything but. My kid has taste, Katie."

Katie's eyes twinkle, and I want to keep putting that light there. "The best taste," she says.

"No doubt. And hey, I'd still think she was the bomb even if she loved Green Day or Nickelback, but whew." I stop to wipe a hand across my brow. "Glad she does not."

"Bless her heart," Katie says, full-on Texas style, then her eyes sweep the kitchen and land on a framed photo of Abby on the edge of the island counter. My little bear is perched in a saddle on a pony, reins in her hands. "That is adorable. Does she want a pony too?"

"She might have mentioned it. But she says she'll name it Mia."

Katie tilts her head, RCA dog style. "That's going to need a little more explanation. Not Dolly, or Cinnamon Apple, or Midnight Ranger, or some other very horselike name?"

Ah, this name might open a can of worms. But what's the harm in bringing it up? I'm not getting my kid a pony, no matter how much of a softie I am. And my kid isn't getting a sibling from me, so the reason Abby likes the name doesn't truly matter.

I turn off the flame, slide the eggs onto a plate. "Apparently, Mia is her *dream* name for a little sister. She has a half brother, so she says"—I dip into my daughter's sassy but sweet voice—"if you won't give me a little sister, I'll gladly take a pony named Mia instead."

An awkward laugh falls from Katie's lips, but she seems to pull it back quickly, rearranging her features into a gentle smile. "Well, I guess Abby knows what she wants."

I'm glad Katie doesn't ask about more kids.

Whether I want them.

Whether Abby's dreams align with any potential reality.

It's not exactly the easiest conversation to have with a woman I just slept with. Or took out on a date. Was tonight a date? It felt a little like one at the costume shop and the lounge.

"She definitely does," I say, then serve my after-midnight guest her late dinner, handing her a red-and-white-checkered napkin and a fork. "Here you go, ma'am, courtesy of the chef extraordinaire at Harlan's Late-Night Diner of Deliciousness."

"Why thank you very much, sexy chef," she says, then adds a little coyly, "I hope there's dessert on the menu."

I scoff as I sit next to her, setting a plate down for me too. "Of course you get multiple desserts, sweetheart."

She takes a bite, then moans. "Mmm. This is delish. Also, you can screw like a very sexy beast," she says with a naughty grin, and I shoot her an approving nod for using the best term ever. "Plus, you can show a woman a good time, and you can change positions on the football field. What's that all about, Mister Running Back Turned Receiver? I read the news reports when you switched, but was curious if you liked it better."

I key in on one delicious detail she just revealed. "Ah, so you read about me? While you were off in Los Angeles being a flamingo in your tree pose or what-have-you, and sassing everyone with your funny yoga sayings?"

Her smile lights up the block. "So you read about me too?"

I shrug, all offhand and casual. "I checked you out from time to time."

She dips her face, hiding a smile. Funny—Katie is not a shy woman. Not at all. But her temporary display of it is insanely adorable.

"I like that image," she says, all soft and vulnerable. That's something she's been a lot of today, but now she's vulnerable about us.

And I like it.

Except, I can't like it too much.

The timing is still all wrong.

As much as I want to ask her out, not only am I leaving for training camp, but she's clearly not in the place for *how about dinner next month when I'm back*?

At least, I don't think so.

"And I like the image of you looking me up now and then," I say, taking another bite of the eggs, then move on to her question. "To answer, I love being a receiver. I played both positions in college, but receiver is way more fun than running back. Plus, there are many, many more opportunities for play-making when you have a passing QB. Which is most of the QBs these days, so it's a helluva good time."

"But is that why the team switched you? So it'd be more fun?"

Laughing, I shake my head. "No, that's just a bonus that I dig. The coach had the idea after a game several years ago against the Hawks. Cooper was throwing to Jones, but he was swarmed by the secondary. I was open. Coop threw to me instead, and I ran it in for a touchdown. About a thirty-yard pass."

"And that did it?"

"Started it at least. The next game we had an injured receiver, so I stepped into the role again. Boom. It was like magic."

She grins, a little bit like she's keeping a secret. "Definitely."

I nudge her with my elbow, quirk a brow. "What's that look for? Like you've got an ace up your sleeve?"

She raises her face, her smile magnetic. "Just that I've seen your games. You and Cooper are definitely like magic."

That makes me feel damn good. Sure, my stats tell me I'm good at my job. The results make it clear. Two rings don't lie either, especially since I was MVP in one of those games. But hell, hearing a woman you're hot for say she admires the way you work elicits a special kind of thrill.

Because football isn't just a game. It's my livelihood. It's my passion. It's the thing that's made me tick my whole damn life.

But...what will I do without it?

All good things come to an end, and eventually, this game will too.

The last thing I want is to overstay my welcome.

I do *not* want to be the guy who hobbles off the field, booed by fans shouting good riddance to an over-the-hill dude.

I want to go out on a high note.

End it on my terms.

But when? That's the question, and it's one I just don't have the answer to.

Great.

Here I am, my mind cycling back to work issues on a night when I'd like to escape them.

"So, what about you?" I ask, since I'd much rather be *her* distraction tonight.

I'd rather be her distraction another night too. And maybe another after that.

But I'm pretty sure that's not in the playbook.

CHAPTER 16

KATIE

Now it's my turn to catch him up on my career.

"I started a yoga brand with my sister, building on the classes I'd been teaching—yoga for people who hate yoga. And boom. Turns out there are a lot of those people who learn to fall in love with it. Our style is a little irreverent, a lot fun."

"And you're the face of it," he puts in.

That's all true. When Olive and I met with the investor in Los Angeles seven years ago, Charlotte liked my style and Olive's penchant for numbers. She invested and helped us grow the concept. Now, some of my classes are available online for a subscription package of videos. Others I do in person, when I tailor sessions for clients and retreats. And others still are taught by the teachers I've trained in our various studios. "We expanded it to twenty studios all across the West Coast. Added clothing and fashion, with T-shirts that have sayings like *Yoga—it's cheaper than therapy; If you think I'm bitchy now, you should see me when I miss yoga;* or *Yoga is my favorite way to pretend to work out.* So that's my story, and Sassy Yoga has been fabulous," I say.

"You became a yoga queen," Harlan remarks as he takes my plate, rinses it, and sets it in the dishwasher.

"Please. I'm a yoga empress," I tease, then roll my eyes in self-deprecation. "That's the term an LA magazine used to describe me, and the nickname weirdly stuck. Now, some of my students call me a yoga empress in the classes I teach."

"A yoga empress running a yoga empire. It's fitting," he says, adding a wink. "Since you're so damn flexible."

And I like the sound of that. "Let me show you what I can do with my legs."

In a flash, he scoops me up in his arms, carrying me again. As he heads to the stairs, I laugh, loving the ride.

Loving this whole strange turn of events.

All this talking with Harlan seems like the second date we never had.

That makes my chest dance with butterflies, but my head throbs too. With confusion.

How is this even possible?

I'm having an amazing time with another guy, the best time I've had in ages. Did Silvio and I ever have this much easy, breezy fun?

Just the thought of the man I was supposed to marry stirs up a bucket of guilt.

Less than twelve hours ago, I was about to say I do to another man. To pledge love and fidelity to an Italian artist who likes opera and ordering tuna tartare at midnight. Instead, I spent the evening with a man who cooks killer eggs and rocks out to one of the greatest country singers of all time.

And I loved tonight.

Is something wrong with me for enjoying it?

As we head up the steps, questions clang through my mind.

Is something wrong with me for craving more hot sex from Harlan, rather than missing...*anything* with my ex right now?

Am I, well, a female cad for savoring that sweet conversation in his kitchen? Loving the tales of his daughter? Wanting to know more about his job? Wanting to share stories of mine?

That felt so date-y.

How can I do that the night of my...

But I stop that train. Tonight isn't my wedding night.

It's a night that seems to exist in its own time and place.

It's a parallel universe night.

That's what I tell myself as we turn into his bedroom—that I'm another me right now.

I'm the me who, evidently, wasn't entirely sure about Silvio.

The me who wonders if maybe his lack of interest in axe-throwing was a sign.

Maybe I don't know how to judge men or anybody else.

Certainly, I trusted the wrong people.

And tonight isn't about forever. It's about fun. It's about an escape. It's about a hot, charming, sexy man who wants to give me everything I need.

He sets me down, closes the distance between us, and cups my cheeks. "I haven't kissed you enough tonight. I need to make up for it now."

I lift my chin, an eager creature, ready and waiting. "I won't object to more kissing."

"Good. You're about to get a boatload of it."

A boatload is my new favorite measurement after Harlan drops his lips to mine and kisses me breathlessly. His pillowy lips sweep over mine as he wraps his arms around me, his fingers sliding through my hair.

Tugging me closer, he kisses me deeper.

It's slow and lush, and it feels like melting into his arms.

My knees go weak as he kisses me with a luxuriousness that makes my bones sing Ella Fitzgerald tunes, that feels like a warm summer day spent lounging under the blue sky.

When he breaks the kiss, he glides his thumb along my jaw, down to my chin, cupping my face.

"Now, I believe I promised you multiples. And your pleasure has always been a favorite thing of mine," he says.

He brings me to the bed, slides a hand between my legs, and strokes me till I'm gasping and calling his name.

Like I do again a little later, when he pulls me on top of him and tells me to ride him.

I oblige, and the pleasure blots out the worries and the questions.

I'm too blissed out to think, as I fall asleep in his arms.

———

But when I wake, I know something sharp and clear—I can't start something with him as much as I want to.

I need time to sort out this mess in my head and heart.

I need yoga and wine.

I need friends and me time.

Especially since he makes me coffee the next morning, and it's life-affirmingly delicious with just a hint of cinnamon.

"You seem like a woman who likes her spice," he says after I drain the mug.

Already, he seems to get me. What a crazy notion. "I do yoga so I can justify my wine and coffee vices," I say as I rinse the cup, then sigh. "I should go," I say, a little resigned.

"All good things must come to an end," he says.

Do I detect a hint of wistfulness in his tone too? Pretty sure I do. And I'm pretty sure I need to do some serious lotus-ing to sort through the last twenty-four hours of my life.

I need to figure out what it means that I nearly married a man who decided to take a honeymoon with my mother less than an hour later.

What it means that I went home with this hunk and had the best sex of my life on my non-wedding night.

What it means that I want to see him again.

"And it was very, very good, but yes, they do end," I say, echoing the sentiment, since I don't want him to think I'm going to Velcro myself to him on the rebound train.

He nods toward the door. "I'll call you a car service now. And I have some clothes for you to head home in." After he makes a call, he strides to the living room, picks up some folded items, and offers me a pair of gym shorts and a Renegades sweatshirt. With a smile of gratitude, I take off his T-shirt and pull on the new duds. I swim in both of them, the shorts slipping down my waist.

He holds up one finger. "I've got something for that." He heads into the kitchen and returns ten seconds later. He hands me an apron with snowmen printed on it. "Take this. Wrap it around your waist."

I grin in approval. "It's a life hack for a belt."

He winks. "You got it."

"It's also a Christmas apron. You own a Christmas apron?" I ask, sort of in awe. It's so freaking cute, I don't know what to do with how sweet it is.

"I own many. I was born on Christmas."

Nothing has made more sense than that. "Of course you were," I say. I tie the makeshift apron-slash-belt and head to the entryway, pull on my cowboy boots, and grab my clutch. "Can you just toss the remains of my wedding dress?"

"Consider it done."

"Thanks for that. And for tearing it off me."

"Oh, I assure you, the pleasure was definitely mine."

"And mine too." I draw a deep breath. Here goes the hard part. I hate to do this, but I have to. "I really want to see you again. But…"

Harlan shoots me a resigned smile. "I know. Wrong timing."

I smile so damn sadly. "Worst timing ever," I say, choking up a little.

Yup, the whirligig of emotions knocks me around again. "I

think I need to sort out everything that's happened." But I can't stand the thought of walking away. "But what if we try again? Maybe in the fall? That feels like enough time. But duh. The fall is for football. You'll be busy with the game."

"I will, but I'd love to see you again. Maybe the third time will be the charm."

I sure hope so.

When the car arrives at the curb, he sets the Indiana Jones hat on my head, then kisses me goodbye. I glance down at my get-up. "I should return all your clothes to you. Do you want me to drop them off later? Leave them on your porch?"

He waves a hand dismissively. "I've got plenty of aprons, shorts, and sweatshirts to keep me busy till the fall. Why don't you return them when you're ready for that date?"

My heart warms at that. I wish I were ready now. But I'm not. "I will."

I leave, decked out in his clothes, my new hat, my old boots, and an apron.

I'm a mess, but I'm happier than I was yesterday evening.

And I'm a little hollow too.

Imagine that.

THE FALL

CHAPTER 17

KATIE

One more lap.

I push through the cool, blue water, burst above the surface, then breaststroke my way to the end of the pool. When I hit the edge of the deep end, I slap my palm on the concrete and indulge in several long breaths.

My father putters at the other end of the pool, organizing floaties in a big basket. I hoist myself out of the water and reach for the towel I left on the diving board. As I dry off, I inhale the quiet.

It's six in the morning on a Sunday, and even though the swim and tennis club my dad owns is open right now, the classes don't start till after nine.

Swimming has always centered me. I suspect my love of yoga started in the pool. They're different, sure, but also *not*. Both rely on that mind-body connection, on breath, on finding your own pace.

I wrap the towel around my waist and circle the pool toward

the shallow end. The scent of chlorine is thick and familiar—it reminds me of home.

As a kid in Texas, I spent afternoons goofing off in the water when Dad taught classes. Later, the pool was an escape for me when Mom left Dad shortly after we moved to California.

Oh, yeah, my mom out-Draper-ed Don Draper. She banged the assistant of the magazine she ran, then she married him. I should have seen the Silvio situation coming.

Dad smiles at me as I reach him, and maybe that's the real therapy—talking to him about Mom and Silvio, sure, but also about life and business, his wife, Janice, and their adventures in fishing and golfing. He'll tell me about the swim classes he's teaching here. I'll update him on the corporate clients I've taken on. He'll give me business advice, and I'll weigh in on what to give Janice for her birthday or anniversary—that lemon pound-cake candle from the wine country vintage shop that actually smells like lemon pound cake, a mug that says *Please cancel my subscription to your issues*, and a weekend getaway trip to her favorite golf resort.

It's been therapeutic, and four months post–Just-Escaped-Marriage Day, I feel centered again.

Calm again.

My mind no longer a discombobulated mess.

One of the things that helped the most? Saying my piece. My mom called me several times after taking *my* honeymoon. She texted me constantly after I unblocked her, and emailed me too. Saying how much she loved Silvio. How she hoped someday I'd be happy for her. Asking if I wouldn't just accept that this was true love.

At first, I seethed over her notes.

After all, I'd had to return all the gifts to the guests.

That was super fun.

Not.

But it *was* weirdly cathartic. The practical act of returning presents was like a daily letting go. Breathe in, breathe out, return this blender to the Fishers, give this set of napkin rings back to the Bloombergs.

And in so doing, say goodbye to the double bastards of Mom and Silvio.

Once I returned the last gift, I found final closure.

I sent her a letter, saying simply: *Enjoy him.*

Then I blocked her number again and her email.

Life is better like this.

I'm happier.

And I'm happy hanging out with my dad after I swim.

"So, what's next on the yoga empress's agenda?" Dad asks as we sink down on the bench at the edge of the pool—our chatting bench. "Are you adding a *Yoga keeps me out of prison* class?"

"Or… *Yoga, because punching people isn't cool,*" I joke.

He holds up a hand as a stop sign. "Wait, wait. I've got it. How about a class called *Flexibility for old people who can't get out of bed without moaning in misery?*" he suggests, grabbing his lower back.

Seems like a demonstration if I've ever seen one. "Gee, Dad. Why do I feel like that's spoken from experience?"

"Just wait till you're sixty."

"That's twenty-five years away. I can't even think about that!"

He snaps his fingers. "'It'll be here in a flash." He sets his palms on his pants, takes a beat. "But seriously, everything is going well? The business is still helping you process all the things?"

That is easy to answer. Business has been a wonderful escape, and a healthy one too, I suspect. I've poured my heart even further into our company in the last four months and it's paid off. "It's going great. Olive and I hired a new VP of business dev, and Zachary's been inking deals left and right for corporate classes. All sorts of companies are hiring our teachers."

"But lots of them want you?" he asks.

I shrug and smile. "It's good to be the empress."

He sets a hand on my shoulder and squeezes. "I'm proud of you, Katie. You've been focused and determined, but you never seem angry about what happened with your mom."

I suppose I have yoga and friends and business to thank for that. And my dad. "Life goes on," I say.

"But seriously, I'm impressed. You seem…healthy," he adds.

"It's time, right?" I've tried to give myself that. In retrospect, everything happened so quickly with Silvio. Perhaps that was the biggest flaw in our relationship. "And honestly, we never seemed completely compatible, but I ignored that, because I was swept up in it."

"It was a whirlwind romance," he seconds.

"When I look back at the last year, I think maybe if I just took more time before we planned our wedding, I would have realized it sooner. That's what I learned. We didn't quite fit, but I was captivated, and I convinced myself it was meant to be."

"I think there's a part of you that wanted to believe in fate," he muses, stroking his chin.

Huh. That's an interesting observation. I didn't realize I was such a fate-centric person. "Why do you say that?" I ask, eager for some insight.

"It's something I noticed in you when you were a teenager. When your mom and I split—well, like most kids, you wanted us to stay together, but that clearly wasn't happening, and you wanted to make sense of it. As you tried, you'd say things like how we never seemed right for each other, or how fate had other plans."

That's surprising, since I'm not a believer in fate now. But maybe I needed it as a teen to see me through a tough time. "Maybe I just *wanted* to believe in it."

Dad nods. "I'd like to believe in it, too, but ultimately I think you make your own fate."

I tilt my head, studying his expression, mulling over his words. "You do?"

He takes a deep breath, lets it out. "I do. I believe in hard work, putting in the time, and listening to your instincts. I haven't always done that, but I sure try to now."

Those are words to live by.

I vow to keep doing that too—pay attention to what my gut says, rather than my heart.

I've taken the last few months to find my balance again, and I've spent lots of time with Olive, Emerson, Jillian, and Skyler. We've started an ad-hoc axe-throwing club, along with a self-proclaimed Snooty Wine Night.

Girlfriend time is fantastic therapy.

So is football. I've watched every Renegades game this season, just as I usually do. Harlan is on fire, and his team is having a great run. They've won five games and lost one. By all accounts, he's killing it on the field, though he did leave the last game earlier in the fourth quarter than usual. That was a little odd, but the team was beating Baltimore by two touchdowns and won, so I suspect they wanted to give their stars a rest.

And maybe it's time for me to see more of that star.

Maybe I'm ready.

"Dad?" I say, giving him my attention. "I'm trying to listen to my instincts, too, and you know what they say?"

"What do they say?"

I go for broke. "That it's time to date again."

He slams his hands over his ears. "Tra la la la."

I laugh—because it's fun to wind him up—until he sets his palms in his lap, muttering, "I can handle this, I can handle this."

"You're such a dad," I tease.

He bumps shoulders with me. "Can't help it. But seriously. I'm happy for you. If you want to date again, go for it."

This choice seems right. Four months ago, I was a mess. But I've straightened that up, and I'm in a good place—a place where I have zero plans to get serious again, and no intentions to give my heart away. Nada. But a good time? Bring it on.

"I will. I already have someone in mind."

A few nights later, I host my besties for wine.

I lift my glass and issue a declaration. "I'm diving back into the dating pool," I announce.

My four friends clink glasses with me. Relief and excitement swirls in my chest. I'm ready to try again, but also a tad nervous. "Dating is a shark tank, right?"

"Full of Moby Dicks," Emerson says drily.

"And hammerheads," Olive adds with a wink.

Skyler sets down her wineglass on my coffee table and mimes banging a drum on the punchline. Then she jerks her gaze to me and goes all business, tucking her stray red strands of hair behind her ears. "Are we going for Tinder? A matchmaker? Bumble? Something else?"

"Because not everyone can meet a fabulous tour guide on a Hawaiian vacation," I point out, since I can't resist reminding her of her ridiculously good fortune.

"Lucky bitch," Emerson hisses as she downs some red wine, then taps the glass. "Snooty Wine Club time out! This tastes like shoe leather."

"Well, that's better than last week's wine. It tasted like a veggie burger," Jillian quips, lifting her seltzer water as she nudges our resident vegetarian.

Emerson's jaw drops in mock outrage. "Take that back. Veggie burgers are the best."

"Says you."

"Exactly. I would know," Emerson adds.

I take a drink of my wine, a different red than Emerson's, then murmur appreciatively. "Mine tastes like cherries. I'm winning."

Emerson laughs. "And you deserve to win. So, tell us more. What's the plan?" she asks, rerouting the conversation back to dating.

Apropos, since cherries remind me of the man I'm finally ready for. I set down the glass and clear my throat. "I'm going to reach out to the guy who got away."

Jillian gasps. We're talking full-on, jaw-drop style. This has clearly been a dream of hers for some time. "Oh my God, I've only been hoping you would for seven years. Thank you for putting me out of my waiting misery."

"It really was all about you," I tease. "And trust me, I wish we'd had our Tuesday-night date several years ago. Would have made my life easier."

But as soon as I say that, I have to wonder—would it? Would I have started Sassy Yoga if I'd stayed here and dated Harlan?

Something else wouldn't have happened either. Something much more important. *Someone.* If we'd become a thing, he wouldn't have had his little girl. Maybe we weren't meant to be then for many reasons, after all.

Except, I don't believe in fate.

I believe in timing, and this timing seems right. *To date.* Just to date.

My friends seem to think so, too, judging from their reactions.

Olive hoots. "Get it, girl!"

Emerson shimmies her shoulders. "He's such a hottie." She turns to Jillian. "And he's single?"

"As far as I know," Jillian says with a light shrug, "but it's not like Jones and I spend all our time talking about Harlan's dating situation." She rubs her growing belly. "We're a little busy."

I roll my eyes. "Making people, sheesh. You act like it's so hard."

"Easy as pie," she deadpans, then asks, "Is this going to be more like an official date?"

"Rather than the sort of impromptu ones we've had so far?" I ask with a laugh.

Emerson chimes in, smacking her palm on the table. "That's how I'd put it. You've been impromptu dating him now and then, and he's been impromptu giving you orgasms."

"He *is* a bit of an orgasm dealer," I admit as a shiver rolls down my spine in memory.

After everyone leaves, Emerson stays behind to help me straighten up. As I wash wineglasses and she dries them, she arches a brow. "So, I have to ask…"

I laugh lightly. This is so her. She's uber enthusiastic but also intensely grounded. I suspect her grounded side is rearing up right now. "Of course *you* have to ask something. Spill."

She sets down the towel, stares at me with intense green eyes. "Are you ready? Truly ready? And I don't just mean for orgasms."

"I'm definitely ready for those," I say as I turn off the water.

She sighs. "Hello, yoga empress who doesn't take herself seriously. Make an exception for this. You know what I mean. I get that you're feeling good and healed, and that's truly awesome. And I know, too, that you feel like it all worked out for the best. That the universe saved you from a bad marriage. And yes, it did. But I also know you berated yourself for being so caught up in a whirlwind romance that you didn't pay attention to the signs that he wasn't right for you."

"Want to read my soul a little more?" I tease. Because she's nailed every detail like the bestie she is.

She just gives a soft smile, then squeezes my forearm. "I regret it too—that I missed the signs. I mean, I even said on your wedding day that he treated you well," she says, her voice catching.

A lump forms in my throat. "It's not your fault."

"And it's not yours either," she says, choked with emotion. But she draws a breath like it steadies her. "I just want to make sure you're...you know...ready? Because every time you talk about Harlan, he seems like not only a god in bed, but also a good guy *out* of bed. And that's pretty easy to get caught up in too."

"But I won't," I insist. "That's what I've learned—to take everything day by day. Not zoom too many steps ahead."

"Good. That's all I wanted to know. That you're looking out for you," she says, pointing at my heart. "Because I definitely am. And I promise to do a better job of it this time around."

"And I love you for that."

She flashes a big, naughty smile. "Then I can't wait to hear how your first official date with the O dealer goes."

Really, it's more like a third date. Every time I've been with Harlan, we've gotten to know each other. We've had fun. We've spent real time together in and out of bed.

Maybe we will again.

That's all I want. That's all I have room for.

Time to enjoy the present. To take a chance at that third date.

Once Emerson has gone, I pick up my phone, feeling good about my plans to reach out. This isn't fate. This is timing. And maybe, finally, the time is right for us.

So, I send him a text.

CHAPTER 18

KATIE

As far as opening lines go, this one should be pretty clear.

Katie: I still have your apron, shorts, and sweatshirt.

And he doesn't make me wait too long. As I wash my face before bed, the phone buzzes on the bathroom vanity.

Harlan: Seven years ago, you left behind a lip gloss tube. Now, you've taken my clothes. You're a variation on Cinderella.

That's good, right? Hinting at fairy tales? Except, I don't know. I press on.

Katie: I'd love to return them to you.

I hit Send as nerves rush through me. I'm asking a man out for the first time since I was dumped spectacularly. How could I not be freaking out? My skin prickles with worry. What if I read him wrong? What if I got the wrong intel? He might be secretly dating someone else and Jillian simply doesn't know.

But I have to put myself out there if I want a chance.

So, I wait another few minutes.

Then a few more.

Ugh.

He's not writing back.

My stomach craters to the floor. What was I thinking? He's too good to be true. It was silly to think he was waiting for me to drop back into his life. Like he'd be ready at a moment's notice when he could be snuggling with Miss Right this very second.

Le sigh.

I wait for the *sorry, you're too late* shoe to drop.

I'll just…find something else to do to pass the time till he officially turns me down.

Maybe I should put on a face mask. Drop into a lotus pose. Enroll in my *Yoga for the dating challenged* class, since it's become somewhat of a regular routine for me.

Harlan: Hey! Abby woke up and wanted a glass of water… so natch, I had to fetch it.

Katie: Of course! That's part of the job, I imagine.

Harlan: Dad apparently = water fetcher, among other jobs. She's back in bed now. But enough about me.

Tell me more about this apron you want to return, Cinderella.

My heart does a cat-cow pose, stretching joyfully. Nerves begone. He's flirting. He's definitely flirting. But still, it's best to ask for pertinent intel.

Katie: I will. But first. Are you still as single as the day is long?
Harlan: Woman, would I flirt with you like this if I weren't single?

And now I can't resist.

Katie: Are you flirting with me?
Harlan: If you can't tell, you ought to be put over my knee and spanked with the whip you left behind.

A shiver runs down my back as I head to my bedroom, flop down on the soft pillows, and bask in his messages.

Katie: Was that an official offer to spank me?
Harlan: Put on that apron and I will make my request official.
Katie: And things are getting hot.
Harlan: But seriously, it is holy fucking good to hear from you. And since I'm a gentleman, I'm going to do something right now.

Before I can tap out a reply, my phone rings.

Settle down, woman. Be cool. Don't let on you're in high school again and the hot guy is calling you. "Hi."

And it comes out like Minnie Freaking Mouse.

Real smooth, Katie.

"Hello, sweetheart. I'd love to administer a good spanking, but first things first. I've got a game this weekend, so how about I take you out for foosball and dinner on Tuesday?"

I nearly dance. "A Tuesday-night redo?"

"More than seven years in the making."

"I'm game," I say.

"It's a date," he says, sounding pleased. I feel pleased. As freaking punch. "How have you been?" he asks, sliding right into chatter again, as easily as we've always talked.

Yup, this is good timing. Good fun.

"I'm pretty darn good," I say, relieved to mean it wholly.

"Yeah?" He asks the question not like he doubts me, but more like he's sure glad I'm saying so.

"I am," I confirm. "I've spent lots of time with my friends and my sister and my dad over the last few months. It's been good for the soul."

"You're close with them?"

"Definitely. All of them. My dad has always been my rock. Ever since I was growing up. He was the one who was there for me whenever I needed someone."

"That's awesome. What's he like?"

Ah, that's an easy question, and one I love answering, since I

147

admire my father so much. "He's great. He's always believed in me, supported me. When I was younger, he told me I was strong and independent. He instilled in me a belief from a young age that I could do anything I set my mind to. Fine, maybe *anything* didn't include flying to the moon or singing opera, but still."

Harlan chuckles. "If you can fly to the moon, I want a ticket on that ride."

"And I'd give you one," I say, right as Harlan slides into a croon, singing a little of Frank Sinatra's tune of that same name.

Oh. My. Stars. The man can sing too. "Now you really have an unfair advantage," I say.

He chuckles. "You and your list of unfair advantages."

"Hey! You started it, having all these pros," I toss back.

"Would you prefer cons, woman? Sheesh," he says, then shifts back to the dad talk. "Also, I like your dad already."

I laugh. "You don't even know him."

"But that's how it should be with a dad and his daughter. That's how I am with Abby. Do I think she's the most adorable creature to ever grace the face of this Earth? Hell yes. Do I tell her that every day? No way."

"What do you tell her instead?"

"That I think she's smart and kind and friendly. That those are the things that matter."

A loopy smile takes over my face. I'm not even sure I want to have kids, so why is it so damn sweet how good this guy seems to be with his girl? But then, the answer lies in why I see my own dad a lot. "That will make a difference for her. I love having a good relationship with my father, and I think it's great that you focus on those things with Abby. My dad taught me to believe in who I was on the inside, not on the outside."

"Sure seems like it worked. You're full of spit and fire," he says, emphasizing each word with his very Harlan-like panache.

"Hey, are you saying I'm a spitfire?"

"The very definition, and that's a damn good thing."

I'll take that, thank you very much. "I believed in myself, too, and I chased after my dreams with the tenacity of a lion going after a gazelle. Sort of like how you are on the field."

He lets loose an embellished roar. "You know that's what they called me several years ago? King of the Jungle? It was my nickname."

I crack up. "No! Really?"

"Swear on the Lombardi trophy. I had long hair. Kind of more golden blond, less brown than now," he says, explaining, and this I can't resist. I turn the call to speaker and search Google for said photos as he talks. "A sports reporter called me a *beautiful lion* at a charity auction."

My search results reveal the animalistic hottie from several years ago—Harlan sporting a tailored suit on stage, strutting his stuff. Gorgeous long locks fall on his shoulders. They're a little lighter too. Mmm, I remember how that hair felt between my fingers. "Found the shots. And look at you. *Rawr* indeed," I say with an appreciative groan.

"You like the King of the Jungle look, Katie?"

I give a pregnant pause, just to goad him. "It's definitely... fluffy. A little Fabio."

He groans. "Woman, you are the worst complimenter ever."

"Maybe I like Fabio."

I can practically hear him rolling his eyes. "Ha. Said no woman ever."

"Said lots of women! But I would think three orgasms would be a better compliment," I say with a defiant lift of my chin, though he can't see me.

"Don't shortchange me. I gave you four. Do not retroactively remove one of the orgasms I delivered."

I slip back in time to the night over the summer, sensual memories flashing hot before my eyes, sending tingles shivering down my body. "Truth be told, you've given me more than that. Let's not forget the bathroom at the wedding seven years ago. So it's five. Five that keep me company late at night," I say, and maybe it comes out as a purr. Maybe because I feel all kinds of frisky for him. He's been the star of my late-night fantasies for the last few months.

"You've been thinking of me?"

"A lot."

He lets out a sexy murmur. "Excellent. I've been thinking of you too. Also a lot."

I'm giddy with delight. Just giddy. My libido wants to throw off all my clothes and ask him to talk dirty to me right now. But there's a voice in the front of my head telling me to slow down, to get to know him anew. To take my time since I refuse to be a fool again.

"And I'll probably jump you when I see you, so maybe we can chat more now," I suggest. See? I can be adult sometimes.

"Let's do it. But I want to see you, Katie. Let's switch to FaceTime."

We do, and he calls back on video. When his handsome profile appears on my screen, my stomach flips. Those cheekbones, those pillowy lips, those soulful eyes.

He just makes me...melt.

He's all the unfair advantages in the world.

The man settles into his living room couch, surrounded by pillows. "So, your dad lives in town?"

I nod, relaxing into my pillows too, feeling cozy and comfy as we chat. "He remarried when I went to college, and his new wife is great. They run a handful of swim and tennis clubs together. He was a competitive swimmer in college and decided to open some clubs, teaching kids, adults, and seniors. I've been swimming again there lately. It's been good for me."

His eyebrows lift. "Yeah? In what way?"

This feels a little like opening up. But that's part of dating, right? Taking your time, letting someone in. Baby steps. "It cleared my head. Helped me let go. Swimming always did when I was younger, and it does again now. Along with yoga."

"Was that what got you through their split?"

Damn, this man can read me like a book. "Definitely. I needed an outlet then, too, because things were always complicated with my mom growing up."

"How so?"

That's a good question. And unfortunately, one that's far too easy to answer. "She was very focused on looks. She works in advertising for beauty magazines, and there's nothing wrong with that, but I think it became her sole focus. Almost like she wanted to preserve her youth at all costs. She kept finding younger and younger men. Like her newest fling," I say, my voice tight, as I imagine it might always be when I mention *him*. "He's the youngest of all. Twenty-two years younger than she is."

"Whoa," he says, his eyes popping.

There's not much more to say than that, though. "So, yeah, I needed yoga. I needed swimming. I needed something not to lose my mind," I say, pushing out a needed laugh. That's something I've learned in the last few months—the power of laughter to get you through the hard stuff. I learned, too, how important it is to keep focusing on others, so I shift to him. "But what about you? Are you close with your mom or dad?"

"My mom is great. She's my hero. She's a baker, and that's where I learned to cook and bake."

"Awww, so sweet. Is she still in Georgia?"

"She is indeed. Atlanta. She runs her pie shop still with my oldest sister, Eva. It's called I'm Just Here for the Pie. Even though she doesn't need to run it to live."

"Because…?"

He smiles softly, his eyes glinting with a touch of pride. "I did the whole *bought Mom a new home* thing when I got my first contract. I wanted to take care of her. Make sure she didn't ever want for a single thing. Our parents are sort of the reverse, yours and mine, Katie. My mom's the one I'm close with. My dad cheated on her when I was thirteen. And he took off. He left, plain and simple.

Didn't pay child support or anything. The man just abandoned his family."

I shudder from the awfulness of that. From the anger and hurt I can hear in Harlan's voice. It's one of the few times he's ever sounded less than fine. Less than fun, flirty, or easygoing.

"That must have been so hard. I'm sorry you went through that. Was he around at all after he left?"

Harlan shakes his head. His jaw is set hard. It ticks as he takes a deep breath. "Nope. Not one bit. The fucker moved to Arizona with his new woman and didn't do shit for his three daughters, his son, or the mother of his children."

"Wow. I had no idea." I wince inside at my tactlessness. "I feel like a jerk for not knowing that. For kind of dumping all my stuff on you every time."

He sits up, instantly softening. "Don't feel bad. How would you have known? I didn't expect you to read my mind, and these are details that I don't share in the press. But yes, that's the story."

"Sounds like it's real important to you to be the opposite."

He nods, his expression solemn. "The most important thing to me."

"Sounds like you are too," I say with a smile.

He smiles back. "I try."

"Did you ever miss him when you were younger?"

"For a little while at first, but I didn't like the way he treated my mom. He talked shit behind her back when they were together. I never thought he deserved her."

His relationship with his father sounds about as bad as mine with my mom. "Is he still in Arizona?"

He points to the floor. "He's six feet under." It comes so evenly and surprises me.

"Oh. I had no idea. I'm so sorry."

"Thank you, but he died fifteen years ago. I'm all good now."

"Was it hard at the time?"

"I was in college, and he had a heart attack." He exhales, then shakes his head like he can't quite believe what he's about to say. "Have I mentioned he was with his mistress when he had the heart attack? He was having an affair with the next-door neighbor and died at her place."

My hand flies to my mouth. "Oh God. For real?"

"Indeed," he says with an ironic laugh.

"And I thought my life…" But I don't have to finish.

"I've got some soap opera in my background."

"Seems we both do."

"And that's just one of many reasons why I'm determined to be the best father I can for my kid. I want to show her what it's like when a man sticks around," he says.

My heart expands, doubles in size. Then it lodges in my throat. "You are pretty dang cool," I choke out.

"So are you," he says, then dials up the flirt in his voice. "And I can't wait to see you. And tie that apron around your wrists. Third time's a charm."

I murmur, my mind shifting quickly to dirty land again, and liking the return trip there. "Can't wait either. But I think tonight was the third time. This feels like a date. A damn good one."

"Then I will see you soon for our fourth date."

And even though this time four months ago, four weeks ago, heck, four nights ago, I wasn't ready, I am now.

I won't make the same mistakes.

I'll take my time.

Get to know him truly.

Take baby steps rather than run full speed ahead.

As long as I do that, I won't be played for a fool again. I'll stay one step ahead of my emotions.

I've got this.

CHAPTER 19

HARLAN

On Tuesday morning, Abby crunches into her peanut butter toast, kicking her purple Converse-sneakered foot back and forth. "What are you doing today, Daddy?" she singsongs around the food in her mouth.

After I take the last gulp of coffee, I set down the mug. Give her a stern stare. "Making sure my little bear doesn't talk with her mouth full."

She casts her gaze down, covers her mouth, chews.

Chews some more.

A little more still.

Finally, she swallows. She gulps loudly. Smiles weakly. "Sorry."

I stifle a laugh. She's too cute when she's contrite. I walk around the counter, ruffle her hair. "Thank you for saying so." I park myself on a stool. "To answer your question, it's a Tuesday, so I'm working out with some of the usual crew after I take you to school."

She lifts her hand, counts off on one hand. "Cooper, Chance, Jones, Jason, and Shane?" She screws up the corner of her lips, relieved. "I think I got them all."

I whistle in approval. "They're not all coming today, but well done. You just named a future Hall-of-Famer QB, a World Series-winning pitcher for the Cougars, my receiver buddy, the quarterback for the city's other team, and the All-Star British closing pitcher. You are fire, and your brain is sharp."

She points at me, a challenging look in her hazel eyes. "But can you name all my friends who are coming to your game next weekend?" My girl pops the rest of her toast in her mouth, waiting for me to rattle off the names of her peeps.

"Ye of little faith. Gabriella, Caroline, and Audrey. Booyah. The Fab Four. Do not doubt me."

Abby giggles, then finishes her toast and smiles. "But I don't want to watch a boring game. Sometimes football is kind of dull and if it is, we might want to watch something else instead. On Mommy's iPad," she says, since her mom brings her to the games when the owner invites them. "Like maybe *Girl Power*, that new show about ten-year-olds who have superpowers."

I scoff. "You might want to *not* come to the game and *not* hang out in the owner's booth if you plan to watch your mom's iPad. Sheesh."

"Or we could do cartwheels in the hall, since my new gymnastics class is awesome," she says, and that makes me smile. The fact that she loves the class, not her suggestion of doing acrobatics at the stadium. "And I love that you love Gym Buddies. But you can't do cartwheels in the hallway at the stadium. Got it?"

"Got it. But maybe we'll watch gymnastics instead. I could watch Simone Biles all day long."

"Understandable. She's the bomb."

Abby's all earnest as she hops off her stool and asks, "But once you've seen Simone, don't you think football is boring?"

She brings her plate to the sink, rinses it, then sets it in the dishwasher as I answer. "Football is fascinating, fast-paced, fantastic, and fabulous. And that's alliteration. So, not only do you get sports knowledge with me, but I'm practically an English teacher too. Now, the first bell rings in twenty-five minutes, Miss I Made My Dad Cry by Calling His Job Boring." I frown, like I'm going to sob.

She runs the few feet to me, grabs my legs, and hugs me hard. "Don't cry, Daddy. Football is fun. Just be careful."

I scoop her up, drop a kiss on her cheek. "I promise. And I'll see if I can get over it…if you brush your teeth."

"I'll do it."

———————

Fifteen minutes later, her redbrick school comes into view on the corner of Octavia Street, not too far from my gym on Fillmore. She tugs on my hand. "You never told me what else you're doing today. After you work out with your friends. What will you do tonight?"

I stiffen momentarily.

This is a quandary.

Do I bring up my date?

She's only six, so she doesn't *need* to know.

I've certainly dated here and there since Abby was born without sharing, since again, no need to. I've even had a couple girlfriends, but nothing that lasted too long. Dating has never been a huge issue.

Except for once.

During the last off-season, I broke up with someone I truly didn't realize I'd been *dating*—a single mom, Cassie, who I met at Abby's old gymnastics studio. Cassie was fun, clever, and the mom of a girl Abby liked in her class, a kid named Izzy. Cassie and I hit it off as we watched the kids cartwheel, so when Cassie asked about meeting for a playdate the next weekend at a local park, I said sure.

We met and the girls clambered up monkey bars as Cassie and I chatted.

She suggested we do it again the next weekend.

Abby liked the idea, so I said yes. More swings and slides for them, then the girls were hungry, so we all grabbed lunch. Cassie got the girls their own table, and the two of us sat and ate grain bowls together.

Hmm.

It felt a little too date-y for my taste, but maybe that was a normal parents-after-a-playdate activity.

And again the next week. The girls were hungry, we went for Thai food, and while we waited, Cassie was flirty, and handsy, and all kinds of suggestive.

At the end of the night, she asked if I wanted to come over once the kids went to bed.

Whoa.

I said no thanks, but I was happy to help the girls get together.

Cassie said I was a dick.

Then she added that she didn't want the girls to have play-dates again. A few days later, Izzy told Abby she didn't want to hang out with her anymore because her mommy didn't like her daddy.

Abby decided she didn't want to run into Izzy again at gymnastics, so she stopped taking classes over the summer, and was, admittedly, a little bummed about both the classes and Izzy de-friending her.

Maybe it was my mistake, or maybe it was a tangled mess of hurt feelings.

But I don't want to fuck up again, especially now that Abby has found Gym Buddies and is having a blast there.

Dating and single dad-dom aren't easy to balance. Hell, some days, finding an opening in the secondary is easier than figuring out modern dating.

So, I'm not sure if I should tell Abby I'm seeing someone tonight.

Weirdly, I kind of want to.

But it's probably too soon.

"Seeing the guys at the gym, then we've got game film at the stadium and a team workout," I say. I give her a kiss, we say good-bye, then I take off for the gym.

I run at a light jog to Fillmore, wincing only briefly when my hamstring protests. I should have stretched better.

Once I reach the gym, I hit the mats on the floor first, stretching out my creaks and sore muscles. Not everyone's here today, but it looks like we've got a foursome. Cooper warms up on the treadmill. Jason racks weights.

When Shane fills his water bottle, he strolls past me, arching a brow, his blue eyes doubtful. "Tell me something, mate. Is it tough getting old?"

Kids today. They think they're so clever. "Yes, Shakespeare. Something you'll find out eventually too," I point out, though it's a way off for the Brit. I've got ten years on the guy.

"Not for a long time. Nor for Jason, for that matter," Shane quips, gesturing to the boy-next-door twenty-five-year-old quarterback for the Hawks, the city's rival team.

"Hey! Don't pull me into your chest-beating battles, Shane," Jason says as he sits on the bench.

I stretch my back. "Let's not forget I have something neither of you have." I waggle my right hand, showing off my two rings to those whippersnappers. "When you win your first World Series, Shakespeare, drinks are on me. Until then, I'll enjoy *these* benefits of age. Same for you, Jay."

The QB nods solemnly. "Of course, Harlan. I'm all about honoring my elders," he deadpans.

I roll my eyes. Sheesh. Can't win. "You two ducklings are in rare form today."

"Why do you wear those to the gym? Your rings. Don't they, I dunno, get in the way when you work out?" Jason asks me as he lifts the bar, almost like he's mocking me for wearing them.

But I have my reasons.

Damn good ones.

161

I catch Cooper's eye as he steps off the treadmill and makes his way to us. "Coop, can you please remind the kids why we wear our rings to the gym?"

My good friend flashes a smile, showing off his twin rings, too, as he scratches his jaw. "Gee. Could it be because we have them… and they don't?"

I sit up and smack palms with my quarterback.

As Cooper and I move to join Shane and Jason in the weight area, the conversation quickly segues to evening plans. Tuesday is usually date night in the NFL—since game weekends are tough for going out.

"I've got a busy night of hanging out with my three favorite people—the wife and kids," Cooper says, a proud, married dad.

Shane's blue eyes glint. "I have fantastic plans with a fetching woman."

I turn to Jason. "And you, kiddo?"

The All-American guy shrugs sheepishly as he presses the bar. "I met a cute guy the other week. I'm seeing him again."

I nod approvingly. "Good for you. Anything serious there?"

He smiles, resetting the bar as he sits up. "We'll see. We're going to work out and get boba at a new place in Hayes Valley."

"That is a maddeningly adorable date," Shane says.

"And it will probably also give you shredded abs if it's your second workout of the day," I add.

Jason wiggles his brow as he switches to free weights. "Shredded is the way to go. But that's not why I do workout dates."

Cooper turns to Jason. "This is a thing now? Workout dates?"

The young guy laughs. "Dude, yes."

"Like, for everyone?"

Another laugh. "Yes, for everyone," Jason says.

I clap Cooper's shoulder, shaking my head in amusement. "Even I knew that."

"Yeah, because you're single," Cooper points out.

"And because I'm not out of touch! Also, please don't tell me you're one of those lame-ass married dudes who can't be bothered to take his wife on a date."

"I take Violet on dates. We go to coffee shops, and we like karaoke," he says a little defensively as he grabs some weights.

"I like karaoke, too, but workout dates are fun. It gives you something to do other than twiddling your thumbs over a cup of joe," Jason puts in.

Shane nods sagely. "Exactly. Coffee is so last century. But I prefer concerts and clubs."

Cooper turns to me. "And do *you*, Mister *So in Touch*, have plans for a date tonight?"

"I sure do," I say with a grin, sliding into lunges to stretch my hammies some more.

"Bet Harlan nicks your idea, Jay, and brings her here to hit the StairMaster," Shane deadpans.

"Yes, that's me. I have zero creativity," I say with a roll of my eyes. "But it's not a workout date, so don't worry, Jason. I won't be stealing your plans."

"By all means, steal them. Workout dates are awesome," he says.

"I'm gonna take your word on that, duckling. I'm more of a get-out-of-the-gym type of guy."

Jason stops his biceps curls and sets down the weights. "One hundred bucks says you wind up doing workout dates sooner rather than later, Harlan."

"Ooh. The kid throws down," Cooper hoots. "You in, King of the Jungle?"

It's not in my nature to turn down a challenge. I cross the distance and shake with Jason. "You're on."

"I can't wait for you to say *you were right*," he says as we place our bets.

"So young. So cocky," I muse.

Cooper chuckles. "We'll take the blame for that. Now, back to you. Who is she, tonight's non-workout date?"

I'm stoked to tell them; I've been hoping for another chance with Katie for a while. Timing has been all wrong—but now, it's just right. Third time's a charm.

"Someone I've been wanting to see for a long while. So don't wait up for this old man," I say with a wink. "Because I can go all night long, and we don't need a workout date for that to happen. Take that, little ducklings."

When we're done, I head to the stadium with the other Renegades, counting down the hours till I see Katie again.

I've got a good feeling about this date.

CHAPTER 20

KATIE

blast The Go-Go's as I zoom around my place, getting ready to kick ass and take names.

I down my green tea, singing along to Belinda Carlisle in between sips and bites of my vegan breakfast sausage.

The music is getting me in the mood to see that man tonight, taking me back to our unexpected evening four months ago.

Not that getting in the mood for Harlan is hard, but I like the reminder of our last night together.

And I'd like to have another night very soon.

When I finish my breakfast, I brush my teeth, cinch my hair in a ponytail, and text Emerson.

Katie: Breakfast of champions! Watched your show and tried one of those vegan sausages you recommended.
Emerson: You've always loved sausage.

Katie: Pot. Kettle.

Emerson: Absolutely. Also, yay for vegan sausage, but tonight I hope you get the non-vegan kind.

Katie: How can you be adorable and gross at the same time?

Emerson: It's a talent.

Katie: Love ya! I'm off to meet a new client. Zachary is killing it with deal-making. He's sending me to work with a venture company to do a stress-release workshop.

Emerson: Go be a badass yoga babe.

Katie: Always.

On that note, I grab my bright-red purse, tuck my phone inside it, and bound down the steps of my building to the waiting car.

"Hey, Saul," I say to the driver.

"Hello, Miss Madigan. You're looking spirited this morning. But then, you often are."

"Only way to be." I flash him a grin. He's my regular guy—I like to use a driver when I have a ton of meetings, and today is one of those days. This way I can work as I zip around the Bay Area.

I slide into the back of the car right as my phone buzzes.

Grabbing it from my bag, I glance at the screen, and a giddy smile takes over my face. A message from the man of the day blinks at me.

Harlan: Question—would a foosball/ice cream shop work for tonight's date? After dinner, of course.

Katie: Two of my favorite things. Three, if you count dinner. But does the shop have a good name? I require a clever name.

Harlan: Darn. The only place I found that offers two of life's greatest treats is called...wait for it...Ye Olde Ice Cream Shoppe.

Katie: I'm so sad thinking about all the missed opportunities there. They could have called it Poles and Cones.

Harlan: Ah, good one. I was thinking Sweet Cheeks and Sticks for my future foosball/ice cream joint.

Katie: And will you serve Libido cones and cups of Desire?

Harlan: Both. All night long. That combo is on the house for you, sweetheart.

The bubble inside me cannot be burst. It's growing bigger and glowing brighter. I clutch the phone, delighting in the messages from him. Taking time to get to know someone is going to be a blast. Bring it on, dating. Come to me, flirting. I am ready to enjoy every step of my brand-new, slow-down-and-smell-the-roses path.

I'm tapping out a reply when my phone trills.

Zachary's name flashes across the screen. "Oh, fabulous dealmaker. Tell me things," I say as Saul slides the car into traffic, heading south on our way to Palo Alto.

"Change of plans," Zachary says, all cheery and caffeinated. "I called Michelle just now. She wasn't scheduled for a class today, but I want to send her to the venture firm instead of you. Because

I need to send *you* to a new last-minute client. Came in earlier this week and specifically requested the yoga empress."

I adjust my imaginary tiara. "It's good to be the queen."

"I'm sure it is, your majesty," he quips, then continues. "I've been sorting through the paperwork. The deal isn't done yet, but they've seen your online videos and researched you, and Lacey—she's the contact—was raving about the class you did last year in Los Angeles for the elite marathoners. The new client is high-profile."

A smidgen of worry digs in, and I hope my plans for tonight aren't about to get completely derailed. "Just tell me they aren't in Los Angeles," I say. Literally nothing can ruin my day *except* the cancellation of my long-awaited date with the man I've had the most chemistry with ever.

Huh.

That's how it is with Harlan.

We have chemistry, in bed and out of it. Our attraction burns hot, and our compatibility seems off the charts.

Zachary laughs loudly. "Nope. The new client is in the city, so you actually don't have as far to go. You're welcome. It's Blaine Enterprises." A fire truck blares its sirens, and I don't hear what Zachary says next, then sirens blast louder.

When they fade for a second, I shout, "Just text me the info."

The volume climbs again, and Zachary booms, "I'll send it to your driver's GPS."

"Thanks," I say, and when we hang up, my phone flashes with the new email icon.

I scan the pertinent details from my VP. The class I'll be teaching is *Ouch! I Can't Reach My Toes—Yoga for Flexibility.*

Ah, that class is so fun. And the deal could lead to more partnerships with other high-profile businesses, Zachary writes.

Sounds good to me.

I tap back a reply.

Katie: On my way.

Then I return to the text thread with Harlan, smiling at the message about his pretend ice cream joint. It's my turn, so I write back.

Katie: Glad to hear your fictional ice cream shop won't charge me. For the record, I am all over a foosball and sweet shop.

Harlan: Someone needs to make that happen. My mouth is watering now just thinking of it. By the way, are you in the mood for sushi, Thai, Italian, Vietnamese, or some other fantastic cuisine tonight? The only thing off-limits is a new boba place in Hayes Valley because my bud Jason is taking a date there, and if we show up too, I'd look like I have no creativity. So don't say boba in Hayes Valley, pretty please.

Katie: Darn. I love boba tea!

Harlan: Ha. Me too. And trying new boba shops is fun.

We text back and forth, picking a location for sushi as the car zips through the city.

"Almost there, Miss Madigan," Saul calls out.

"Thank you for the heads up," I say, but I don't glance away from my phone because talking to Harlan is too fun.

Harlan: Fair warning. I plan on kissing the breath out of you as soon as I see you tonight. Miss those lips of yours, sweetheart.

My stomach flips. Warmth winds through me.

Katie: I definitely volunteer as tribute for that.
Harlan: Excellent. Now, I need to turn my phone off. We have game film today, and my Lyft just dropped me off at the training facility.
Katie: We just drove past the stadium. Have fun!

Only, instead of going by the stadium, Saul pulls into the parking lot behind it. That's odd. Why are we here?

But Saul doesn't know. The email says to go to the South Entrance of Blaine Enterprises, so I do, even though it looks suspiciously like the training facility for the San Francisco Renegades.

Before I can knock on the door, it swings open, and a woman greets me. She's petite and peppy, full of energy. "I'm Lacey, and we're excited to have you here. Your online video on how to balance a crow pose in ten days? Changed. My. Life." The tiny brunette brims with enthusiasm as she escorts me to an exercise room. I quickly get the room set up with mats and Lacey turns to me and says, "And here is our Super Bowl–winning team."

My head spins.

No effing way.

My new client is the San Francisco Renegades.

Which means I'll be teaching downward-facing dog to my date.

CHAPTER 21

HARLAN

Coach Greenhaven clicks off the big screen, takes a deep breath, then says to the team, "And that's what you need to know about the Seattle secondary. They are as ruthless as Baltimore's."

"My right thigh will vouch for Baltimore," I say, patting my leg. A collision with that team's cornerback last month led to a strained hamstring, but thankfully, it didn't put me out of commission.

With a stern look in his gray eyes, the head coach turns his gaze to me, then nods to the rest of the fifty-three-man roster, parked in leather chairs scattered around the room. "And that's why I took Harlan out of the last game there at the end. Don't want that thigh to turn into an injury for him, and if anyone else sustained a similar injury, I'd do the same." Coach takes a beat, surveys the team. "And that's also why we're implementing some new protocols. Our team trainers are on top of the latest sports medicine research and exercise. Studies have shown that athletes heal faster from injuries and have fewer injuries, too, if they practice yoga regularly."

I sit up straighter, my interest piqued by the mention of yoga. Katie's profession. Maybe I'll learn an interesting tidbit to share with her tonight. Bet she'd dig that.

"It improves strength, balance, and flexibility, and it's proven to help top athletes speed up their recovery time and stay off the injured list. Something you all want to do, I presume?"

Nods and grunts of agreement echo in the spacious room. I sit on the edge of my chair, eager for more info.

"And starting today, you'll all be taking yoga classes," he says.

Some of the noises of agreement become groans and whines.

I turn around, giving the guys a *c'mon* look. "You all just said you wanted fewer injuries. Now you don't want to do yoga? Man up, Renegades."

"Yoga is for girls," someone mutters.

"Yoga won't help me tackle."

"Yoga is weird."

I roll my eyes. "You wish you played as well as a girl." I will defend girls till my dying day.

Probably from the grave too.

Coach lifts his hands to settle down the naysayers. "Enough. You're doing yoga from now until the end of the season. No griping. You want a nice, long, healthy career? You'll practice warrior pose, tree pose, and whatever else the teacher says. This is not optional, Renegades. This concludes the meeting." He points to the door.

"Head to Exercise Room Three and get into child's pose. Which ought to come easy to some of you."

Oh, this is even better. I'll have so much juicy goodness to share with Katie tonight.

I head out of the film room with Cooper. "I love yoga," he says. "Violet took me to a class last year, and it was awesome."

"So, you *did* do a workout date," I say as we stroll down the corridor.

He scratches his jaw, seems to consider this. "Huh. I guess that was a workout date. Damn good one too. Guess Jason is onto something."

"Seems he is, but I'm still opting for dinner and foosball tonight instead," I say as we near the exercise room. But I switch gears away from dating as I point to my hamstring, nerves in my voice. "I could use something to help with this old leg here. I don't want to pull a muscle and be out of commission."

Maybe yoga will be my savior. Maybe it'll help keep me at the top of my game in this critical season.

Critical, as I figure out what the hell to do with my football future.

Cooper claps me on the back. "Dude, I need you on the field. You're one of my favorite targets."

"And I want to keep being one," I say intensely. Since that's the goal, no matter what. I still don't know what happens at the end of the season. But whether this is my final year or whether I try to get an epic deal in free agency, the last thing I want is to be down for the count. *At all.*

Stats, games, and playing ball—that's what I want to do.

I draw a soldiering breath, point to the door and the room beyond. Ready to handle whatever the team throws at us. "If yoga helps me, I will be Namaste-ing day and—"

I stop in the doorway.

Whoa.

A smile spreads at the gorgeous sight.

Who knew I'd be getting an early preview of my date tonight? She's the last person I expect to see, but damn, it is good to set eyes on Katie.

Lucky me to get a sneak peek.

Except.

Wait.

Hold on.

What the hell is she doing here in the exercise room? With mats spread out on the floor, and yoga straps and stuff?

Plus, she's in her yoga clothes, and she's talking to Lacey, one of the team trainers.

Well, shit.

The answer comes in a flash, and it sucks.

She can't be our new yoga teacher.

And yet, I'm sure she is.

I groan inside. Pretty sure, too, that a date with Katie will violate the team's no fraternization policy—no dates or hookups with personnel like team trainers, team docs, team managers, or team anythings.

Katie swings her gaze to me. For a fraction of a second, her eyes flicker with excitement, but resignation quickly replaces it.

Frustration swirls in my gut. I try not to let things get me down, but I am more than bummed.

I am seriously disappointed.

All these years, all this time, and now this twist of fate before what was supposed to be our third time lucky?

Jaw tight, I grab a mat, flop down, and listen to our new yoga instructor for the next fifty minutes as she guides us through a series of poses.

These are the poses I want to do *with* her.

Only, I can't.

When class ends, the guys filter out, but Lacey calls me over to the front of the room.

What's that all about? Does she know I already have a thing with Katie? Are we going to be put on some kind of notice?

I haul in a breath, steeling myself for a reprimand for something I couldn't foresee. I do my best to stay cool, flashing a smile at the blond bombshell I want to take home with me and the brunette pipsqueak in charge of our physical fitness.

The trainer bounces on her white sneakers. "Harlan, I want to personally introduce you to Katie Madigan."

Lacey, that won't be necessary. I personally introduced myself to every inch of her delicious skin a few months ago when I hand- and cock- and tongue-delivered four orgasms, but thanks for the formality, anyway.

"Pleasure to meet you," I say, extending a hand to Katie.

Her blue eyes twinkle with a cocktail of mischief and regret as she takes my palm. "Pleasure to meet you, too, Harlan. I enjoy watching you play."

"And I enjoy posing like a flamingo," I say, still holding her hand. I don't want to let go. This may be the only time I'll get to touch her all day.

Hell, maybe all season.

I whimper inside.

My dick wails a song of sorrow.

My libido curls up in the corner.

I've been cock-blocked by my own damn team.

"So," Lacey continues, her brown-eyed gaze straying to our joined hands. Quickly, I let go. "The receiver's coach and I met earlier today about you, Harlan."

I jerk my gaze to Lacey. "You did?"

Lacey, a former cheerleader, nods enthusiastically. Lacey does everything enthusiastically. "We did, and we thought, given the hamstring strain you sustained the other week, we should make sure your flexibility and balance are at peak levels."

For a guy who puts in the extra work, the suggestion sure bristles me. "You're saying they're not?"

Her smile is wide. It usually is. "I'm saying your performance is indeed peak, and we want to keep it there. We think yoga can do that. What do you think?"

I flash back to my jog this morning. To the wince I felt. Sure, I spend plenty of time lifting weights, running plays. But stretching? I suppose it wouldn't hurt to improve ye olde flexibility.

I let go of the momentary annoyance. "Let's do it."

She wipes a hand across her forehead in exaggerated relief. "Whew. I'm glad you agree. Because we'd like you to set up some one-on-one sessions directly with Katie. We need our star receiver corps to be in fantastic shape. Maybe tomorrow morning you could meet up at Katie's studio? Obviously, the team will cover all the expenses. So, if you two can just exchange numbers and handle the timing?"

Lacey's eyes widen as she waits for an answer.

Katie chimes in first. "Absolutely. I welcome the chance," she says.

I clear my throat, hiding the chuckle working its way out. The situation isn't funny, but the idea that we need to trade numbers is.

Though, maybe funny isn't the word. More like devastating to my dick and heart, since both are into Katie.

Lacey spins on her heel, leaving me alone with the woman I want but can't have.

I glance around. Coast is clear. My chest weighs a ton. I hate doing this...

"So, about tonight," I say heavily.

Her shoulders hunch. "I know. I figured as much."

She's already on the same page, but I need to be clear. It's important. "I shouldn't date someone who works for the team." It'd look bad, especially in this critical season. I'd look like the playboy I once was. I'm not that guy anymore, and I don't want to put the team in an awkward position. The potential for a social media blowup is too high.

"And I can't date a client," she adds, sadness in her tone. Her eyes sweep the exercise room, then return to me. "It could hurt our reputation as we're growing the business. I worry it would look like I'm sleeping my way to deals, especially with such a high-profile one. This is a big opportunity for Sassy Yoga."

She sounds wracked by guilt, and I'll have none of that.

"Katie, I want this deal to go well for your company, so don't apologize. I understand completely. Truly, I do." Especially since it's harder for women in these situations. Society often gives top athletes a slap on the hand when they mess around with women they work with. But the fairer sex? They usually get the jagged edge of the judgment knife. I hate the thought of that happening to Katie.

"Thank you for saying that. And please know I would ask for someone else to fill in, but my business manager made it explicitly clear that Blaine Enterprises hired *me*." She still sounds like she's in the worst funk.

Same here.

"You're the face and brand," I say with a sad smile. "Everyone wants you."

She dips her head, laughing wistfully. "But I would otherwise have switched. Because I really wanted to see you tonight," she says, so sweet, so vulnerable.

I step closer, daring to get near to her, to inhale her scent. "I really wanted to see you too."

Instead, we make plans for the morning.

Professional plans.

Even so, when I hit the sack that night, all I want is for the sun to rise.

CHAPTER 22

HARLAN

Seeing Katie in her cute blue yoga pants, that tight pink yoga top, and that sexy, swishy ponytail? Well, let's just say it frazzles my brain.

But I'm a good boy.

I'm in the zone.

The cat, cow, dog zone.

We are just a yoga teacher and a client, not the man and woman who cancelled a hot date last night.

In a private room at her studio, designed for one-on-one sessions, Katie takes me through several poses, then says it's time for a lunge twist.

"This is critical for a receiver. It'll help as you lunge for catches," she says.

I've done plenty of stretches over the years, just like this one. But Katie studies me like a scientist, then shifts my body like a sculptor, setting her hands on my hips, urging me to deepen the rotation.

I'd like to deepen other rotations.

"There! That's perfect. Now just hold it," she says, so damn encouraging as she sinks into the same pose, twisting her elbow against her thigh, looking supple and flexible and all sorts of bendy.

"Show-off."

"I just like to move my body," she says with a smile.

And that's not helping, because I like all the ways she moves *my* body, as well.

Like when we switch to a frog pose. "On your hands and knees," she says.

"Things I'd like to say to you," I mutter, and dammit, that's not the cat-cow zone. That's the naughty zone.

Must stay out of it.

"Harlan Taylor," she admonishes, but there's a sexy note in her voice that tells me she, too, is savoring every flirty morsel we allow ourselves.

Which isn't much, but I'll take what I can get.

"Then you need to slide out your knees a little bit, like a frog."

I settle into the awkward AF pose. "I look like a dork."

"Yes, but who cares?" she asks with an easy shrug, a sexy jut of her shoulder. I swear, everything this woman does is sexy to me.

But I also like talking to her.

Chatting with Katie is one of the easiest things I've ever done. Always has been, ever since the first night at that wedding. We just clicked. She's a kindred spirit.

"Doesn't matter if you look dorky. Or silly. Just...laugh," she suggests.

"Aren't you supposed to say...I dunno...*om* or *namaste*?" I tease.

She settles onto her mat next to me, getting into the same pose, first on her hands and knees, then sliding her knees out to the side. Looking like a frog, obvs. "I take the poses seriously, but I don't take myself too seriously," she says, then her lips curve into a sly smirk. "Ribbit."

I chuckle. "I've got some animal noises for you right here." As I hold the weird pose, I give her my best roar. "Rawr!"

She cracks up, falling face-first to the mat as she slaps the floor.

"What? Was I not fearsome as a lion?" I arch a brow.

She turns to me. "You're as fearsome as the king of the lion frogs, Harlan!"

"See if I ever entertain you with animal sounds again," I say, but I'm laughing too.

Especially since we're definitely not in the naughty zone anymore. That has to be good for our brand-new working relationship.

"Moo," she says, quickly zipping out of the frog pose and into a bovine one, bowing her back. Seconds later, she's arching like a cat. "Meow."

I whimper.

Katie is a very sexy yoga cat.

"Meow-zers," I say.

Hopping out of the position, she moves behind me, dropping her hands to my hips and wiggling them. Her tone is teacherly again, the yoga instructor who believes in what she does. "If you can hold the frog pose for at least a few minutes every day, that'll help release the groin and inner thigh. Those are locations for a lot of injuries. You want to keep the groin nice and soft."

"No, I don't want my groin soft," I blurt. Because I can't not go there.

She laughs, giving another slight adjustment. "There. Just hold." But her soft voice and her gentle hands are having the opposite effect on me.

This one-on-one is *not* helping my dirty brain. I can't stop thinking about the one-on-ones I crave with her.

Yup, hands-on is leading to hard-on. I cast about for neutral topics. "So, is it true yoga is cheaper than therapy?"

Her blue eyes twinkle. "Guess it depends on what I charge the Renegades," she says with a wink.

"I like your capitalist side."

"Nothing wrong with wanting to make a good living," she says, lady boss and owning it. Damn, that's hot too.

"I couldn't agree more." I cycle to another of her yoga sayings from her clothing line. "Is yoga your favorite way to pretend to work out?"

She's quiet for a beat, then sits next to me, meeting my gaze. "Are you just quoting me back to me now?"

I flash a grin. "Seems I am. I researched more about your business before these sessions. Still love the cute sayings."

Her smile is magnetic. "Thank you. I'm flattered you did that."

"I like your style. I like what you've built."

Her eyes shimmer with happiness. I love that I put that look there. "That means a lot to me. And you know what?"

"What?"

"I like watching you play. I'm having a big ol' watch party this weekend with my girlfriends. We're talking charcuterie boards, wine, nachos, and Jillian's special guacamole mix. And we'll be rooting for you."

Pride suffuses my whole being.

There is something fulfilling about playing a game you're good at for a woman you like.

Even if you can't have her.

I wish this could work. I wish we could move forward, earning first down after first down. But it seems the universe's defensive line is tougher than us right now, and we're punting rather than picking up where we left off.

Not now, and not for the foreseeable future.

But maybe at the end of the season? Coach said we'd be doing yoga for that long, but when we're done, maybe our timing will finally line up.

I tuck that thought away. I'll hold on to it until the moment is right to bring it up.

———

On Thursday after our team workout, I do one of my favorite things—I pick Abby up from school.

She bounds down the front steps of the school building, alongside a curly-haired blond, and barely gives me a chance to say hello.

"Hello—"

"Can we go to the playground around the corner? Audrey and I want to do the rock-climbing wall, and it'll be so fun," Abby says, then wraps an arm around her friend, who flashes me a gap-toothed smile.

"Please, Mister Taylor," Audrey puts in. "My mom said it's okay and you can drop me off in an hour," Audrey adds quickly, gesturing to her mom who's talking to another parent by the school entrance.

"And she only lives four blocks away," Abby says at the speed of light.

Laughing, I finally get a word in edgewise. "Well, it seems you two have already plotted this whole playground playdate."

"We did," Abby says. "So, it's a yes?"

"I'll just check with Audrey's mom." I make my way to the school entrance, and once I confirm Audrey's mom is cool with the plan, I return to the girls. "Rock-climbing time," I say, grateful my life and my job allow me this sort of flexibility in the middle of the week.

But there's only so much flexibility I have.

The next day is also *technically* my day with Abby, but I won't be able to spend it with her. I don't spend any weekends with her during football season. I'm either flying to another city or we're in the team hotel, deliberately away from family. That's just how it goes in the league.

In the morning, we grab the two most excellent apple pies we baked last night, then I take her to Danielle's house around seven, since we have a 9:00 a.m. flight to Seattle for our game this weekend.

Danielle lets us in, and I step into the foyer.

"Thanks again for taking her to school. And having her this weekend and all the other weekends," I say with a smile, and a little bit of sadness too.

"Easy-peasy," Danielle says, and that's my reminder to sweep away the pang of longing for weekends. Truly, I'm damn lucky to share this kid with a mom who's so chill about, well, everything.

"And we made you two pies," Abby announces, thrusting the pink boxes at her mom. "One's for us to take to the gymnastics showcase on Saturday, and one is for you and Jamie to take to the hospital."

Danielle's eyes light up with culinary delight. "The parents will love it at Gym Buddies. And I guarantee the nurses will love this one too." She turns to me. "They seriously appreciate it when doctors bring them pies baked by their favorite player."

"You're famous at Mommy's hospital," Abby says.

"Especially since you've been playing like you're about to *own* the heck out of free agency," Jamie calls from the kitchen, then pops his head in the doorway, waiting expectantly.

Like now is when I'm going to decide my off-season plans.

My entire career plans.

Truth is—I still don't know what I'll do in January.

No clue whatsoever. Maybe I'm waiting for a sign. Is my good health—knock on wood—a sign to keep playing? Or is it a sign to quit while I'm ahead?

I wish I knew.

Danielle rolls her eyes. "Jamie. He's not going to just tell us one morning in the entryway."

"A man can dream," Jamie says with an easy shrug.

"And the answer is—I'll keep making you pies," I tell him, like that's a satisfying answer.

But it's the only one I can legitimately give.

I bend to scoop up Abby, giving her one more hug. "I'll miss you, little bear. Good luck in your gymnastics showcase," I say, since that's another thing I'm going to miss this weekend.

"Good luck in your game." She gives me knuckles, and her fist explosion is legendary, but it breaks my heart all at the same time.

We fly to Seattle to vie with one of the toughest teams in the league. That Sunday it's the game of the day, a marquee matchup between two top teams in the west.

When we run through the corridor of the stadium and hit the field, that familiar rush of energy blasts through me.

Always has.

Ever since I was a kid and touched the gridiron for the first time, I've felt it. The thrill. The excitement. For nearly fifteen years, I've been playing the game I love for a living.

Will I still feel this way next year?

Who knows?

Right now, though, it's game time.

And I'm in the zone.

Trouble is, so's Seattle.

Their defense is on fire, and I don't get a chance to make a single play during our first possession. I run a quick route right, but the secondary is all over me like flies on honey.

The game's a tight one for the rest of the quarter, with both teams putting up zeroes.

When we get the ball with three minutes left before the end of the half, I'm raring to break the scoreless streak. Hell, we all are.

Cooper gives us the play, and I head to my spot on the line of scrimmage. I'm in motion, and once he takes the snap, I race off down the field, slip behind the linebackers, and catch a beautiful twenty-five-yard pass at the edge of the field.

And hot damn, I would love to sail away with this baby into the end zone, but Seattle's about to steamroll me. I scramble two feet to get out of bounds, spinning around before the linebackers tackle me.

I land just so, and for a smidge of a second, I wait for that wince in my hamstring.

But I feel fine.

Completely fine.

And that makes me feel good.

Now, I know Katie didn't cure my hamstring strain in a couple sessions. Sports and training don't work that way.

But every little bit helps, and I'll happily enjoy this moment, especially since it turns into a touchdown before the clock runs out and we head inside at the half.

The seven points is energizing, as it fucking should be.

And *this*—this is what I'll miss if I retire.

The buzz, the intensity, the utter joy in making plays as a team.

That's what we do in the second half, too, hunting for a chance to put more numbers up on the board.

It's not easy, but Cooper slings another pass my way right before I spin out of bounds. But I haul it in, whirl around, and put my fleet feet to use to bring it all the way home.

I feel great when I reach the end zone.

The kind of great that makes me want to run to the stands and kiss the girl I like.

Too bad she's not here.

And, more so, that we're not together.

CHAPTER 23

KATIE

That happened fast.

I lift a glass of Wild Chemistry at The Spotted Zebra. "Let's toast to Zachary's deal-making skills," I say on Monday night. My VP lifts his glass and clinks mine, then Olive's.

"To the best, most fantastic exec there is," Olive chimes in, with a grin she can't seem to contain.

Our whiz kid is the man of the hour. The day. The week. First there was the deal with Blaine Enterprises last week, and now he's moving on to bigger and shinier contracts.

He shakes his head. "Just doing my job," he says, but I can tell he's pleased. Since he joined Sassy Yoga a few months ago, the bespectacled wunderkind has been on a tear, inking deals left, right, and upside down. "Besides, it's all on the two of you. The Renegades loved you, Katie, and Lacey was quite impressed. And they love the terms that Olive presented to them," he says, giving credit to the business genius that my sister is.

Gotta love this guy. He often deflects praise—such a rarity in business. But the man deserves it. His cheery attitude and nice-guy approach work so damn well when striking deals. Sort of the opposite of the conventional wisdom on how being a prick can land you better terms. Zachary snags the deals we want by actually—gasp—negotiating with a smile and making sure everyone wins.

And I want him to know that. "We need you. We think you're fabulous, and you're, what, one deal away from the bonus we didn't think you'd earn till the end of your first year? Credit given where credit's due," I say, then take a drink of this delish cocktail the bartender whipped up. Mmm, it's tropical with a splash of tequila, and it's fabulous. Like Sassy Yoga right now.

"And Zachary," Olive prompts, shooting him an appreciative smile, "don't hold back from Katie. Tell her what you told me in the office earlier today."

Zachary straightens his shoulders, sets down his glass. He pushes his glasses up on his nose. "We're in talks with the San Francisco Dragons. It's early days. But I'm hopeful. I've been talking to the new owner, and she's amazing," he says. "And, just like the Renegades, they like the idea of having a high-profile yoga expert teaching the team. I'm telling you, YouTube has turned yoga teachers into celebs, practically, and you're one of those."

I dip my face, both embarrassed and proud.

He's not wrong, though.

The online videos we've created have raised our profile, and I lead most of those videos.

But there's another emotion swirling in me too—regret. For

what might have been with Harlan. I wanted the chance to explore possibilities with him. To take my time getting to know him. Is there a way to have it all? Or maybe…eventually?

I shift in my chair, feeling a little awkward asking, but needing to anyway. "So, how long is the Renegades contract for?"

Part of me hopes he says it ends when the season does, and I can seize the chance to see Harlan then. Another part hopes he doesn't say that at all.

Surely, this is the universe's way of telling me to slow down, right?

Universe, why are you so hard to read? Just give me a sign.

Zachary clears his throat. "Till the end of the season, with an option to renew for next year. But they already expect to renew it. The contracts department said as much."

Olive claps gleefully. "See? You've already impressed them."

I fix on a big grin, grateful the client is happy, even though my silly heart already wrote a reunion scene for Harlan and myself at the end of the season. Best to get my red pen out and slash that possibility. Perhaps that's the sign. The universe is slamming the brakes on my hopes. The universe knows I was going too fast.

Fair enough. Message received.

"And the Dragons would be a huge coup," Olive puts in. "I would love to add them to our client list."

My business brain snaps me back to the deal-celebrating moment. "Absolutely. You're going to get us deals with all the major sports. This could be huge expansion-wise," I say, imagining our potential if we add a pro baseball team to our list of corporate clients.

That's where it's best to focus. Not on my Prince Charming fantasies. Besides, I learned the hard way where too much attention on a man can lead. Especially a man you don't know really well.

"Just keep being an awesome yoga empress, Katie. And I'll keep getting the deals. You make it easy," Zachary says.

The three of us toast again, then order appetizers and brainstorm the next steps for the business.

When the meal is over, we say goodnight to Zachary, and Olive and I wander through Hayes Valley to our favorite ice cream shop.

Which makes me think of Harlan and our Sexual Tension Swirl ice cream.

Which makes me miss him.

Which makes me wish our timing was a little better.

Damn.

I sigh in the San Francisco November air, the fall breeze whisking by us.

"Hey," Olive says, linking her arm with mine. "How do you feel about this partnership? Are you truly okay with it?"

I whip my gaze to my mind-reader of a sister. "Was it that obvious?"

"Obvious that you were thinking about your guy who got away? Yeah," she says, with a bob of her shoulder. "I can kinda read you. Sister intuition."

If only she'd seen me yesterday when I lost my mind over Harlan's big play in the Seattle game. She wouldn't have needed intuition, that's for sure. But she was doing a long bike ride in wine country to prep for a charity century ride, and now's the first time we've had a chance to truly connect.

"To answer your question, I'm all good with the partnership. It's huge for us, don't you think?"

"Definitely. And it's already leading to more. But I feel bad for you that you had to cut off your thing with him. That's why you asked about timing, right? To see if the contract would end at the end of the season?"

Way to read me like a book.

I scoff like it's no big deal. "We barely even had a thing. It's fine," I say as we bound up the steps to the ice cream shop. "And this is for the best."

She arches a questioning brow, her piercing blue eyes boring into mine. "Are you sure?"

"Positive," I say with more conviction than I feel. Whatever was brewing with Harlan was more than a *thing*. But I don't want to ruin Sassy Yoga's expansion plans on account of my romantic interests. I already had to clean up a wedding that went bust. Kick my ex-fiancé out of my apartment. Get rid of his stuff. Return countless gifts. It was a man exorcism, and I don't want to go through anything remotely similar again. Getting involved with a client, and then Roomba-ing my business life would be even messier, and that's saying something.

Best to let those romantic hopes go. "We didn't truly have a date, so what am I even giving up?"

Just the best chance I've had in ages.

That's all.

We head inside and order ice cream.

A consolation prize.

CHAPTER 24

KATIE

The next day, I work with the team at the training facility. A cornerback grumbles as I lead fifty-three men through the lizard pose. As we move into triangle, cat, then cow poses, some of the linemen shoot me dubious looks.

But I'm used to it, and the skepticism doesn't bother me.

Plus, I try to meet them on their terms.

Competitive terms.

Saying things like: *Bet this helps you protect the quarterback more, bet this will help you evade the secondary, bet you'll dodge and dart past linemen faster.*

And the handy caveat that motivates most athletes—*bet this helps your…stamina.*

Lacey weighs in from her post at the back of the exercise room where she watches over the class. "We all love stamina," she says.

"Hey, Lacey. Why aren't *you* doing all the yoga poses?" The question comes from Erick, the backup quarterback, and it sounds like he wants to see Lacey on all fours.

"Same reason I don't get into the huddle on Sundays. I'm—wait for it—not on the roster." She's all deadpan and fabulous with her comeback. I kind of love her.

"C'mon. If we have to do this, you should too," Erick shouts.

With his bare foot tucked against his calf, Harlan calls out to Erick. "Yes, that's logical, Erick. Completely logical," he says.

"Who said anything about logic?" Erick quips.

I cut in before the place turns into more of a zoo. "The tree pose is one of the best things you can do for your balance, and I suspect balance matters just a little bit out there on the field. Harlan, you're doing a great job with the tree pose," I say, gesturing to the receiver who's mastering the poses in no time.

"Ooh, Harlan, teacher has a crush on you," Erick catcalls.

My cheeks redden. Maybe it wasn't the best idea to single out the guy I'm into.

Smooth move, Katie.

"Let's keep things professional," Lacey cuts in.

The reminder is useful for me too. I step away from Harlan and move over to Cooper, who's also looking pretty damn good as he holds the pose. "Your quarterback does an excellent flamingo impression," I say, using him as my example instead.

Because I'm not here to focus on only one guy.

I'm here because it's my job.

A booming voice carries from the doorway. "Looking good, men."

I whip my gaze in that direction, where the head coach surveys the guys. It's Coach Greenhaven, one of the best in the NFL, a man both feared and revered. "Keep up the good work," he says to his team.

The men all stretch a little deeper, hold a little longer for him.

When the class ends a minute later, the guys filter out, but Lacey and the head coach stay behind.

Then, his intense eyes land on me. "Lacey says you're making an impact."

I stand taller, enjoying his praise. It's not often the head coach of a Super Bowl–winning team doles out praise for me. More like, well, *never.* "It's early days, but I hope so," I say.

"Good. Just don't go work for the Hawks now," he says drily.

I smile. "I promise to stay away from your local rivals."

"That's all I can ask for," he says, then strolls out.

Lacey's eyes shine. "He's not easily impressed."

That's a damn good thing for Sassy Yoga, and that's why I'm here.

The next day, I prep the private room at my studio, eager for Harlan's arrival.

Maybe that makes me a junkie, but I'm getting hooked on these regular doses of him.

This whole teacher-student thing was definitely not on my vision board, but still, I look forward to every session with him.

I set down the mats, a purple one for me, a green one for him.

Then, a strap for each of us, and my mind only briefly flickers to other uses for straps. Next, I place yoga blocks on each mat.

Step back.

Consider the scene.

Do I need anything else?

Should I play some Ed Sheeran?

And I scoff.

What the hell, Katie? Are you setting the table for a romantic dinner? Want to add candles and roses?

I do my best to eject the swoony thoughts from my brain. I'm just a teacher and he's just a student.

When Harlan arrives, I'm professional yogini Katie. "I have a full menu of exercises for you. I'm going to work you hard."

Work, work, work.

With a sexy smile, he lifts a brow. "Make me your pretzel."

I do just that for the next thirty minutes, and then we move into downward dog variations.

I show him the pose I want him to do.

He imitates me, but a line of concentration digs into his forehead as he adjusts his hands. "Not sure I'm getting it right. Can you help me out?"

My heart flutters. It's so endearing the way he asks without any macho bravado.

"Of course," I say, then move beside him, running a hand down his spine.

And all the swoony thoughts I pushed away boomerang back to me.

Sure, this is not how I wanted to be touching Harlan's back. Ideally, I'd be naked.

Under him.

But touching him while his clothes are on is still a thrill. The man has muscles for days, and I am not immune to a hard body.

Though, I am *supposed* to be immune to his.

"Keep your legs as straight as you can," I say, pressing gently on his lower back as he holds the pose.

"Admit it. You want to check out my ass," he quips as he pops his butt higher.

Gah. I love a tight rear end.

Or, really, I discovered I did with Harlan. I discovered a lot of things in those two very sexy times with him.

Times that can't happen again, Katie. Stop daydreaming.

"It's a very nice booty," I concede. "But I'm more concerned with making sure you press your hands into the mat and tuck your toes. That's when you'll find the biggest benefit."

He cranes his neck, looking up at me. His eyes twinkle. "I'd like you to find my biggest benefit."

I roll my eyes.

This man is the biggest flirt I've ever met.

Well, besides me.

Maybe that's why we get along so well. We are birds of a flirty feather.

Setting my hands on his hips, I wiggle him into a slightly better position. "Just making an adjustment for you."

"That's not the adjustment I was hoping you'd make," he says, injecting a little more gravel into his tone.

I laugh. "You are relentless today. And you said we were off-limits."

"We are, but apparently I woke up on the naughty side of the bed this morning."

"That's both sides for you?"

"You know it," he says with a laugh.

"Not surprised at all."

"Bet your bed has two naughty sides just like mine," he says.

I'm getting firmer abs just from laughing with him. "Maybe it does. Now, let's switch to warrior one pose. But I want you to transition from downward dog and flow right into it. I'll show you." I drop onto my feet and hands with my butt in the air, then I raise my torso, lifting my arms toward the sky. "See?"

A low rumble comes from his chest as he stares shamelessly at mine. "Sorry, did you say something?" His eyes widen like a cartoon character catching sight of a delicious plate of goodies.

My goodies.

And you know what? I honestly don't mind him ogling me.

Still, it's best to segue to tamer teasing. I shake a finger at the NFL's sexiest player ever. "Tsk, tsk. And I thought you'd be a good student."

"I thought I wouldn't want to bang the teacher," he says with zero guilt, only desire.

It's an enticing sound that I like far too much.

I, too, like that Harlan truly is a good student, and a devoted one. He's been doing yoga on his own at home since we started, and he's making strides in our one-on-one sessions. Once he shifts into warrior pose, I move behind him, sliding a hand down the outside of his thigh.

"You want your spine erect," I say.

"That's not the only thing erect," he mutters.

"If it makes you feel any better, this is torture for me too. Teasing and torture."

He meets my gaze, a sparkle in his warm brown eyes. "Mmm. *Yoga for Sexual Teasing*. New class for the yoga empress."

"I'd only offer that class to you," I whisper as a spark sizzles down my chest.

"And I'd take that class all day long, since being with you like this is delicious torture. You're like a cherry pie I just want to devour."

Oh, my.

That's quite a dart of lust rushing through my veins right now. I don't think I've ever been compared to a cherry pie. I'm not sure I want a man to ever compare me to anything else.

Harlan makes me feel wanted in a way I never did with my ex. Or, honestly, any other man. None of the men I dated in Los Angeles. None of those guys floated my boat this much, this soon.

Except him, especially since the way he looks at me is incendiary.

And hard to resist. "I bet you'd savor every bite," I whisper, then want to smack myself.

I'm pushing the limits.

Harlan is a client. Sure, my business belongs to Olive and me, but that doesn't mean I can do whatever I want. Sleeping with a client is risky no matter what. Word could get out. Our business could suffer. We employ yoga instructors up and down the coast, as well as office support staff. My choices impact many more people than just me. I'd do well to remember that. Monday night's celebratory evening should have reminded me.

I refuse to be my mother.

I will not let my choices hurt others—not my sister, my employees, or the business I've built.

There's a right way and a wrong way to do things.

I need to do things the right way because I personally know how deep the wrong way cuts.

I stop, take a breath, and treat this moment with the gravity it deserves. "Harlan, do you want me to switch you to another teacher? I can do that. I know Blaine Enterprises hired me, but I can say it's not working out. I can find an instructor for you. I can say someone else is better suited to your needs."

But I don't know if I can make good on my offer. I flash back to Zachary's words on the first day—the team asked for me. Then Monday night—this deal's already leading to others. Would I even be able to step aside as per the contract? And if so, could I walk away from this opportunity?

I brace myself for Harlan's answer and the question of whether I can deliver on it, whatever he chooses.

He scoffs, then raises his arms so his hands are parallel to the floor, showing off how well he knows our routine by transitioning into warrior two. "Look what I mastered in one week with you. I am

not a quitter. I can do this. And I can handle this cherry-pie lust."
His eyes hook onto mine, and mischief flickers in them. "Though,
you *are* irresistible."

I feel the same way about him.

Thirty minutes later, we finish our session. As we gather our
water bottles and towels, Harlan sighs like he's throwing in the
towel. "You know how I said you were irresistible? That's why I have
to take you to lunch right now."

What harm could come from one meal between a yoga teacher
and a client?

Nothing.

Yes.

Lunch is safe.

Lunch is totally safe.

CHAPTER 25

KATIE

Since Harlan is too easy to flirt with, my only option is salad.

No one orders salad on a date—the risk of dressing down your blouse or snagging spinach in your teeth is too great. But what's even riskier than a regular salad? A salad tossed with micro greens and kale. Add in arugula for good measure. Sprinkle some chia seeds.

There.

This won't feel like a date because that's not date food. That's girlfriend-do-I-have-anything-stuck-in-my-teeth food.

This salad will help me see Harlan like a friend.

I place my order at Harvest Haven, a new café off Polk Street that Emerson recommended. Harlan orders a protein fiesta wrap, something football-y with chicken, tofu, beans, and garbanzos. Basically, a recipe for muscle building.

Happy sigh. I love muscles.

Wait. Stop. No muscle thoughts, Katie.

I swipe away all thoughts of big, toned arms that can hold me down hard and any other images that make my lady parts do the samba.

Cha cha cha, indeed.

Instead, I'll focus on…*this place*. Yeah, that'll erase the smut from my head.

I swing my gaze around the hipster joint.

The walls are concrete.

The chairs are butcher block…well, blocks.

The tables are steel.

"It's not terribly inviting decor," I remark as we walk away from the counter.

"It's possible this place is too hip for me," he says, grabbing a table.

I try to get comfortable on the exceptionally uncomfortable chair. "I almost feel like this place is trying too hard."

He frowns as he sits. "It's official. This is the worst chair ever."

"It's not even a chair," I second. "It's a pain-delivery mechanism."

He chuckles, then his eyes flicker. "There's a park a few blocks away. Want to get our grub to go and eat there? It has *picnic tables*," he says like he's dangling gumdrops in front of Hansel and Gretel.

"Yes, please," I answer before it hits me that a picnic in the park is the very definition of romantic.

That's what I'm trying to avoid with Harlan.

Dammit.

But then, a picnic is only romantic if I let it be romantic.

And I won't.

C'mon, chia seeds. Lodge between my teeth.

After we grab our order to go, we head up the street, and I focus on non-romantic, non-flirty topics. "I'll have to give Emerson a hard time about Harvest Haven's get-the-hell-out-of-here vibe. She was raving about it on her show the other week, and she told me I had to check it out. I try to support her as much as I can."

He tilts his head, his gaze curious. "What's her show?"

I tell him the name of Emerson's bona fide online hit. "She's a vegetarian, and several years ago she started reviewing the places where she ate. At first, it was just for fun. She was having a good time, giving reviews like, *No, this vegan meat doesn't taste like chicken, and I don't want it to taste like chicken. It tastes like yummy grainy goodness dancing on my tongue.* Then her videos took off because she's so accessible and real and people love it."

"Good for her. Sounds like she loves what she's doing," he says as we reach the top of the hill.

"She says that's the key to a happy life. Doing what you love." We cross the street into a tiny park ringed by trees and tall hedges. It's a hideaway here, an escape from the rest of the city. Birds chirp, a light breeze blows, and the sun—rare in November—warms my shoulders.

"That seems like a pretty good gauge of happiness," he says as we find a picnic table and settle in. "Sounds like you agree?"

Briefly, I let the last few years run through my mind, from the highs of building a business with my sister to the low of being left at the altar and betrayed by my mother. I focus on the joys and the pain, but ultimately, the triumphs. Olive and I love Sassy Yoga fiercely, and it feels like *ours*, not only because it is, but because we truly love what we do.

"I do. I worked in fashion before, doing retail buying. And while I love the fashion line we built at Sassy Yoga, I adore sharing something that's helped me with many others."

"You do seem pretty intent on helping. I've noticed that when you're with the team. With me, too, but especially the team. You take time to make sure everyone gets it, knows what they're doing. To add a compliment or a quip. You make it fun," he says with a smile as he unwraps his sandwich. "You've always been a yoga person?"

"No. Not at all. I was very much an eye-roller back in the day."

Harlan tosses his head back, laughing. "Love that term. That's perfect."

"Because so many people are, right? Basically, the world breaks down according to those who love yoga, and those who go full Robert-Downey-Jr.-eye-rolling GIF at the practice."

He bites into his sandwich, nodding as he chews. When he's done, he says, "That's spot on. So, you were a Robert Downey Jr.?"

"Absolutely." I pop open the lid to the salad, then grab a fork.

"What changed for you?" he asks, eyes intent on mine. Harlan is a fantastic listener, I'm learning. He stays on topic; he asks questions. It's refreshing.

"My friends and my sister," I say after I take a bite. "I was resistant to it, but Skyler and Olive—my sister—had started going way back when." I flap a hand over my shoulder toward the ancient history of my life.

"Way back when? In the dark ages?" he teases, his eyes alight with self-deprecation.

"Yes. It was eons ago. Seriously, though, it was shortly after college. They both went to yoga at the gym and told me to try it. Olive, the perv, said it was good for sex. Skyler, who now prays at the altar of eight hours of sleep a night, said it helped her insomnia. So, I went. *Reluctantly.*"

"I think you just described half of my team," he adds.

But their mixed reactions don't faze me. "They'll realize the benefit over time," I say. I believe in what I do, and I'm confident it'll help the guys. "And you? Are you reluctant? Skeptical? Totally devoted to the bennies of shavasana and wine forever and ever?"

His smile catches me off-guard. It's so magnetic, but it fades quickly. He takes another bite, sets down his sandwich, then sighs. "I'm open to it, but I'm in a different place than some of the young guns, you know?"

Ah, the age conversation. I figured it was coming with Harlan. I'm aware of the chatter about whether or not this is his last season. "Because you're thinking more about the future?"

He nods decisively. "I think a lot about what's next. Worry about it. Wonder. I love football the way your friend Emerson says you should. The sport is like air to me. I've loved football since I was a kid, and it's hard to imagine *not* playing."

There's wistfulness in his voice. It's a sound I rarely hear from him. He's usually so playful and upbeat. But now and then, he reveals the things that seem to weigh on him. *This* definitely seems to.

"But I also really like taking my daughter to school, and teaching her to read, and letting her sneak-polish my toes when I conk out on the couch when her friends are over. I love seeing her as often as I can, and I *don't* love spending every weekend from August to December pretty much unavailable. Know what I mean?"

My heart catches in my throat and thunders there. A man who wants to be there for his kid is so damn appealing. His affection for parenting makes me all kinds of mushy. Makes me think about things I haven't thought about in ages. "I don't have kids, but I can imagine." I say it casually; I'm not opening a kid convo, and I doubt he wants to have one. That's not what today is about.

He sighs, his brow knitting. Sounds like he's gearing up to say something hard. "Did you want to? With your ex?"

Or maybe that *is* what today is about. The question of kids pushes me out of my comfort zone, and I answer with another question. "Have kids?" It comes out a little squeaky. "With Silvio?"

"Yeah. Did you?"

The intensity of his gaze says he's genuinely interested. I'm not sure why it matters what I wanted with my ex when he's so far in the rearview mirror. "We never talked about it," I answer honestly.

"Hmm."

He leaves it at that, but I don't drop the subject yet. With time and distance from my ex, I've learned more about myself. What I want. What I hope for. And kids are part of that. An unanswered question, but still a part.

"I suspect that was yet another reason why it didn't work out with him," I say. "Looking back, we didn't have a lot in common.

We didn't talk as much as we should have. I suppose I wasn't sure how to tell him the truth."

"That you don't want to have kids?" Harlan asks, his voice speckled with nerves.

A stone wedges in my chest. This is hard to say. I do want kids, if the timing is right, if the relationship is right, if I'm with someone who feels like my forever. But that sounds so *fairy tale*, so I answer more plainly. "I worry that the opportunity has passed me by. I'm thirty-five. I don't know if I'll have the chance." I glance around the park, not sure what I'm searching for. Maybe just the courage to voice the rest. His vulnerable eyes give me that strength. "I'm still single. So I don't know if it'll happen, and that's the truth." I hold up my hands in surrender.

To time.

"Do you want it to happen?" he asks.

"If it's right. The right man. The right relationship. I won't force it. If I've learned anything, it's that life comes at you on its own terms, in all sorts of unexpected ways. You have to roll with the punches."

He takes another bite, nods like he's absorbing what I said. When he's done chewing, he says, "That is definitely true. The key is to adapt."

"Like you did when your daughter was born," I say, returning to the center of his world. "It must be hard when you can't see her as much as you'd like."

He takes a steadying breath. "It is, but hey, we make it work. I don't get to see her on weekends during the season, but when I do, we have a blast together." He flashes me a smile, almost like he needs to slap it on for bravado. "But hey, my weekend job isn't too shabby. I'm hanging in there at thirty-six."

I want to ask him more about Abby.

About being a dad.

But he's returned to football now, and that seems where he wants to stay. Maybe wise for me, too, given the way my heart flips when he talks about being a dad.

So, I keep the conversation in *that* zone.

"I'd say you're doing more than hanging in there." I tap my temple. "You have all the advantages up here. You have wisdom and insight. You have instincts. As well as moves on the field," I say. "Hello! Did you see your game last weekend? You had that gorgeous twenty-five-yard catch at the end of the half. And how about the fifty-six-yard catch when you were nearly out of bounds?" I lift my arms high in the air, then stretch to the side, doing my damnedest to imitate his grace and power on the field. "And you grabbed it before it hit the ground, then you spun around and ran into the end zone." My voice pitches higher, my excitement spilling over as the instant replay flashes before my eyes. "It was glorious, and my friends and I were shouting your name in my living room."

I pick up my fork and dive into the salad again.

Harlan's eyebrows rise and his brown eyes glimmer with… delight.

Utter delight.

And pride, too, it seems. "You liked that? My play? You cheered hard?"

"The hardest," I say emphatically.

"The hardest, you say?" It comes out a little dirty, a touch suggestive.

"Yes, you sexy beast. I cheered the hardest."

Oops, I objectified him again.

And he seems to love it, judging from the sly smile gracing those full, gorgeous lips.

Lips I want to taste desperately.

Harlan's eyes never stray from mine. He stares at me darkly. Speaks seductively. "And did your friends want to know why you were cheering so hard?"

That rumbly voice sends a shiver down my spine. "They know I'm working for the team," I say, teasing him, playing it coy.

"That's the *only* reason they think you cheered hard?"

"Fine, fine. They know you're an orgasm dealer," I add, with an over-the-top huff and a puff.

A laugh bursts from him. "That's what you called me?"

"That's what you are," I say, squaring my shoulders, owning it. "Wait. Am I objectifying you for being spectacular in bed? They also know you're a sweetie pie, a funny guy, and a good dad."

He waves a hand dismissively. "Back it up to spectacular between the sheets."

"Ha. Is that all you care about?"

With utter intensity in his eyes, he nods. "At the moment, yes. I'm into this nickname. *A lot.*"

A flush races across my chest. "Well, it's the truth. I speak the truth. And I also got a wicked thrill watching you use those hands so expertly on the field, knowing what those hands had done to me." I take a beat, let my eyes drift down his chest. "Your whole body."

Oh hell, I'm terrible at not flirting.

Harlan leans closer across the table. "Do you have any idea how much I want to take you home, toss you on my bed, and make you feel incredible?"

A pulse beats between my legs. I ache for him.

So much for arugula's help.

"As much as I want you to?" I toss back, since flirting with him is too fun.

"That much," he says, then we stare at each other, a lot heated, and all kinds of heady. The air crackles, and I want to forget the rest of the world, screw the day, and spend the afternoon in his bed.

In his arms.

But I've got to have some self-control.

Deep breath.

I take a bite of my salad, trying to let the lettuce do the trick. When I set down the fork, he chuckles under his breath.

"What?"

"You've got a chia in your teeth."

Saved by the seed.

CHAPTER 26

HARLAN

That weekend, Danielle and Jamie bring Abby and her friends to the stadium.

They watch the game from the owner's suite, and I wish I could pop up there and see my girl before kickoff.

But that's not in the cards.

The team has rules about no distractions, and the rules work.

They put us in a football-only mindset.

On the field, Cooper is unflappable in the pocket, marching the team closer and closer to the end zone with every play it seems, trading off throwing to his favorite targets—Jones and me.

The two of us combine for three touchdowns when the game ends with a win for the Renegades.

I yank off my helmet after the clock runs out and knock fists with my bud. "Good game, and don't forget I had one hundred one receiving yards to your ninety-nine."

Jones rolls his eyes. "Hope those two extra yards keep you warm at night."

And…he has a fair point.

But the most important point is this—we've only lost two games this season, and we're in playoff contention again.

Something that makes the owner very happy.

Once I've showered and talked to the press, I head to Wilder Blaine's suite.

The billionaire team owner waits at the door, wearing his custom suit and game-winning grin. "Excellent work, Taylor," he says.

"Thank you, sir. And that is a most excellent suit."

He laughs politely, his green eyes glinting, then claps me on the shoulder. "I know our GM is looking forward to talking to your agent."

Ohhhh.

That's a sign if ever I heard one.

"That's great," I say, buoyed by his words, since it's not often the owner himself makes it clear he wants you.

"And your family is welcome anytime in my suite," he says.

It's a great offer. Truly it is. "I appreciate that, Mister Blaine."

"And we appreciate you," he adds, punctuating his praise.

I make a mental note to pass on his words to my agent, since I'm pretty sure they're a guaranteed offer in free agency.

But I'll do that tomorrow, because once I head inside, my favorite person rams into me. "I saw your catch. Also, Simone Biles did the coolest thing ever and you need to see that too," Abby tells me.

We watch gymnastics on Danielle's iPad, Abby in my lap, until it's time to go.

———————

On the way to school one day next week, we pass Fog City Bakery. The shop catches Abby in its tractor-beam scents of sugary sweetness and pillowy bread.

A sign on the glass beckons, and she moves trance-like to it. "Mun-kee," she reads, sounding out the word. "Monkey bread!"

I clap a few times. "Well done."

She tugs on my shirtsleeve. "That's what smells so good. Can we get some?"

"Before school?"

She stares at me like she can't believe I'd question her request. "Why not? It looks yummy and smells good."

I peer through the doorway at the shelf of treats, zeroing in on the cinnamon-y, caramel-y pastry calling our names. My stomach rumbles. "It does look tasty, but you just had breakfast. How about we make monkey bread this afternoon?"

Her smile spreads across the city. "Deal." We resume our pace. "But, Daddy, do you know *how* to make monkey bread?"

I roll my eyes. "I know how to research recipes and buy ingredients."

She pats my arm. "You're so smart."

"So are you."

When we reach the school, a dark-haired dynamo whirls into Abby from out of nowhere, smash-hugging my kid. "You should come to *my* gymnastics class today," the kid declares when she lets go.

My girl beams. "Sure, Gabriella!"

"It's after school. My dad is taking me. Can you come with me?"

Abby swivels around. "Can I go? She said her class is doing balance beam, and I really love doing the beam. Please, please, please."

And the monkey bread afternoon falls by the wayside. "Of course, little bear. But I bet you don't have a leotard, so why don't I drop one off for you after my yoga session?"

She snickers, then turns to Gabriella. "I call him Daddy Yoga, like Baby Yoda from *The Mandalorian*," she whispers to Gabriella.

The little brunette giggles.

"Bring leotard, I will," I say in my best Yoda voice.

Both girls laugh, but then Abby smacks her forehead. "I have a leotard! There's one in my bag from my last class. And we can make monkey bread when I get home."

"Seems you have the whole afternoon planned."

Abby smiles proudly. "I do."

Gabriella looks up at me and presses her hands together. "Mister Taylor, next time I come over, can I paint your toes again?"

I arch a brow. "Were you the culprit who made them pink and blue last time?"

A deep belly laugh comes from nearby, and I turn to the source of it—a guy in glasses with a thick beard. "She does drive-by pedicures when dads fall asleep." The man extends a hand. "I'm Arturo. Gabriella's dad. Good to meet you."

As the girls scurry off to the playground before the bell rings, Arturo gestures to them. "Gabriella said she wanted Abby to come to gymnastics today. Is that cool with you? It's kind of last minute, but I'll take the girls."

"Absolutely. I appreciate you doing that," I tell him. "Let me know where to pick her up?"

He waves me off. "Nah. S'all good. I can drop her off when they're done."

"Works for me," I say with a smile. "You're a full-service dad."

Arturo smiles. "That's me. I'm a stay-at-home dad," he says, looking supremely satisfied with that.

"Good on you," I reply, and I mean it.

He glances around like he's checking for eavesdroppers. When he finishes his sweep, he says, "Also, that catch the other week in Seattle. Epic, man. Epic." He holds up a hand for a combo high-five, fist bump.

"Thank you."

"You're killing it this year. Don't retire. We need you around for a long time. And don't you dare sign with anyone else in the off-season. Hey, how about a deal?" He points at my chest. "If you re-up, I'll always take the girls to gymnastics. I've got an extra booster seat in my car."

"You should be my agent. I like that deal," I tell the guy, then thank him again for ferrying the kids around, and we exchange numbers before I skedaddle.

But honestly, his situation doesn't sound too bad either. He seems pretty happy doing what he likes.

I make my way to the gym, join the guys for a workout, and shoot the breeze. But my thoughts aren't entirely on the here and now.

They're on the future—a year ahead and a couple of hours from now when I meet Katie at her studio.

I've seen her five times since our cancelled date—from the classes to the private sessions—and each time I want to see her again a little bit more.

Seeing her is terrific and tempting at the same damn time.

I resist because the last thing I need this year is a whiff of a scandal. But, even more so, I don't want to bring that on Katie.

The Renegade and the Yoga Instructor—Caught Downward-Doggie Style. Yeah, that's not how I want to cap off my career—by putting a black mark on hers.

But also, I want more than doggie style with Katie.

More than sex.

I just like her.

A whole helluva lot.

And I sure wish we didn't have the worst timing in the world, because all I want is to take her out and treat her well.

———————

Katie circles me as I lie on my back near the wall, my legs going up it and forming an L.

For the record, I hate this pose.

It's hell on the hammies.

"Shimmy your booty," Katie tells me. "A little more. Just a smidge closer to the wall."

The waterfall pose is fuck-all hard. As I wiggle my butt closer to the wall, she laughs, tugs my legs up, then bends to adjust my butt.

Nice.

This is just so damn nice...

I mean...distracting.

This is crazy distracting.

But I wouldn't change a thing as I indulge in the view of her. "I like hands-on yoga instruction. I'm gonna keep this up," I say, shamelessly staring at her fantastic chest.

While she stares at my...toes.

She flicks her fingernail against the big one. "Too cute."

"Happens to me once a week. I'll take a catnap when Abby has friends over, and they conduct pedicure ambushes."

"The pastels are fetching," she teases.

I wiggle my toes. "Why, thank you. Does it turn you on?"

She leans over me, a little closer. "So much."

A groan rumbles out of me, unbidden. Everything she does gets me going. Hell, just the view of her chest fires me up. Her tits in that sports bra are so damn tantalizing. The tease of them, the peek at her flesh.

I want them, dammit, but I can't have them.

Or her.

I whimper.

She tilts her head. "You okay?"

I clear my throat and sweep away the dirty thoughts. "I'm all good," I say, and hone in on the poses.

Whatever Katie's been doing to the team, and to me, it's

working. In just a couple of weeks, I feel better, I'm playing stronger, and the hammie strain isn't bothering me a bit.

That feels like winning.

The only thing I wish were different is the time I spend with her. I wish I could see her at night, especially after that picnic lunch. Every night, every hour, every second we spend together seems to tug me deeper into her orbit.

And I like her orbit a lot.

Because...I like her.

When we finish and make our way to the exit, an idea takes hold, gripping me. It feels necessary.

Important.

And it's a chance to spend more time with her.

"Katie, do you like monkey bread?"

She swings her gaze to me. "The bread that ought to be cake? The bread that's dessert for breakfast? The bread that's like a cinnamon roll?"

I tap her nose. "Show-off."

"Yes. Yes, I do like it."

I toss out the next question, hoping she also likes what I'm offering. My hope for her yes is more intense than I expected. "Abby wanted to make some, but she's going to gymnastics with a friend. I thought I would get started, and we could finish when she comes home. Any chance you want to shop for monkey bread supplies with me, and then we can make some with Abby?"

I just asked a woman to hang with my daughter and me.

I ought to be terrified. And I'm honestly not sure why I chose now to ask Katie this big question.

But something about this seems just right.

This afternoon is all I can give, but maybe it will be enough for now.

CHAPTER 27

KATIE

I wasn't jonesing for this invitation, but now that he's offered it, there is only one way to RSVP.

"I would love to shop with you and make monkey bread," I say, and his suggestion feels worlds better than any night with my ex.

And it feels just as good as dancing to 80s tunes, shopping with a drag queen, and making eggs with *this* man.

Being with Harlan in any little way feels good.

That's scary as hell, but wonderful too.

It's making me think about timing, and steps, and possibilities.

About the future, and how to make it happen.

Risky thoughts I probably shouldn't entertain, given my past. Given my heartbreak.

And yet, I am.

That means there's monkey bread to make.

"Let's hit it, handsome," I say.

Harlan shoots me a sexy-and-sweet smile that melts my heart—and all the rest of me too.

So much for being *only* teacher and student with him. His smile just crossed the don't-break-me line of my heart.

"And we're off to the store," he says.

And maybe to something unknown.

How is it possible that grocery shopping can be fun?

Tell me that, universe.

I have never enjoyed shopping for food. Food buying is functional.

But shopping for groceries with Harlan is a blast.

I grab a box of brown sugar and waggle it. "Confession time—as a kid, did you or did you not sneak spoonfuls of sugar from the pantry?"

He scoffs. "Obviously. Brown sugar was my gateway drug into sweets."

"Right? Same here. Never turned back. I'm convinced brown sugar ignited my lifetime love affair with yummy things."

He sweeps the box into the shopping basket. "My words to live by: you can never have enough brown sugar, good tunes, and"—he stops to glance around the bougie gourmet store in Pacific Heights, then lowers his voice—"good sex."

Mmm.

Those words rumble from his lips. They're about more than the physical. "I like how you added an adjective before sex. It's important to specify. Because bad sex is *not* worth having," I say as we reach the spices, and I grab some cinnamon.

"You're a woman after my own heart," he says, and I want to shout, *Yes. Yes, I am.*

But I should slow down, so I zip my lips as he talks.

"If you're going to do something, you might as well do it right. Football, yoga, parenting," he says, listing the things that matter to, well, to us. "Friendships, musical taste, baking—pies in particular—and yes, sex."

I swear, this man wants the same things I do. Feels the same things. Is this what a real connection is like? Maybe.

We wander past the frozen goods. "Honestly, there's no reason to have bad sex," I say. "If you're having bad sex, that means you're not trying. Good sex isn't magic. You don't wave a wand and have it. You've got to listen to your partner, pay attention, and, most of all, to want it."

His eyes lock with mine in the relative seclusion of the refrigerated section, and in his brown irises I see as much want as I feel.

This conversation is dangerous, but I don't want to let go of it yet. I like talking about sex with Harlan. I like talking about *why* the sex is so damn good with him. Because something is happening, and something has *always* been happening with us. It's not magic— it's effort. Good, hard effort that pays off. We vibe in bed because we vibe out of bed.

We've vibed every time we've been together.

That's why we can't seem to resist stealing every little moment.

I'm not sure I want to resist much longer.

Maybe he doesn't want to either. "I loved reading your cues, Katie," he says. "Figuring out your needs, and then delivering. That's what made it so damn good."

In the span of a few seconds, this conversation has shot from our childhood memories to why our intimacy rocks.

Our intimacy that we're *not* having.

But tell that to my body. The shiver that runs down my chest and settles between my legs feels wildly intimate.

"You think so?" I ask, a little breathless as I stand next to the butter.

"Don't you?" He sounds breathless too.

"Sometimes, but I also think we read each other's cues out of bed too. Like the way we interact—that's part of it. Part of why it's so good," I say.

This is hardly the place for this talk. But we've never been in the right place at the right time. Why should today be any different? Maybe I'm learning to embrace the moments with Harlan, to take them as they come.

When they come.

Even if I try to halt them with a pump of the business-minded brakes here or there, the moments don't stop.

They keep happening, from seizing the night at the wedding seven years ago, to making the most of my anti-wedding night this past summer, to our yoga sessions, to lunch…to today.

He inches closer, latching on to my words. "I do think the way we are together is why the sex has been so damn good," he says, and I am buzzing. "But *everything* with us is so good."

My entire body hums with arousal and longing.

With need.

With hope that I can somehow rewrite the future. That I can discover an opening to what I want where I'm not hurting the people I work with. Where I'm not behaving like my mother in business.

I *need* to find that way.

And I need to find it soon.

I'm not even technically involved with this man, but it sure seems like I am.

Here goes the next thing—putting my feelings out there, taking the steps to let him know. I should be cautious about those things, but I can't be bothered right now. "I can't believe I'm saying this by the nine-dollar eggs, but I was really looking forward to seeing you again. To all of it. To everything."

If I'm going to look for a way forward with him, it should start with speaking from the heart. So, I do. "I was looking forward to dinner and ice cream and foosball and sex, and also just…getting to know you more. I still am. I look forward to getting to know you more each day because I like everything I've already gotten to know," I say, reaching for the side of the cold case like I need to hold on or I'll stumble.

But I'm pretty sure I've already fallen.

CHAPTER 28

HARLAN

My head is spinning.

I feel woozy, too, almost like I've been knocked hard out of bounds.

But I like this feeling. It's new and different, but it's all good. And I want more of it. "I was looking forward to spending more time with you," I say softly. "I wanted all of it. The sex and the dates and just…*you*. I still do. I like you so much."

My heart slams against my rib cage. I'm dangerously close to dropping this red basket on the floor, shoving her against the yogurt and eggs, and kissing the breath out of her, no matter what it brings.

For all our flirting, all our teasing, all of this red-hot sizzle, she's on to something—the reason our first kiss went to my head. Hell, I can still remember how it felt to taste her lips for the first time.

Spectacular.

I like this woman.

I like her so damn much.

The last few weeks have fueled those feelings. The time with her *not* kissing, *not* touching, and *not* fucking has only fanned the flames.

Even though I can't touch her, I *can* use my words like she just did. "Katie Madigan, I'm so into you, it's kind of crazy."

Her smile is one I want to remember for a long time. Here, by the organic eggs in the grocery store a few blocks from my home, she smiles like I've made her happy.

Just happy.

And isn't that what a man should aim to do for the woman he wants? Treat her right and make her feel good? It's that simple.

But whatever is happening between us isn't simple. It's complicated by downward dogs and deals with the team. A tryst would be risky, but much more for her than me. Whether I finish football now or in a few years, I'm at the end of my days. I've achieved the greatest highs in the game. Her career trajectory is rising, shooting higher every day.

I'd just be another jock who messed around with a trainer, a teacher, a woman stretching him. Though not the way I want to cap off a career, I'd be forgiven in a heartbeat.

She'd be the woman who slept with a client, and I don't want that for her.

So she has to stay off-limits, and I have to stay hands-off.

She sighs wistfully. "So now what?"

That's a good question.

I drag my hand along the back of my neck, then shoot her a rueful grin. "Want to go prep the monkey bread supplies?"

"I do," she says.

We check out and head to my place. As we head up the steps, I'm keenly aware this isn't the first time Katie has stepped into my home. The first was on her non-wedding night, when I brought her here to sleep with her.

But now she's stepping inside playing a different role in my life.

A colleague of sorts? A teacher? A partner?

None of those terms feel right.

She's coming into my home as a friend. Yes! That's why I invited her over today. Katie's a friend at the moment, and that's why it feels like the perfect time for her to meet my daughter.

Bags in my hand, I unlock the door and hold it open for her. "After you," I say in my best Southern gentleman voice.

"Why, thank you, sir," she says in her Texas twang.

Once the door closes, we head straight for the kitchen.

"Tunes?" I ask as I unload the groceries.

"If it's Ed Sheeran, Dolly Parton, and Adele, we're golden."

I chuckle. "How about I throw in some Frank Sinatra and Eric Clapton, and we can call it a day?"

She lifts the sugar from the bag, shakes her hips, and gives me an approving hum. "We'll get along just fine, sir," she says, still playing with the accent.

"Darling, we always have." I hit Shuffle on some tunes, and Ed Sheeran's tones fill my home, making Katie happy, judging from the twinkle in her eyes. Then I drop the accent and say something that's a little bit hard. "Hey, Katie."

"Yeah?"

I square my shoulders. "I don't introduce women to my daughter. It's just not something I've done." I swallow roughly as I lay the truth on the line like she did in the store.

I want her to know that this thing between us is becoming much more for me.

More than I expected.

More than it's supposed to.

It's turning into something that feels a little inevitable.

She receives my words like a beautiful pass, catching them with a smile and warm eyes. "I'm excited to meet Abby. She sounds amazing. And I'm glad you want me to meet her," she says in a kind, inviting tone that underlines, black-Sharpie style, why I like her so much.

She's open and honest and caring and fun.

"She is amazing, and so are you," I say, and it feels like a weight off my shoulders. I'm glad I put that out there.

Maybe we're a lot inevitable, Katie and me.

My hands twitch. The desire to touch her, to pull her into my arms, rockets higher in me. I'm eager for all the next things with her.

Is there any way to have them?

I keep my hands to myself as I measure the sugar and butter.

Sure, we have terrible timing, but the timing doesn't always have to be bad, does it? Her contract with the team can't last forever.

Maybe dating is like a recipe. Maybe it's monkey bread. It takes time for all the ingredients to come together just right.

As I pour the sugar into a bowl, I stop and hit end on the song. Turn to meet her gaze. "Katie, I have this idea. Call me crazy."

"Crazy," she says playfully.

I step closer to her. "What if…"

She laughs softly, clearly liking things so far. "What if…?"

I go for it, run like hell with a brand-new plan. "What if we agree to date at the end of the season when your classes with the team end? I know it's a couple of months away, but I'm not seeing anyone else, and I'm not *going* to see anyone else. You're the woman I want, and these last few weeks have only solidified that more. I don't want to let you get away. I want to lock you up as my date," I say, putting that out there and hoping she likes the plan too. I sure do. It feels like the *only* answer to the *what can we do* question.

Her smile is radiant. Her hand flies to her chest, and her eyes well up with something like…joy.

"I want that, Harlan. I do. Truly, I do." But her smile disappears in a heartbeat, replaced by resignation. "The trouble is, the team has already said it plans to renew the contract."

CHAPTER 29

HARLAN

I'm sadder than the time we lost the championship game five years ago.

I thought I'd erased that awful memory, but it comes roaring back right now. I felt like shit the day we lost by a field goal to Baltimore, erasing our Super Bowl chances.

Now, I feel worse.

I should be able to fix this. My job is to find openings. It's to solve problems on the field. It's to dodge two-hundred-fifty-pound obstacles in the form of linebackers and quicksilver tight ends champing at the bit to slam me to the ground.

I can move like a cheetah on the gridiron, spinning and whirling away from threats. But I can't get out of the way of a problem like this.

"That is…awful but awesome," I say like I'm chewing on sand.

"Yeah," she says with a sigh. "You took the words out of my mouth."

I can't even make a joke. "Well, I get it. You're a great teacher. Hell, you've helped me. And I mean that from the bottom of my heart and my hamstring."

The smile that curves her lips is both tender and wistful. "I'm very glad it's working. That makes me...*professionally* happy."

"But personally?"

She takes a beat and moves the mixing bowl with the sugar in it a few inches away, then the brown sugar bowl. They don't need moving.

Letting go of the bowl, she turns to me, strength in her blue eyes. "But personally, I want everything you said. And I feel like I should be terrified because of what happened last summer...but I'm not." She blows out a breath of obvious relief. "Whew. I kind of can't believe I just said that, because for the last few weeks I was so dang worried. Worried about taking my time, going slowly, doing everything differently. Making sure I wasn't caught up. But everything with you feels right, and I want what's next. I want to pursue a relationship with you. But that's not what worries me."

My heart beats faster. Never has a relationship sounded so good as it does on her lips. I want a relationship with her more than I want to win my next game.

And I really like winning games.

Trouble is, her thoughts are unfinished.

"But what does worry you?"

"I don't want to hurt people," she explains. "I don't want to do in business what my mother did in love. I don't want to go behind anyone's back and hurt them through my actions."

Why is integrity so damn sexy? Oh, because it fucking is. "I understand," I say, my heart sinking once more, up and down like a yo-yo.

Katie nibbles on the corner of her lips, then takes a deep breath. Like she's fortifying herself. "But what if I work to find a replacement? I would search through our roster of teachers and talk to Zachary—he's our business dev guy—and also Olive. And tell them at the end of the season, I need to step back. I'll say the Renegades can't have me next year."

And it's happy yo-yo land.

Excitement buzzes through my veins. "So the Renegades can't have you, but I can?" I ask, all flirty again.

She grins, then giggles too. "I like this plan. I'll make it work. I'll figure it out."

"I fucking love it," I say. "Let's do it. Whenever it works for you, I'm by your side. Know that, okay?"

She nods, her eyes a little shiny. "That's kind of amazing."

"I mean it, Katie. You call the shots here. I'll just be waiting to kiss you on the field whenever you're ready. I know our timing has been all wrong, but let's *make* this our time, once and for all. And thank you. I know this falls on you, when to do this, how to do this, so thank you."

"You can thank me by showering me with orgasms in January."

I growl, holding up a finger to admonish her. "Super Bowl is in February, Katie."

She rolls her eyes. "Fine, I can wait till then."

I close the distance, sweep her into my arms, and hug her tight.

It's risky, but so's chasing a ball the safeties don't want you to catch. So's running in a touchdown. Holding Katie close is terribly risky but absolutely necessary.

When we pull apart, my hands still on her waist, I don't want to let go. "You feel too good in my arms," I tell her.

A breath shudders past her lips. "I sure like being here," she whispers, all soft and irresistibly sweet, her arms still looped around my neck.

So damn sweet that I'm not sure I want to resist anymore.

Can I? Yes. But I don't want to. "What if I steal a kiss right now?"

She runs her fingers along the ends of my hair. "Don't have to steal it," she murmurs. "You can have it."

"It'll keep me going until the end of the season," I whisper as I inch closer, then drop my lips to hers.

Her breath hitches as I kiss her the way I want to right now—tender, gentle, but with a promise.

Like this kiss is sealing our promise for next year.

It goes to my head in an instant. My mind slides into a Katie-induced euphoria as I explore these lips I've missed desperately. As I kiss the corner of her mouth. As I flick my tongue against her bottom lip. She opens for me, a sensual sigh mingling with my own murmurs.

I'm keenly aware of the ticking clock.

But I take what I can get for the moment—a little more of this woman I'm falling for. I deepen the kiss, savoring every secret second. It'll have to sustain me for the next two months, so I let myself get lost in the kiss, and in her, and in my hopes for what's next.

Soon, though, it must end.

I break the kiss.

Her eyes glimmer. Her lips are swollen. "Wow," she whispers.

"Yeah, I'll say."

We let go, and I can't wait for the calendar to jump to next year. But for now, I check the time. My kiddo will be here soon.

I'm nervous and excited for the future…but mostly, elated.

Once she enters the living room, Abby views Katie with studious eyes. "So, you're the yoga lady?"

"I sure am," Katie says. "It is a pleasure to meet the little lady of the house."

Abby giggles. "Lady of the house. I like that," she says, setting her backpack by the couch and running to the kitchen sink to wash her hands. "Hey, yoga lady," she says as we follow her, "do you know what yoga pose pirates like to do?"

Katie taps her chin like she's deep in thought. "Could it be… the plank?"

Abby tosses her head back and laughs. "How did you know?"

Katie beckons Abby with a crook of her finger. "I know all the good yoga jokes."

"Ooh, tell me another," Abby demands, and I park my butt on the stool at the counter and happily watch them.

Katie bends to six-year-old eye level. "How does a T. rex feel after practicing yoga?"

"I don't know," Abby says, nearly bouncing with excitement. "Tell me."

Katie rubs her knuckles against her lower back. "A little dino… sore."

"Ohhh. I like that." Abby wheels around to the counter. "Monkey bread. Can you do a monkey impression like my dad?"

Katie turns her gaze to me. "I've only heard your lion, Harlan. I'd love to hear the monkey. Don't hold back."

I roll my eyes. "You ladies act like you've got me cornered. Like you've tricked me. 'Course I can do a monkey. Ooh-ooh, ahh-ahh," I say, imitating a chimp.

They clap and cheer.

"You know what I can do?" Abby asks.

"What's that?"

"I can be a baker. I've been thinking about this all day."

Abby grabs a wooden spoon and gets to work.

The three of us make monkey bread in the kitchen, listening to Dolly Parton and Adele while Abby tells us about gymnastics and her friend, and Gabriella's dad's funny jokes, and how awesome the balance beam is.

When the bread goes in the oven, Abby stares at the clock. "I don't know how to wait. It's going to be so long." Then she spins around and points at Katie. "Can I paint your nails?"

"Do you have fuchsia? That's my favorite color."

"I do," Abby declares, then runs to her room.

For the next fifteen minutes, Abby gives Katie a manicure, and I count down the weeks till the end of the season.

———————

That night, I read Abby four stories, including one about a girl who gets a pony.

"That girl is so smart. She convinced her daddy to give her a pony," Abby says, snuggling under the covers.

"Gee, Abby. Are you trying to tell me something?"

She flashes a *yup* grin. "But I'd also take a hedgie, a cat, or a dog."

"Named Dolly," I say, repeating her plans as I drop a kiss onto her forehead.

"Or Katie. I like Katie." She yawns, so big it's the size of a pie.

"I'll let her know you plan to name a pet after her."

A line creases her forehead. "Is she your new girlfriend? She seems like it."

Well, kids know everything, don't they? "Why do you ask?"

Another yawn takes over. "I could tell you liked her and she liked you."

I ruffle her hair, glad to tell her the truth about this. "I think she will be soon," I whisper, then I press my finger to my lips. "Secret."

"I'll keep it a secret. Do you think she liked me?"

"I'm sure she loved you."

"Okay," she says as her eyes flutter closed.

I leave her room, shut the door, and head downstairs to finish cleaning up. But before I tackle the kitchen, I grab my phone and sink onto the couch, clicking open my text app.

Harlan: The verdict is in. She loves you.

Katie: The feeling is mutual. She's fabulous.

Harlan: Well, that was easy.

Katie: Some things are. You're raising a good kid.

I return to Katie's words from the picnic lunch about whether she'd want kids. *With the right man. The right relationship.* I'd love to talk to her more about that, but via text message hardly seems appropriate. End of season feels like a better time. But I can at least say this…

Harlan: You were great with her.

Katie: Yeah?

Harlan: Hell, yeah.

Katie: It makes me happy to hear you say that. I want to be good to her.

Damn. This woman is doing all the things to my heart.

Harlan: She asked if you were my girlfriend.

Katie: And what did you tell her?

Harlan: That I hoped you would be soon. Feels close enough to the truth.

Katie: What's the truth?

Harlan: I see you as mine already. I just do. Call me possessive.

Katie: Possessive :)

I don't want to end the conversation just yet, so I spend a little longer texting…*my girlfriend.*

The kid called it.

CHAPTER 30

KATIE

I need to talk to someone.

I can't keep this to myself much longer.

My friends have been my rocks, my gems, my everything.

I *should* tell my sister, but I'm not ready yet. Besides, I'm closest with Emerson. She also *isn't* my business partner, so that helps.

That Friday afternoon, after I teach a class to a local financial firm, sub for one of Michelle's *Ouch! I Can't Reach My Toes—Yoga for Flexibility* classes, and visit another teacher's session, I meet up with Emerson in the Sunset District to "recon" for an upcoming episode of her show. Her word, not mine.

We trek up a staircase of 163 mosaic-covered steps, each one a different design of colorful tiles. It's a hidden gem in San Francisco, but I'm not sure why we're here.

"How exactly does this help you with a food show?" I ask, gesturing to the gleaming steps.

"Because this new burger place is so off the beaten path, it's at the top of the steps."

I scan the environs. Houses tower up on either side of the staircase. "Um, this is residential. Are they even zoned for a restaurant here?"

Emerson tuts, patting my shoulder. "You're so cute. I love your municipal concerns. This is a food truck we're scoping out. It's parked here today. Banging Burgers. It's got all kinds of veggie burgers. I want to eyeball it before I come here officially, and the bonus of exercise ticked another box."

Ah, that makes more sense. Emerson loves to prep so she's not surprised when she shoots an episode. She's the queen of doing her homework. I bet she was a straight-A student in school.

As my foot lands on a shimmering light-blue tile, I decide now's as good a time as any to dive into my dilemma. "So, I need your take on something. Remember that night at my house when I said I was ready to date Harlan again?"

She whips her gaze to me as we walk, those curious green eyes already sparkling with questions. "The date that never happened, right? You said he became a client when you started teaching the Renegades. I've seen the pics on the team's Instagram." The Renegades' social media shared photos of me teaching the guys, which looked great shared on Sassy's Insta feed. "Did that change?"

I answer her honestly. "Yes."

She freezes mid-step. "Whoa." She thaws, setting her foot down. "Are you seeing him?"

That's a good question.

"Sort of?" I say, my voice pitching up.

"How is it a sort of?" Her voice hits the stratosphere.

"We're not really seeing each other, but we made a plan *to* see each other." Finally, I just rip off the Band-Aid. "Ah, hell. I like him so much, Emerson. And everything with him is so good. It's driving me crazy, but in a good way. But you said you regretted missing signs with my ex, and I'd feel like the worst friend if I didn't tell you about Harlan. And I know you'd want to know."

My words spill out in a messy heap on these incredibly beautiful, Instagrammable steps. Emerson is clearly ready to bombard me with questions, but a pack of tourists—judging from the Nikons and *I Love San Francisco* sweatshirts—are fast closing in on us.

She tips her forehead to the top, and we trudge up the rest of the way, duck down the street, and stop in front of a pale-yellow house. "Start at the beginning," my friend instructs.

I tell her everything, starting with the first one-on-one session and finishing with baking with Harlan and his daughter.

"Monkey bread and manicures!" She grabs the sides of her face. "That's too cute. I die!"

"I know, right?" I clasp a hand to my heart. "His daughter is amazing. Such a strong, bright, fun girl. And she likes me too."

"Obviously. You're super likable. And clearly, he's crazy for you if he's introducing you to his kid. That's a big step."

It felt huge to me too. Meaningful, bringing Harlan and me even closer. "I really like him. Falling-hard like. Falling-in-love like."

"Oh, babes," she says softly, nodding sagely. "I can tell."

I grab her hand, squeeze it. "What do I do?"

"I wish I could say *oh my God, he's amazing*, but I don't know a thing about him," she says with a helpless shrug. "But I know you. If you're going to do this, you'll only feel right about it if you do what you said. Find the replacement for the classes, talk to Olive and Zachary, and just be open and honest. You're not like your mother, but if you go into a relationship feeling like her, I worry you'll beat yourself up. I'd hate for that to happen."

My throat tightens with emotion. "You're right. I checked out two classes today, and some others yesterday. And the receptionist at my main studio is amazing, helping me search for options, coming up with lists of who to check out in the Bay Area. And I'm determined to do this right," I say, squaring my shoulders.

She drapes an arm around me. "Good. Then you will. Now, you want to check out this Banging Burger food truck?"

"Yes, but do the burgers make you want to bang? Or do they make you want to bang Nolan?"

Her eyes pop. "Hush. Do not mention him."

I press my finger to my lips. "I won't mention the total hottie who you work with. The guy with the piercing eyes and delish muscles and great smile. The one you were looking at like you wanted to lick sriracha off him. I know you love sriracha."

She crinkles her nose. "Now who's adorable and gross at the same time?"

I point two thumbs at myself. "This woman."

"You know yourself so well."

"Also, is it hard to resist him?" I tease.

She shoots me a *don't you dare go there* look. "I'm supporting you in *your* resistance plans. You ought to do the same for me with Nolan. I bet you, too, are battling temptation every time you see Harlan."

"Oh, I am. I definitely am."

But I won't let temptation win.

CHAPTER 31

HARLAN

Time takes on a glacial quality.

Every day is an *X* on the calendar. Every night, I wait for the dawn to come.

I see Katie at the stadium, and it's wickedly thrilling having our little secret, more so than it was before. I take these little hits of Katie-time to pass the days.

When yoga class wraps up one Tuesday in November, Coach Greenhaven strides in, surveys the lot of us in triangle pose. "Excellent. We'll have to rename you the Pretzels when we host New York this weekend."

There's a collective groan from the Renegades.

At the end of class, I leave as Katie straightens up. The coach stops me at the door. His gray eyes laser in on me, and he clears his throat. "Harlan."

I straighten, reflexively. The coach has that effect. "Yes, sir?"

I ask, hoping he hasn't gotten wind of my plans with Katie. But then, how could he? No one knows. We don't go out in public. We're cautious.

Unless those rumors about phones listening in on your conversations are true. You never know with modern technology.

He claps my shoulder. "You're looking good this season. I keep telling that to the GM," he says.

"Thank you, sir," I say, grateful as always for the compliment.

"GM agrees completely," he says, and the message is loud and clear—*we want you to stay.*

"Thank you," I say, relieved that's the focus of our talk. Even though I don't have anything more to tell him.

"Hope you will," he adds.

"Thank you." It's all I can say, my head nodding like I'm a bobblehead of myself. And I've seen those bobbleheads in the team store. Not my best look.

Later that afternoon, she texts me. I'm in a Lyft heading to meet my agent, so I write back right away.

Katie: Is it hard for you when the coach says stuff like that?

Harlan: How can you tell?

Katie: You never answer.

Harlan: Ha, you're astute.

Katie: You just say *thank you*. Nothing more.

Harlan: I don't know what else to say.

Katie: You're really torn, aren't you?

Harlan: I am. Completely.

It feels good to tell her, to unburden myself of some of these thoughts, so I keep going.

Harlan: I don't want to give up the game, but I also don't know what makes sense for life beyond football.
Katie: You could open a foosball and ice cream shop.

I laugh as I type.

Harlan: I'll mention that to my agent. I'm heading to see her now. She asked if I was going to open a pie shop like my mom. What do you see me doing?
Katie: Whatever makes you happy :)
Harlan: Good answer.

When I reach my agent's office, I don't know that I'm any closer to deciding, but I feel better after talking to Katie.

Harlan: I'll see you tomorrow for our session. I promise I won't steal any more kisses.

She sends me a sad face.

———————

"Beat you," Jason calls out from one hundred feet in front of me the next morning.

"I let you beat me," I shout as we make our way down the

winding hills at the foot of the Golden Gate Bridge, headed toward Crissy Field by the bay.

He slows to a walk, and I catch up with him, having finished our four-mile sunrise run.

"So, you *let* me beat you? That's how you're spinning this?" he fires back.

"Kiddo, I give it all on the field, so I don't need to beat your young ass on a weekday jog."

His brow knits. "Dammit. You have a good point there."

"I usually do."

We pass early-morning exercisers spread out on the fields— boot campers doing burpees, serene groups of older men and woman swaying through tai chi moves, and then a pack of fit twenty-somethings just...shaking their hips.

What the hell are they doing?

I peer more closely as the attendees bend and pick up hula hoops from the grass. "Ah, a hula hoop class," I say, then tilt my head when one of the gals in the class drops a quick kiss onto her neighbor's cheek.

"Looks like a workout date too," Jason adds as we walk past them.

"Speaking of, how was yours from the other week? Anything come of it?"

He shrugs. "We went out a couple times, but I dunno. There wasn't a spark. Not the kind I want. Know what I mean?"

I picture Katie and our yoga sessions. The fire that flames between us. I chuckle knowingly. "I do know what you mean. Very much so."

Jason turns to face me. "Spoken from experience?"

I don't need to blab. I've got to protect my woman. But Jason's a cool guy, and he doesn't know Katie. He plays for the other team, so he's not her yoga student. "Yeah, the woman I was supposed to go out with a couple weeks ago. Didn't quite happen, but it's still awesome." Even without naming her, that feels good to admit.

"Wait. You were supposed to go out with her, but it didn't happen, so how can you say you're sparking and it's great? I'm a little confused."

I'm not sure I can untangle it for him or anyone yet. "Let's just say it's complicated. She's someone I, well, I work out with."

He cracks up, grabbing his belly. When he collects himself, he says, "I told you workout dates were great."

"I suppose you did. I suppose that's what we're doing," I say, and talking to a friend about what's happening feels fantastic.

Holy hell, I want to tell him more. I want to tell everyone about Katie.

Not yet, of course. Not today.

But soon.

I want to go out with her, to paint the town red, to take her dancing at the 80s club. I want to shop for crazy costume parties at Daisy's Duds, and, hell, to take her to the playground with my kid.

I stop in my tracks, struck dumb by a realization.

I'm thirty-six, and I'm pretty sure I've never fallen this hard for a woman before.

"Wow," I mutter, awed by the awareness of what's happening to me.

"You okay, man?"

I shake my head like a dog shaking off water, trying to collect myself. "I'm great, actually. I just realized something kind of mind-boggling."

A sly smile spreads across his face. "And are you going to tell her you're falling ass over biceps, triceps, and delts for her?"

I jerk my gaze to the relationship expert by my side. "How are you so wise at twenty-five?"

"It comes with my good looks," he says with a wink. "Also, maybe don't wait too long."

That's excellent advice.

———————

Later that day at her studio, as Katie and I work on variations of the warrior pose, I ask her, "How are you feeling about…?" I point from her to me.

She shoots me a sassy smile. "Am I still hot for you, do you mean?"

"No, I consider that a given."

"So cocky."

"And you should take it as a fact that I'm still hot for you. I meant, are you still feeling okay about our plans?"

As I stretch my arms ceilingward, she answers, "Yes. I've been checking out other teachers, visiting their classes, working on some suggestions for replacements."

She tells me more about what she's been up to as we move through other poses, then drop to the floor, stretching side by side on our backs.

I flash back to Jason's words from this morning. *Don't wait too long.*

I don't want to wait *any* longer, but I don't want to pressure her either. Hell, I feel the pressure from my team, and it's no fun, so I don't want to do that to Katie. But I *can* let her know where I'm at in other ways. "I wish time would speed up," I say, turning my gaze to her as I stretch.

"Me too," she whispers, sounding sexy and hopeful at the same time.

"What do you want to do first?" It's wild, secretly planning this romance we'll have when our careers are no longer in the way. "Every time we've planned a date, it's fallen through."

She wiggles her brow. "Then we won't plan a typical date. No foosball and dinner. No bowling and ice cream."

"We have no luck when we plan like that," I agree.

She takes a beat, reaching her arms high over her head on the mat. "I think you should just come over the night you win the Super Bowl."

I shift to my side. "I like the way you think."

"You do?" Her eyes lock with mine.

The air between us crackles.

"When we win, I'll fly home, and then I'll get in a car and go straight to your house."

She shifts to her side too, propped on her elbow. "I'll open the door wearing a naughty grin, because I'll be so excited to see you. You'll probably throw me against the wall."

I breathe out hard, my skin heating up. "I fucking will."

She slides her hand along her side, over her hip. "You'll tear off my yoga pants."

My eyes drift down to her chest. "I'll rip off all your clothes."

She licks her lips, lets out a shuddery breath. "We can go bare, Harlan. I'm on protection, and I have a clean bill of health."

"Me too. Clean bill of health," I rasp, my dick rock-hard at the thought of feeling her slick heat against my cock. "I bet you'd feel incredible."

"Bet you would too," she murmurs.

Fuck waiting.

I reach for her, running a hand down her side, sliding closer to her sexy-as-sin body. "I need to steal a kiss now. It'll get me through missing you this weekend."

"Take it," she says, then seals her lips to mine. She crushes my mouth in a consuming kiss. It's the opposite of our last kiss in my kitchen. This one is wild and desperate, tinged with jet-fueled need. It's rough and messy, the kind of messy that leads to hands roping in hair and teeth clicking and me yanking her against my erection.

I flop to my back, pull her on top of me, and rub against her. "Katie," I groan.

She whispers my name with the same urgency as she rides the hard ridge of my cock. She rocks and sways, then consumes my lips again as we grab at each other.

Everything feels electric and intense. Whatever faint hold I had on control spirals away.

She swings her gaze to the door. This is the moment where we should break apart. Smooth down our clothes. Settle our jackhammering pulses.

A glance at the door is the kind of break in the action that can jolt you back to reality.

To consequences.

To promises.

Instead, Katie says, "Let me make sure it's locked."

In a heartbeat, she hops up from me, scurries to the door, and locks it. She's back in seconds, straddling me again.

"Are you sure, sweetheart?"

She rocks against me, pressing her hands to either side of my face. "So sure," she murmurs.

I grab her ass, cup those cheeks, and tug her tighter. Now is the time. "I want you so much. I'm so crazy for you. I'm falling for you so hard."

She gasps, then smiles softly. "I'm falling for you too," she says, sounding utterly lost in the passion.

Just like I am.

CHAPTER 32

KATIE

He's too hard to resist.

I want a taste of him, this man I've fallen for.

So in my yoga studio, I shimmy off my pants, shove down his shorts. My mouth waters when his cock says hello.

Oh yes. I have enjoyed every encounter with him, and it is so very good to touch him again.

To touch my man.

Because he feels that way—*all mine.*

I wrap a hand around his hard length, and he shudders. "Katie," he moans, sounding desperate, sounding lost. It's the sexiest sound I've ever heard.

And it's all for me.

I've tried to take my time with him, to learn my lessons, to go slow. To do everything right.

But *he's* what feels right.

And he's all I want. I want all of him naked against me.

"Take off your shirt," I tell my guy.

He sits up and does that sexy move where he tugs it off in one quick sweep.

"I want to be under you," I say with a moan, since I'm wildly aroused already. "Want to feel this whole gorgeous body against me."

"You should have everything you want," he rumbles.

In a split second, we shift. I'm on my back on the mat, and he's kneeling between my legs, rubbing the head of his cock against my wet, aching center.

Pleasure rushes through me at the delicious feel of him. It pulses through my core as I reach for his hips and pull him closer.

He slides in an inch, and we both groan at the same time. Needy, hungry cries.

My hands loop around to that fantastic ass, and I grab him. He heeds the call, sinks all the way into me, then stills.

Ecstasy throbs through my body.

I'm shaking everywhere.

Pleasure and longing and emotion swirl inside me as I hold him tight. Wrapping my legs around his firm ass, I whisper, "Missed you so much."

"Missed you too," he groans as he rocks his hips, finds a pace, and moves in me. He lowers his chest to mine, keeping me close, swiveling his hips.

He grunts, then lets out a long, plaintive, "God, you feel so good."

I feel more than good. I feel wanted. I feel worshiped.

I feel all the things I told myself to wait for. I feel *everything*.

Most of all, I feel like we're not just falling into each other, but falling deeper in love with each thrust.

It's more than sex.

It's connection and intimacy.

As he moves in me, roping his arms around my shoulders, holding me tight, he whispers sweet nothings.

How good I feel.

How much he wants me.

How incredible this is.

It's all so wildly wonderful that I swear I'm flying off Earth and rocketing to another plane of bliss. My toes curl. My pulse surges. I am bathed in endorphins as we rock and thrust and move together.

Sweat slicks down his chest. His breath rushes fast, telling me he's getting closer. "Katie, need you to come soon," he says, practically begging.

And that's all I need.

His desire.

His lust.

It unlocks my climax, and I soar to the edge, gasping and panting. My orgasm coils tight, then rocks through me in blinding, beautiful waves.

"Oh God," I gasp. The sound of my voice jars me, and I bite down on his collarbone to shut up.

That does it for him, and he fucks me through his release, murmuring my name as he shudders, coming hard inside me.

A minute later, we're both loopy and sweaty, and we need to deal with cleanup at my yoga studio.

But I don't care, and I don't think he does either.

He snuggles against me, kisses my cheek, then says, "I'm falling in love with you."

And it's so right with him. It's more than right. "I'm falling in love with you too."

Later, after we straighten up, I walk him to the door, then wave goodbye. "Good luck with practice tomorrow," I say. He's got an all-day practice and prep for the game this weekend.

"See you soon," he says with a wink, then heads up Fillmore.

I watch him the whole way with a dopey smile on my face.

When I return inside, the receptionist drums his purple-polished fingernails on the counter. "He's such a cutie. Thank you again for having eye-candy clients."

"It's my pleasure," I say with a laugh.

He slides his finger across his iPad screen. "Now, don't forget tomorrow morning you have the videographer coming so you can shoot *Ten Days to Half Moon Pose.*"

"I'll be here."

"And you want to stop by Leilani's class in the Mission. I took it yesterday, and her tree poses are to die for."

"I can't wait."

He fixes me with a pout, narrows his winged-eyeliner eyes, all the more stunning against his dark-brown skin. "Are you ever going to tell me what all this research is about?"

"Someday," I say breezily, still high on sex, on falling, on love.

But the next day, I wake up with a smidgen of guilt wiggling through me, and it's not about the half-moon shoot.

As I shower and get dressed, I keep asking myself if maybe I shouldn't have given in with Harlan.

Should I have waited till the end of the season?

I wait for the universe to answer, but instead, there's a knock on my door.

I head to the peephole.

My mother is waiting on the other side.

CHAPTER 33

KATIE

'd be less surprised to see Ed Sheeran.

I turn into a statue with my mouth hanging open. How do I talk? Think? Act?

My brain goes sluggish.

The woman who ruined my wedding is here at my home. She hasn't reached out to me since August when I sent her my "Enjoy him," note.

But now she's here on a Thursday morning.

Knocking.

This makes no sense.

I stare at my hand like it's not even attached to my body. Like it's been injected with novocaine and I can't move it.

Do I let her in?

Ignore her?

Tiptoe to the bedroom and hide until she goes away?

Just like that, I know what to do.

I am *not* hiding. I grab the knob, open the door, and meet her gaze for the first time since she took my almost-husband from me.

"Hello," I say. I don't have time to fashion a quip or a zing.

She flashes a red-lipsticked smile at me. "Darling."

It's said without fear.

There is no hint of repentance in her voice. No sense she was ever in the wrong.

Her confidence unnerves me. I'm not sure how to handle her. My jaw tics, and I grit my teeth as I wait for her to speak.

Her eyes widen, and she peers inside. "Well, can I come in? Would you like to invite me?"

No. I would not like to.

But I'm morbidly fascinated with her chutzpah.

Also, she's my mother. When I'm around her, I snap back to how I felt growing up.

Small.

I'm the gnat on her shoe, one of the kids she didn't stick around for, and she's the master of the universe. Curiosity wins. I open the door wide. I need to know why she's here.

She sweeps in, scans the walls emptied of Silvio's art, and surveys the couch strewn with colorful pillows. "The couch looks better now than in those neutral tones. Pinks are so very you…" She waves airily, and right is wrong and up is down, and why is my mom complimenting my taste in color, which is so vastly different from her man's taste?

"What can I do for you?"

She spins around and presses her hands together like in prayer. "I'm here to ask you for a favor. An absolutely delicious one." Her tone is imploring, her eyes wide—and I'd even say guileless if I didn't know her better. But I do know better.

Whatever she's about to ask is all about her.

Everything's all about her.

"Okay," I say evenly, trying hard not to lose my cool. I don't want her to know she still affects me. That seeing her rattles me.

How was I able to sass her when she swept into the suite before my wedding? Oh, right. Because that was *before* she capsized my plans.

Now I know fully what she's capable of, and I hate that I come from her, that we share DNA.

She squeals, then gasps. "Katie! I'm engaged!"

I blink and jerk away. It's like a blast of frigid air has whipped into my home and assaulted me. "What?" It comes out like it has ten syllables.

She flaps her hand, brandishing a fat ring. It's shiny, gaudy, and so very her. "He asked me to marry him! Silvio did. And I said yes."

I stumble backward, grabbing the kitchen counter behind me so I don't fall.

Is this my life?

Is she truly here to show off her engagement ring?

But she steps closer, waggling her diamond at me. "He asked me to marry him on the Golden Gate Bridge." She clasps her hand to her chest. "It's so romantic. Isn't it?"

She waits for an answer with expectant eyes, like my opinion on engagement locations matters.

"It's great," I say with zero emotion.

Why do I feel nothing? It's eerie, this flatness in my heart. This nothingness.

I should be…livid.

Destroyed.

Why do I feel like I'm floating above this scene?

"That's where we had our first date," she adds, still giddy, still bouncing on her toes.

What did she just say? Their first date? She's mentioning their first date? It had to have been…

"When he was with me," I say, but it doesn't come out enraged. I sound offhand, and I'm not sure what's going on inside me.

She tilts her head. "C'mon, you're not still upset about that, are you?"

Truthfully, I'm…*not*.

I'm not upset.

I'm not bothered at all.

I am, admittedly, mystified that anyone would brag to the ex about getting engaged. I'm amazed that she would think I'd want her to share this news.

"I'm not upset," I say in the same flat tone—a tone that seems to vex her.

She flicks her wine-red locks off her shoulder, adopting a haughty expression. "Aren't you happy for me?"

Is that what she wants? For me to be happy for her? With a surprised chuckle, I shrug. "I have no opinion, honestly."

She furrows her brow, stomps her foot.

I laugh. Foot stomping? Is she serious?

"Katie, love, I want you to be happy for me," she pleads, her big eyes begging.

"I'm sure you do," I say, revealing nothing, feeling nothing.

Not a thing.

And it feels…great.

At last, I understand my emotions. What was confusing is now clear. Feeling nothing for her feels utterly fantastic.

"But you don't seem happy," she adds, stepping closer, waving her hand at my face again. "You're all frowny. Talk to me."

There's nothing to discuss with her. If I'm frowny, it's because I'm making a plan for the day. I have things to do. Yoga classes to check out. A replacement to find. A tough conversation to have with my sister. And a DNA donator to kick the fuck out of my house.

I smile, deep and delighted at last. I draw a fulfilling, gorgeous breath that fuels me, then lock eyes with her. "I don't actually care about your engagement or your wedding, Mom. Or your life, for that matter. So if you're wondering what I'm thinking, it's this—I don't care. And I feel great about that."

I am wildly thrilled to say all that. It's not a zinger. It's just the truth.

Her jaw drops. She is the definition of aghast. "And to think I came all this way to ask you to be my maid of honor."

I bark out a laugh, clasping my belly. Truly, that's hilarious. So damn funny I can't wait to tell Emerson and Olive and my dad.

"The answer is no. Let me show you out." Now my tone isn't flat, isn't empty. It's wickedly amused.

She's more selfish than I ever imagined, and I no longer feel small. I no longer feel betrayed by her decision to romance my former fiancé.

Thank God she took him from me.

If I'd gone through with that dumb decision, I'd have said *I do* to the wrong man, a man who wasn't right for me.

And if I'd walked down the aisle, I'd never have run into Harlan again. Harlan—the man who makes my heart and body sing.

There is no convincing, no tricking, no uncertainty with Harlan.

If my mother hadn't snagged Silvio, I wouldn't have found all my own strength—the strength to live entirely differently from her.

I owe her nothing.

I owe myself so much more.

Thank you, universe, for showing me that.

I stride to the door, yank it open, and sweep out my arm. "I believe we're done."

The second she leaves, I grab my phone and take the next step—something I should have done a week ago.

CHAPTER 34

KATIE

I don't like to bail on appointments, but I have to. As I snag a Lyft, I call Elliot at my yoga studio.

"Hey, Ells. I need a favor. Big time."

"Anything for you, doll," he says brightly. "Do you need me to grab you a hot tea or a lemon cookie from Doctor Insomnia's?"

"Both sound delish. Get them for yourself and put them on my tab. But actually, I need you to reschedule the videographer. I'm so sorry, and I'll pay his fee for today, of course. But something came up and I have to take care of it."

"Of course, love. Everything okay?"

I smile, unsure of the answer, but hopeful. "That's the goal."

Then I call Olive to tell her I'm coming to see her, but she doesn't answer.

Oh well. I'm going in anyway.

I'm rarely here at our corporate office in Hayes Valley, but I still know nearly everyone, so I say hi to our employees as I walk through the cubes.

As I head for Olive's office, nerves thrum through me.

Should I have said something to her sooner? Let her in on my plans?

The nerves take flight as I reach her door, ajar as always. Whether I picked the wrong time or not, I still need to do this.

Deep breath.

I've got this.

I rap my knuckles on the wood, peeking around. She's stretched out on her couch.

She and Zachary are pointing to his laptop, laughing hard at the screen. "And then it goes like this." He lifts a hand and mimes swatting something…off a counter, maybe?

Ah, they must be watching cat videos. Olive is addicted to evil cats.

Olive looks up, laughing still as she waves me in. "You have to see this one. This tuxedo is such an asshole. She knocked over the coffee maker for literally no reason."

Zachary stares at her. "Olive, there's not *no* reason. She's a cat. That's reason enough."

"True, true."

I join them on the couch, watching the video of a dastardly cat swatting mugs, vases, shot glasses, and more to the floor in a cacophony of sound and feline destruction. When the demolition is complete, Zachary shuts his laptop, winded from laughter.

Olive is his twin in chuckling. I'm not sure if this means she'll be in a better mood to receive my news or if I'm about to burst her bubble.

Zachary pushes his glasses up his nose, then stands, clutching the silver laptop. "I've got a conference call, so I better take off. Good to see you, Katie. Don't be a stranger." Then he leaves, shutting the door.

Smart guy.

Olive sighs happily, then meets my gaze and roams her eyes up and down my frame. "It must be a special day. You're hardly ever here. Are you going to whisk me off to test that new chocolate shop that just opened today? Because I had plans already to eat my lunch there."

"No," I say, steeling myself to tell her the truth, the full truth, and nothing but. "Listen," I begin.

In a nanosecond, she sits up straighter, her expression shifting to intensely serious. "Oh."

Images of my mother flicker before my eyes. Her pop-in this morning. Her assumptions. The way she's lived her life. My deep, potent desire to be the opposite to her. I haven't entirely been that way these last few days, but I have to be now. If I want to have the life I desire, I can't operate like her at all. Not one bit. "Mom came by this morning."

Olive cringes. "What did she want?"

"To ask me to be her maid of honor. She's marrying Silvio."

Olive's jaw clangs to the center of Earth, then back up. "Oh, Katie. I'm so sorry."

I shake my head, quickly dismissing any sympathy. "It's fine. I'm not upset. I don't care about her or him. But the thing is, I don't want to be like her. Not at all. And I have been. I haven't been truthful with you."

Confusion crosses her face, lining her brow. "Okay. What do you mean?"

With my head held high, I begin. "I fell in love with Harlan while working with the Renegades. He's wonderful and amazing, and I'm going to start seeing him. We were going to wait till the end of the season, and I've been looking for a replacement to recommend for the classes I teach them, and I had this whole plan to find someone who they'd want and be impressed with. I was going to finish out the contract and then tell you," I say, and sadness flickers in my sister's eyes.

"You were?" She sounds devastated.

I'm such an ass for hurting Sassy Yoga. But I have to do this. No matter what.

"I'm so sorry, Olive. I know it probably seems selfish, and I'm about to tank a deal. But I can't be this person who's ridiculously in love with this guy and making plans to be with him and not tell you. And not tell them—Lacey at Blaine Enterprises. I feel like I'm deceiving everyone, and that's wrong. I hope you can forgive me, but I can't work with them anymore. And that has to start now."

She shakes her head and doesn't stop shaking it.

My heart plummets, knowing I've disappointed her so terribly. Tears well in my eyes, and a lump forms in my throat.

"I'm sorry," I say past the hitch. "I'm sorry I messed up this deal you and Zachary worked so hard for. But I just can't lead a double life. I need to be honest about this—fully honest. So I'm truly sorry."

She gets up, scoots closer, wraps an arm around me.

Huh.

That's not what I expected.

"Um, I thought you were upset. You were just shaking your head like crazy," I say, flummoxed.

She laughs into my hair. "Because I'm so happy for you, you dork." Then she yanks me in tighter for a hug.

Second out-of-body experience so far today, and it's not even noon. But I go with it, hugging her back. "You're happy for me? You don't hate me? You don't think I'm terribly selfish?" I ask against her shoulder as tears slip down my cheeks.

She shakes her head once again, then breaks the hug but clasps my shoulders. "No. I think this is incredible. I'm happy for you. And telling me takes guts. Being willing to walk away from a deal takes big ovaries. Going after love takes so much courage."

Oh, hell. The tears fall even faster. "Really?"

"Yes, really. You're not at all like Mom. You're brave and gutsy, and I think this is fantastic. You could have sneaked around for two more months, but you didn't."

It's my turn to wince. "Well, we did sneak around yesterday. We had sex at the yoga studio, and then when Mom showed up this morning, I knew I couldn't wait any longer."

She smacks my thigh. "Sex at the studio! Oh my God, you dirty, racy girl. I want to hear how it was."

I grin, all hopped up on endorphins again. A tingle races down my chest from the memory. "Amazing," I say.

But I'm not only remembering the physical side of our relationship.

I'm recalling all the emotions.

And the words.

And the connection.

And I can't wait to share those details with my pack. "He's a good guy with a big heart, and he's in love with me too," I say, feeling all dreamy and warm. "Like, one hundred percent. You and Emerson and Jillian and Skyler have nothing to worry about. He's worthy."

She bounces on the cushion and claps her hands with glee. "Dish. *Now.* Everything. You've been holding back. I demand every swoony and dirty detail."

So, I tell her, sharing how we got to know each other better, how we fell for each other over yoga sessions and lunches, over conversations and monkey bread. How all that went down before we smashed into each other again yesterday.

"Clearly, resistance was futile at that point." She can't stop grinning and grabs my hand, squeezes it. "He sounds great. You seem happier than you ever have been. And I know you wanted to see what could happen with him." Her lips curve into a knowing grin. "Honestly, I had a feeling when you asked about the contract at dinner a couple weeks ago."

I tilt my head, grinning. "Yeah, I kinda sensed you did."

She rolls her eyes, giving me the most *duh* of *duh* looks ever. "Hello! It wasn't that hard to figure out."

"I've been researching replacements like crazy. I've gone to a ton of classes, and I want to find the perfect person to—hopefully—fulfill the contract. I know the Renegades might say no, and that's on me. I'll do whatever you need me to do to find new clients to make up for it. Hell, you can dock my profits until we sort this out."

A wild snort emanates from her. "Oh my God. You're hilarious. *Dock your profits?* Give me a break. It's our company. Yours and mine—equal ownership. I'm not docking your profits. We both took on the risks, and I'm not going to punish you."

"You're not?"

"Did you think I would?" She pokes my chest, then hisses. "Now I am pissed at you."

I sigh, but I'm smiling and she is too. "I just want to do right by you and the company."

"And you are," she says, then winks. "But don't you worry. I've got your back."

Intrigued, I arch a brow. "What do you mean?"

"Like I said, I had a feeling this might happen. So I've been scouting replacements for you too."

I squeal now—full on, through the roof. "Oh my God. You have?"

She taps her temple. "Sister intuition."

"I'll say."

Olive's not the only one I need to talk to, though. I square my shoulders. "I really want to let Lacey know today. I don't want to pretend any longer."

Olive pops up. "Let's do it."

My sister heads to her desk, calls Blaine Enterprises, and asks for Lacey. They set up a time to meet tomorrow, and Olive says she'll come with me.

Funny, how I pictured going it alone—doing this whole fix-my-mess-by-myself thing.

But my friends and my sister have been by my side all along.

Especially when Olive settles in next to me and we discuss her options, then mine, reviewing teachers and putting together a new plan. It feels amazing to have this kind of support.

But then, that's what we've always done—support each other.

And it feels so damn good to have her here with me today.

CHAPTER 35

KATIE

There is someone else who supports me too.

Who's a big part of this situation.

Who's the very reason for it.

I ring Harlan, but I don't expect him to answer. He's in practice most of the day. Still, I want him to know what's going on.

When I reach his voicemail, I end the call and click to text. Better to just tell him everything.

Katie: Hello! Can you say *busy day*? It's been one. My mother showed up unexpectedly at my place this morning, and it was kind of eye-opening. She asked me to be her maid of honor at her upcoming wedding. I said no. And I felt great. Amazing. Because I felt nothing for her—no anger, no hurt, no annoyance. I felt lucky to be on the other side. But I also realized, I don't want to be like her one bit. So, I'm not asking you to change anything, but I don't want to do this secretly any longer. I told Olive today, and we're working together to find the best replacement for me to present to Lacey. I know this is all happening sooner than expected, but... I didn't feel right pretending anymore. Especially after yesterday. I am falling for you, and I can't keep working with the team and you this closely, knowing how I feel. I hope you understand. I'm working at the office with my sister today. Call me or text me or something!

Before I hit Send, I review the message, a new dose of anxiety running through me. Have I stepped out of bounds with Harlan? Assumed too much? Am I going all Lone Ranger?

But then, I replay what he said in his kitchen as we made monkey bread: *whenever it works for you, I'm by your side.*

I need to trust that he meant it. That he's able to handle this change in plans.

That's part of his job—to react to split-second shifts on the field. To his quarterback calling audibles. To getting open when other receivers are swarmed.

Harlan, I sure hope you're open to catch this pass I'm lobbing your way.

But whether he is or not, I need to do this for me.

This is the right way to live. This makes me happy.

And I'm doing it.

———

My phone is silent the rest of the afternoon as I go for a swim to calm my nerves, then still as Olive and I bring Zachary into the plans and finalize our ideas with him.

They *might* also watch a few more cat videos.

As a big orange cat leaps onto a piano on Zachary's screen, I check my phone again, hoping for a reply.

But there isn't one.

I refocus on work. We make calls and come up with a pitch that we hope Lacey will love. I try not to stress about not hearing from Harlan.

Besides, there's time. I'll surely talk to him tonight, and we'll be all set before Olive and I see Lacey tomorrow.

But at four thirty, my sister sighs a heavy, "Oh."

I snap up my gaze from my phone, tension tightening in me. "What is it?"

She hums thoughtfully at her desk, then raises her face from the screen. "Lacey just emailed me. She says she has an all-day meeting tomorrow, but she lives in Hayes Valley and wants to grab a drink in an hour."

My heartbeat races to the moon.

It's fine, it's fine, it's fine.

I repeat that over and over.

I call up my yoga mantras too.

Yoga and wine and coffee and something. Yoga is how I pretend to be calm…and fuck! I'm not calm. I can't settle down.

But I need to. I need to trust Harlan meant it when he said he'd be by my side.

I need to trust I'm not hurting him.

I take a deep breath, set a hand on my chest, and will my heart to quiet.

I send him one more message as we leave the office.

Katie: Hi!!!!! I'm freaking out. Is everything okay?

But I don't hear from him as we head to the bar to meet Lacey, and I do my best to be the cool, collected businesswoman I am.

Or should be.

When I reach the lobby of our building, I'm anything but cool and collected. Especially not when Harlan walks through the revolving door and straight toward me.

CHAPTER 36

HARLAN

That was an exhausting practice.

But a damn good one. I knock fists with Cooper, then Jones as we leave the field. It's been a long-ass day of stretching, game film, drills, and playbook review.

Then lots of time with the receiver's coach.

"I feel good and ready for Sunday. You guys?" I ask.

"Hell, yeah," Jones says.

"Bring on New York. If we win, we'll clinch a playoff post," Cooper adds.

"Gee, I hadn't noticed," Jones deadpans.

"Smartass," Cooper says as we head down the corridor. "The wife is coming, and the kids, and I cannot wait to give her a kiss at the edge of the field once we secure our spot. It's my lucky tradition, and I won't break it."

"I'll do the same with my woman," Jones adds.

"You two are too cute," I say, shaking my head in amusement at their romantic antics.

But inside, my heart squeezes a little harder than I'd like. I want what these guys have. Want it badly.

Took me long enough to find the woman I want to share those moments with. But I've found her, and I can't wait to start up with her for real.

In public.

In the light of every damn day.

The possibility of that someday, maybe next season, brings a smile to my face.

"What are you grinning about, chuckles?" Cooper asks when we reach the locker room.

"Just thinking about games and stuff," I say. It's sort of true, and sort of not.

I hit the shower and get dressed, and once I'm buttoning my shirt, I grab my phone from my locker.

"See you all tomorrow," I tell the guys as I take off, powering on my cell as I go.

Once I'm in the hallway, I order a Lyft, then my notifications light up.

I check to make sure Danielle's got Abby as planned.

Yup. All set.

Abby even texted me from Danielle's phone with an I love you!!!!!!!!

Complete with eight exclamation points and, also, nine heart emojis.

I write back, telling my girl I love her too, then I find a text from the woman I'm crazy for, and I slide it open.

Whoa.

I read it twice.

Holy hell.

She did this?

She. Did. This.

She fucking did this.

Katie is brave and gutsy and sexy and all mine.

Also, she sounds worried AF.

That is not okay.

I pick up my pace through the hall, texting her back as I go.

Harlan: Is everything okay, you ask? Everything is amazing. You're amazing. And that sounds like more than a busy day. I'm coming to see you.

NOW.

Do not worry about a thing with me. EVER.

I google her work address, and when I get in the Lyft, I change my destination, giving the driver the address to Katie's corporate headquarters instead.

As we weave through traffic, my mind time-travels to yesterday in Katie's studio. How incredible it felt to make love to her. It slips back further to the days we've spent at my home, the conversations we've had. I wind all the way back to more than seven years ago when I met her.

How we clicked instantly.

But then fate threw obstacles at us left and right, up and down. Timing has always vexed us.

But look what Katie did today. She sped up time. She took it in her hands and said *I'm doing this*.

I grin as I think of her, my tough and sweet and sexy and strong Katie.

She made this happen.

She made *us* happen.

When my mind leaps ahead to this weekend, and the next one, and the one after that, I know what *I* can make happen.

I have no more questions.

Only clarity.

I text her one more time.

Harlan: Can't wait to see you. Can't wait to tell you something big.

CHAPTER 37

HARLAN

I only have eyes for her.

I march straight over to my Katie, sweep her up in my arms in the lobby of her building, and kiss the breath out of her.

She melts into my kiss in seconds, murmuring and sighing as I sweep my lips across hers.

It's been twenty-four hours since I touched her, and already that feels too long. That only confirms what I'm about to do.

I set her down, and she gazes at me, woozy and happy. "Whoa. That was quite a greeting."

I can't wait a second longer to tell her. "I know what I want to do at the end of the season. And you're the first person I want to tell," I say with a newfound certainty.

And a calmness too. My brain is no longer full of questions—only answers.

But the sound of clapping reaches us. With Katie still in my arms, I swing my gaze to the right. A woman—I presume her sister—is cheering us on, and a guy in black glasses claps along with her.

Meanwhile, Katie grins at me, then holds up a finger. "I'm dying to know, but I do have to go see Lacey. We have a meeting with her in about ten minutes to let her know what's going on and that I need to step back."

Damn.

My heart craters.

I want to spend the rest of the night with Katie.

A throat clears, and the blond who'd been cheering now closes the distance, stretching her hand out to me as I set Katie down.

"Hi. I'm Olive Madigan. You better be good to my sister or I will kick your ass," she says.

I flinch, which I don't do even when linebackers steamroll me. But there is something hella scary about that sister bond. Plus, I'm pretty sure Katie delivered a similar warning to Jones all those years ago. It's just…hot when women look out for each other.

"I will be so damn good to her. You have my word, Olive," I say from the bottom of my heart.

Olive lifts her chin and holds my gaze. "Good." Then she turns to Katie. "Now, you're excused from the meeting. Zachary and I can handle it. We've got this. Go be with your man."

Katie gasps. "For real?"

Olive rolls her eyes. "For real. Seriously. Go."

"Tell Lacey I'm so grateful for the opportunity. That I loved it," Katie says, her voice brimming with excitement.

"Tell her I loved it too," I say drily.

"Somehow I doubt the team will be upset with you about a thing." Olive's tone is equally dry.

"Tell her anyway," I add.

"I will," Olive says.

"You guys are the best. You really don't mind?" Katie asks.

"We'll take it from here."

"We've got this covered," the guy in glasses chimes in. Then to me, he says, "Good luck Sunday. I'll be rooting for you to clinch."

"We all will," Olive says, then grabs the guy's arm, and they take off.

I return my gaze to Katie, but not before I do a quick sweep of the lobby. A receptionist tries to keep herself busy at the desk, but I can tell she's also trying just as hard to listen.

The elevator stops, lets off passengers. Someone enters through the revolving door.

"Let's get out of here," I say.

———————

Fifteen minutes later, we're at my home, since it's closer.

The second the door shuts, Katie parks her hands on her hips. "Spill. I waited during that whole Lyft ride. And it was hard. *Really* hard."

I laugh and loop an arm around her waist, tugging her close. "I'm so proud of you, my sexy, impatient, brilliant, tough, gutsy woman."

She rolls her eyes. "Flattery won't get you anywhere. *Talk.* I am dying to know what you decided. I updated you on my day the whole ride over. I told you every detail."

I swipe my thumb along her jaw, laughing at her greedy heart. It matches mine.

And my greedy heart doesn't want to wait a second longer. I won't let timing rule my choices. I'm done with waiting, and planning, and hoping.

"Sometimes, you have to make your own time," I say, turning more serious. "That's what you did for us today, and I love it. And I love you, Katie."

She shudders out a breath, roping her arms tighter around my waist. "I love you too, Harlan. So much."

"And I love what you did. Because I learned you have to stop looking for the perfect moment and just seize it, instead. So that's what I'm doing now." I take a big gulp of air. Dear God, I hope she likes my plans. I truly do. I hope they aren't presumptuous. But here goes. "At the end of the season, I'm going to retire."

Her mouth falls open. Goose bumps rise on her arms, and her eyes widen to saucer size. "What?"

I smile, feeling so damn good about this. Feeling resolute. "I've had a great career. I'm healthy and injury-free. I've won more games than lost. I have two rings, great stats, and amazing memories with incredible teammates." I take a beat—my throat tightens with emotions, but I push through them. "But the thing I don't have that I want more than anything, more than football, more than winning, is time. Time with my little girl, and time with the woman I love."

Her lips quiver, and her eyes shine with tears. "You're not going to open…?"

"Open a pie shop?" I supply.

"Yeah?"

I shake my head.

"An ice cream/foosball place?"

Another shake.

"Are you going to be, I dunno, a broadcaster, or a play-by-play analyst?"

I laugh, shaking my head, holding her tight. "No. I just want to be…" My heart expands as the words take shape. I hope this doesn't freak her out. "A dad."

She lets go of me, her hand flying to her mouth, tears streaking her cheeks. "Oh my God."

But I'm not done. "And if you'll have me, I want to be your man. I want to spend my time with you and my girl."

"Stop, just stop."

My brow knits. I freeze. "What did I say wrong?"

She shakes her head, grabbing me harder, pulling me closer. "That is the sweetest thing."

"Yeah?" I ask, my smile returning.

"So sweet. I love it."

"You do?"

"I do. So much. It's perfect for you."

"I just want to have weekends with Abby. And you. I want to go to her gymnastics showcases, and I want you to come with us. I want to take her to the playground, or whatever she wants to do, and bake pies with her and you, and not worry about traveling to New York or Dallas or Seattle. I just want…time. I want it with her, and I want it with you."

And I'd really like to have kids with you.

But I don't say that yet. I don't want to scare her off. Soon, I'll tell her. Very soon.

She swipes her fingers across her cheeks, wiping away tears. "I think that's a perfect post-football career."

I run a hand through her hair, kiss her eyelids, her cheek, her jaw, then return to her lips. I kiss her with newfound freedom, with the sense that we can kiss again tomorrow and the next day, and then again on Sunday.

When I break it, I toss her onto my shoulder and head for the stairs. "If memory serves, you liked this fireman's carry," I say.

"Mmm. Loved it," she says as I take the steps two by two. "Are you taking me to your room to do bad things to me, handsome?"

"I'm going to do very good things to you," I say as I reach the landing. When I set her down, I look into her eyes. "Hey. You want to come to the game this Sunday?"

She nibbles on the corner of her lips. "Can I kiss you when you clinch?"

Oh, yeah. She knows me so well. "You better. I want a hot, sexy sideline kiss from my woman."

She tap-dances her fingers up my shirt. "Then you better win, handsome."

"I plan to."

I make quick work of her clothes, and football falls completely from my head. In seconds, we're naked, tumbling onto my bed, and rubbing and pressing against each other.

Her hands slide up my chest, her fingers sending a rush of pleasure through me. "Can I ride you?" she whispers.

A groan works its way past my lips, coming from deep inside me. "Yes. The answer to that is *anytime*."

I shift to my back, and she straddles me. She dips her face to mine, kissing me as she rubs her sweet, hot pussy against my throbbing cock.

And I am pretty much helpless, lost in desire for her.

She sinks onto me, taking me all the way, and my body crackles, electricity sparking everywhere.

My hands loop around to her soft ass, and I grab her cheeks, knead and squeeze her flesh.

She raises her chest, sliding her hands up to my pecs, setting a wild pace.

She looks like the woman I wanted in my bed the night I met her.

And the woman I wanted to please the night I met her again.

And the woman I can't live without now.

She is all of those women, and I'm crazy for every side of Katie.

She's the one I want now, and for all time.

I'm certain, and certainty feels incredible.

So does she as she rides my dick and rocks her body against mine, her moans growing louder, her pace quickening, her breath coming fast.

Her sounds and murmurs light me up, and soon we're both chasing the edge, then coming together.

In that regard, we've always had great timing.

Later, after we shower, I ask if she's hungry.

"Starving," she says.

"How about I take you out to eat?"

The sparkle in her blue eyes is the best thing ever. "Yes."

Once we sit at a trendy restaurant and order, I go for it, tackling the next item of business. "So, you said you and your ex didn't talk about kids. And you and I talked about them, but in a sort of roundabout way. So, this is my way of being direct."

I'm pretty sure I know her answer. But I don't want to assume. "Would you like to have kids with me someday? Because I would love to have kids with you."

I don't have to wait long for her answer. It comes in Katie reaching across the table, cupping my cheeks, and saying yes.

Yup, I like these retirement plans a whole helluva lot.

That night, we bake a thank-you pecan pie for Katie to take to her sister in the morning.

"Bet she spent the night with Zachary," I say as we put it in the oven.

"You naughty man," she says.

I scoff, knowing I'm close to right. "I saw the way he looked at her. And how she looked at him."

"And how was that?"

I undo the apron around my waist, close the distance between me and my woman, and pin her arms behind her back. "Like he wanted to tie an apron around her wrists."

She shoots me a dirty grin. "Tie that around mine. Then maybe spank me and fuck me in your kitchen?"

"We have just enough time while the pie bakes," I say, and I do as she asked while the pie rises.

In the morning, Katie leaves after we enjoy the shower together, and a text pings on my phone an hour later.

Katie: All went well! Lacey is good with a replacement and the pie was a hit.

Harlan: I'm going to tell the team today I'm retiring. Can you come back then?

Katie: Honestly, I'm pretty happy with this solution. There are many other clients I can work for, and this way, everything is neat and tied up.

Harlan: Tied up. Sounds like what I'll do to you next time I see you.

Katie: And that's another reason! If I were to go back to the Renegades, I'd be the teacher who their Hall-of-Famer receiver ties up at night.

Harlan: I'll tie you up in the morning, too, if that makes you feel better.

Katie: I'm game. And I'm good with how it all shook out. Every single thing.

Harlan: Me too, sweetheart. But what about your sister and that guy?

Katie: I need to get her alone to discover those details. But she does have that just-been-fucked glow on her face.

Harlan: Like sister, like sister.

CHAPTER 38

KATIE

Fifty thousand fans stomp their feet.

They chant the team's name.

I'm like a Kermit the Frog nail-biting GIF, a nervous wreck, staring at the game clock. I can't take my eyes off it. "C'mon, Renegades," I shout. "Put some numbers up."

My dad pats my shoulder. "Bet your guy scores."

"I don't care who scores from the Renegades. I just want them to win," I say desperately.

"We all do," Dad says. "Have faith."

But faith doesn't win football games. Talent and timing and skill do. The score is still tied with hardly any time left.

With tension threading through every muscle, I perch on the edge of my seat as the Renegades get in the huddle with only a minute left in regulation.

"C'mon, my daughter's boyfriend," my dad shouts amidst the din of voices. I cast him a glance, roll my eyes.

"What? No one can hear me over the crowd."

"And I don't care if they do," I say.

"Go, go, go!" he cries.

When Cooper takes the snap seconds later, Harlan shoots off down the field, going long. Holy smokes. He runs like the wind as Cooper cocks his arm, takes aim, and hurls the ball downfield.

I hold my breath as it arcs twenty, thirty, forty, fifty yards.

Harlan leaps, arms high in the air, wrapping around the ball and cradling it. Then he runs like hell into the end zone.

I lose my mind, along with the rest of the fans and the team itself.

My dad and I high-five, and hug, and he holds me close for longer than two football fans normally embrace. "You did good. I'm proud of you, Katie," he whispers in my ear, at just the right volume for me to hear.

"Me too," I say, emotion tight in my voice.

"But then, I've always been proud of you."

"Love you, Dad."

"Love you, sweetie."

When the game ends, the Renegades celebrate on the field, but the man who made the game-winning touchdown yanks off his helmet and rushes over to me. I make my way to the edge of the stands, racing closer to him.

His grin is elated. His brown eyes are lit up like sparklers.

When I reach him, he lifts his arms for me, and I climb over the stands and into them.

He tugs me close, kisses me, and says, "Playoffs, sweetheart."

"Get that third ring, handsome."

He smooches me hard, and when he lets go, a reporter strides over and asks for a minute.

"Sure," he says.

She thrusts the mic at him. "How did it feel to make that game-winning touchdown catch?"

He glances at me next to him.

I squeeze his hand, letting him know I'm by his side. He told the team his news already, but he hasn't told the fans. "It felt great, Erin. Especially since this is my last season."

Her eyes widen. "Oh. You've decided to retire?"

He nods, resolute, making his announcement official. "I have. This will be my last season as a Renegade, and I hope we go out on top. I'll do everything I can to make that happen."

"And what will you do when you retire?"

He shrugs happily, lifts our joined hands, presses a kiss to mine. "Spend time with my girlfriend and my daughter. Maybe take some trips." He turns to me. "Hey, Katie, want to travel in the off-season?"

"As long as the timing works out," I say with a smile.

He winks my way, and I catch it.

"We're a good team," he says.

Yes, yes we are.

CHAPTER 39

EMERSON

EARLY FEBRUARY

I whistle with approval as Katie holds up a sparkly fuchsia Renegades sweatshirt. "Is this the winner?"

It's the top for her to wear tonight, for many reasons. "Perfection. The sparkles are so very you. Plus, you totally look like a WAG," I tell her as I kick my foot back and forth in our Vegas hotel room.

"I'm not a WAG for much longer," Katie says, but she doesn't sound wistful. She sounds happy, like she's been about, oh, say, pretty much everything these last few months. She turns to the other person in the room. "And I guess you're not a...*what*...much longer?"

Abby giggles. "I'm not a KAP after tonight. Kids and pets," she adds as she ties the shoelaces on her royal-blue Converse sneakers, the team colors.

"Wait. Kids and pets of sports stars go together like wives and girlfriends?" Katie asks the cutie-pie perched on the end of a king-size bed.

"Yes, because pets are important too. Like the pony you and my daddy might get me someday," she says, batting her lashes.

I hold up a hand to high-five the seven-year-old. "Work it."

"I'm trying. I swear I'm trying," Abby says.

Once she tugs on her sweatshirt, Katie goes over and bops Abby on the nose. "You sure are trying. And trust me, I'll campaign pretty hard too, once your daddy retires."

Abby pumps a fist. "Yes."

I point to the bed. "Sit," I tell my best friend. "I need to touch up your makeup."

Katie's eyes turn serious, her forehead creasing. Hmm. Is she remembering the last time I did her makeup? Her wedding day that never happened?

Well, today couldn't be more different.

I can't wait.

"I'm just going to make you pop for TV. You know the cameras are going to be on us," I tell her and Abby. But I shake a finger at the adorable kiddo. "No makeup for you."

"I know," Abby says, then stares intently as I powder Katie's nose, dust on some blush, and give my friend a smoky eye.

"Are you excited for today?" I ask breezily, doing my best to keep my tone casual.

"I'm excited and insanely nervous," she says, fiddling with a friendship bracelet in Renegades colors that Abby made her. Abby wears a matching one. "I can't even imagine how he feels, playing in his last game." She flashes me a smile. "Except, I can. He's told me."

"And how does Mister Harlan Taylor feel?"

"Ready," she says with a crisp nod and a smile. "Like the timing is totally right."

Abby pops up from the bed. "I need to use the little girls' room. 'Scuse me." She rushes to the restroom and shuts the door.

"And speaking of timing, thank you again for babysitting her in your room tonight," Katie whispers, nodding to the bathroom. "Tonight might be the night."

She has no idea.

I just grin. "Happy to help."

"And what about for you? How's everything with you and Nolan? You looked so cozy in your last episode." She says it like she's leading a horse to water and wants me to drink up a whole stream.

As I swipe on her mascara, I smile softly. I'm not drinking from that river. No way. "We're just friends. The show is going great. We're landing new sponsors. He's my friend and my co-host."

"That's what you say now," Katie teases.

"That's what I'll always say," I add.

But when Nolan, all broad shoulders and smoldering gaze, joins us as we head to the stadium for kickoff, I wonder how long *always* will be.

It's like he gets better looking every day.

Sexier every night.

More dangerous by the hour.

"Hey, gorgeous," he says, then drops an arm around my shoulders.

A friendly arm.

Since he's a friendly guy.

A friendly guy who, every now and then, makes me think dirty thoughts.

I shove those all out of my head, though, because it's game time, and I've got a job to do.

EPILOGUE

KATIE

FOUR HOURS LATER

I've lost my voice, and I don't care.

We are all going wild in our fifty-yard-line seats. If I thought the noise at the December game was eardrum-crushing, that has nothing on the Super Bowl.

Pretty sure half the noise is coming from our crew.

Harlan offered to get us all a suite, but we opted for a row instead. So I'm cheering as the clock winds down. Abby's by my side, along with Emerson, Nolan, Jillian, Olive and Zachary, my dad, and Harlan's buddy Jason—Jason's team didn't make it to the big game—as well as some of my new favorite people—my boyfriend's mom and his sisters.

His mom is a fabulous Southern gentlewoman, all sass and manners, with lungs the size of a hot-air balloon. No one has shouted louder for her son.

"C'mon, run it in, sweetie pie," she shouted when Harlan caught a pass in the third quarter.

Sweetie pie.

I nearly fainted from cuteness. But I will not faint, because we have plans for tonight. Timing matters when it comes to baby-making, and I stopped taking birth control in December. I'm moving in with him when we return to California, but tonight—fingers crossed—I'm ovulating.

We decided, why wait?

We both know what we want.

To grow this family.

I squeeze Abby's hand harder as the Renegades' defense holds the other team to only a yard.

It's third down.

The game is nearly over.

My man's team is in the lead.

If the Renegades' defense can shut the other team down for good.

On the next play, the opposing quarterback lobs a Hail Mary pass that makes my heart crawl up my throat.

But there's no one open, and just like that, my boyfriend wins his third Super Bowl!

"Daddy!" Abby shouts, thrusting her arms in the air.

"He's the best," I cheer, elated and euphoric, along with the rest of my friends.

Confetti falls.

Music blares.

And the winners rush to celebrate on the field.

It's wild and exhilarating, and since I feel like I'm dancing in the sky, I can't even imagine the emotions swirling through the man I love.

A few minutes into our sideline celebration, Emerson grabs my arm, then nods at Abby.

"Look who's here."

Emerson tugs me, and Abby by extension, to the sidelines. In a flash, I'm grinning and I can't stop.

My guy is there for us, waiting, like he was a few months ago after the game in San Francisco.

Harlan reaches for me, and I hop down into his arms. Emerson lifts up Abby, and Harlan scoops her into his arms next. "Hey, little bear, what did you think? Was that boring?"

"Not at the end when you won," she says, matter-of-factly.

As he holds his little girl, he turns his gaze to me. "Did I go out in style or what?"

"You sure did," I say, beaming. "I am so proud of you."

"Good. Because this is the perfect time to ask you something."

What on earth does he have to ask me on the field teeming with reporters and teammates and Gatorade and noise and music and…

My hand flies to my mouth.

Harlan has set Abby down and dropped to one knee.

Abby squeals.

The sweaty, game-winning guy of my dreams has a velvet box in his hand, and I've no idea where it came from. Emerson? But who cares, because he's talking.

Loud and clear.

"I love you so much, Katie Madigan. And I planned to ask you this whether we won or lost, because you're what I want beyond this moment. For all time. For always. I love you madly. Will you marry me tonight?"

I blink, stunned.

Utterly stunned.

"Tonight?" I croak.

Abby cheers. "Say yes, say yes, Katie!"

I laugh, and the sound is chased by sobs, and holy hell, I'm crying.

"Yes, Katie. Tonight. We're in Vegas. Our friends and family are here. I want you to be my wife, and I want us to be a family, and I don't want to wait any longer."

You know what?

He makes the most excellent points.

I fall to my knees, joining him on the grass, and wrap my arms around him. "Yes. I say yes. Let's do it."

Abby jumps up and down, and we both pull her in for a hug.

Sometime after midnight, we make it to the chapel at The Extravagant with a yawning seven-year-old and the whole crew.

"Told you the pink sparkly sweatshirt was the way to go," Emerson says with a wink as I walk in wearing a simple white dress.

The sneak.

She'd packed the dress and handed it to me when we returned to the hotel to shuck off my game clothes so I could put on *this*.

Now, she's holding a bouquet of tiger lilies. "And these."

I clutch them close to my heart, then walk down the aisle and pledge to love Harlan Taylor for the rest of my life.

When the justice of the peace turns to the groom, decked out in one of his tailored suits, and asks if he'll love, cherish, and honor me for the rest of his days, he says, so easily, so happily, "I do."

He says it with love and passion and trust.

That's all I could ever want.

EPILOGUE

HARLAN

MORE THAN A YEAR LATER

whip up eggs for my wife. Brew her some coffee. Slice her a peach. Set the goodies on the breakfast plate as she nurses the baby.

What a sight.

Katie looks so good as a mom. Who would have thought?

Well, this guy.

Katie looks good doing pretty much everything.

And she's aces at doing most stuff, too, so she's mastered parenting already.

"Look at you. Such a pro in no time," I say when the baby finishes, and Katie burps her on her shoulder.

"Yes, sign me up for five more," she quips as she pats our daughter's back.

"Don't tempt me," I say drily, then set the plate in front of her.

"Gimme Mia. I need some snuggles." I make grabby hands, and Katie gives me the baby.

Our five-month-old makes the sweetest sigh as I hold her close. "There. Wasn't that delicious?" I glance at Katie, nodding to her plate. "Now, eat your breakfast, sweetheart. You have a busy day teaching those ballplayers downward dog. Bet they're not as fun as football players."

"Of course they aren't." She takes a bite of the eggs. Once she swallows, she holds up her fork to make a point. "But I'm also not in love with any of them."

"Good, let's keep it that way."

"I will," she says as the rush of Converse-clad feet echoes from upstairs.

"No running indoors, Abby," I call out.

The sound slows. "Sorry. Just getting ready."

"Well don't run the forty-yard dash."

"She's excited for school today," Katie says as she clears her plate. "She and Audrey and Gabriella and Caroline are doing a presentation on why gymnastics rocks. She practiced it with me last night. It's about three PowerPoint slides long, and it's awesome."

I smile. "That does sound awesome. I can't wait to hear how it goes."

Once Katie sets the plate in the dishwasher, she moves behind me, plants a soft kiss on my hair, then scurries upstairs to our room to get ready to teach yoga to the San Francisco Dragons.

After that, she'll make some videos, and then work with Olive and Zachary.

When she rushes downstairs, she calls behind her, "You'll do great, Abby! Love you."

"Love you, Katie," Abby shouts.

Then my wife returns to me, kisses my cheek, and gives Mia a big hug. "Miss you already, sweetie," she whispers to our little girl.

I walk Katie to the door, hand her her purse and phone, then steal another kiss—a lingering, sweet kiss that makes me think of the dirty things I'll do to her tonight.

"Mmm. Later, I want to strip you out of those yoga clothes," I say, eyeing her salaciously.

She leers right back at me. "Do you have any idea what you do to my ovaries when you talk dirty while you hold our baby?"

"I do," I say. "I definitely do."

She grabs one more quick kiss. "I love you."

"And I love you."

She leaves, and I shut the door behind her. After I clean up, I grab a BabyBjörn, strap it on my chest, and put Mia in it as Abby bounds downstairs.

"I'm ready for school!"

"Let's do it, little bear."

Abby grabs her backpack and slings it over her shoulders, and we leave the house like that. With Mia on my chest and Abby holding my hand, I walk my oldest child to school.

And then I'll spend the day with my youngest.

And the night with the love of my life.

Now *that's* winning.

ACKNOWLEDGMENTS

Thank you so much to Deb, Jocelyn, Cid, India, Annabelle, Susan, Michelle, and the team at Sourcebooks for bringing this book to your hands!

ABOUT THE AUTHOR

A #1 *New York Times*, #1 *Wall Street Journal*, and #1 Audible best-selling author, Lauren Blakely is known for her contemporary romance style that's cute but spicy. Lauren likes dogs, cake, and show tunes and is the vegetarian at your dinner party.

Website: LaurenBlakely.com
Facebook: LaurenBlakelyBooks
Instagram: @laurenblakelybooks

MOST VALUABLE PLAYBOY

FALLING FOR HER WASN'T IN THE PLAYBOOK.

Cooper Armstrong entered the Most Valuable Playboy charity auction with one goal in mind—be the player who goes for the most dough. But when trouble shows up in the form of an unscrupulous journalist who wants Cooper to marry her, he needs a whole new play.

Enter Violet Pierson. With a smile as sweet as cherry pie and a mind that runs quicker than the forty-yard dash, Violet saves the day with the highest bid. To seal the deal, Cooper smacks a kiss on her and announces in front of the whole crowd that she's his girlfriend.

It was only supposed to be one kiss, but now Cooper's agent says it's better for his contract negotiation to keep up the act. Soon, the boyfriend-girlfriend scrimmage quickly turns into a full contact sport. But even though most of their kisses are for show, the world seems to disappear when their lips touch.

"A LAUREN BLAKELY BOOK IS A GUARANTEE OF A GOOD TIME."

—Meghan Quinn, *New York Times* bestselling author

**FOR MORE INFO ABOUT SOURCEBOOKS'S BOOKS
AND AUTHORS, VISIT: SOURCEBOOKS.COM**